W9-BSY-886

Portia Da Costa is one of the most internationally renowned authors of erotic romance and erotica, and a *Sunday Times*, *New York Times* and *USA Today* bestseller.

She is the author of eighteen *Black Lace* books, as well as numerous short stories and novellas.

Also by Portia Da Costa

The Tutor

PORTIA DA COSTA

BLACK
LACE

1 3 5 7 9 10 8 6 4 2

Black Lace, an imprint of Ebury Publishing
20 Vauxhall Bridge Road,
London SW1V 2SA

Penguin
Random House
UK

Black Lace is part of the Penguin Random House group of companies
whose addresses can be found at global.penguinrandomhouse.com

Copyright © Portia Da Costa, 2003

Portia Da Costa has asserted her right to be identified as the author of this
work in accordance with the Copyright, Designs and Patents Act 1988

This novel is a work of fiction. Names and characters are the product
of the author's imagination and any resemblance to actual persons,
living or dead, is entirely coincidental

First published in 2003 by Black Lace
This edition published in 2015

www.eburypublishing.co.uk

A CIP catalogue record for this book is
available from the British Library

ISBN 9780352347824

Typeset in Janson Text LT Std by Palimpsest Book Production Limited,
Falkirk, Stirlingshire

Printed and bound by CPI Group (UK) Ltd, Croydon, CR0 4YY

Penguin Random House is committed to a sustainable future for our
business, our readers and our planet. This book is made from Forest
Stewardship Council® certified paper.

MIX
Paper from
responsible sources
FSC® C016897

1

The Best of Times?

It was the best of times, it was the worst of times.

Rosie knew it was a Dickens quote, but for her it always conjured up visions of *Star Trek*. Of Kirk and Spock and a time that had been both good and bad for them. A time like that night, a week ago, when she'd had probably the best sex ever; then the worst of all let-downs afterwards. That night when Geoff had made love to her like a Mills and Boon hero who'd just read *The Joy of Sex*; then told her, five short minutes into the afterglow, that 'it', or more precisely 'they' were finished.

I should have known it was too good to be true when he brought roses, she thought now, a sad, wry smile on her face.

'Roses for my Rosie,' she echoed, more in self mockery than genuine bitterness. A canny northern lass like her should have smelt a slippery southern rat from the outset. A smooth, blond, southern rat with a pin-up's face and a strong sexy body to match it. Fool, Rosie! Fool, fool, fool!

The trouble was, if every trickster and let-down artist could do the things that Geoff could do, then Rosie knew she was going to go on being a fool, putting up with all kinds of chauvinist piggery for the tunes that they – or in this case, he – could play on her nerves and her senses. The way he'd touched her and teased her and brought her alive; tuned her to a pitch of pleasure she'd not thought her body capable of; taught her she was sexy, even though she suspected his motives in doing so and realised now that he'd made little conscious effort to educate her.

Those bloody roses!

'For you,' he'd said, whisking them out of her hands as soon as he'd put them there; just so he could grab hold of her, kiss her and start running his hands over her body. The fact that she was wearing just a thin silky dressing gown made the process all the easier.

'God, you've got a great body on you, northern girl,' he said roughly, sliding the thin, slick stuff over the rounds of her full, fruity buttocks. 'Those super-models look great in magazines, but there's something to be said for a girl with some flesh on her bones.'

Such observations as those had hurt her when they'd first started seeing each other, but for a while now she'd been more sanguine. She *was* a rounded girl, and there wasn't too much she could do about it without making her life a misery; but she'd noticed of late that a lot of men shared Geoff's viewpoint. She'd seen plenty of hot looks aimed her way, undressing eyes studying her full breasts and her curvy bottom, and she'd started enjoying the feeling.

She certainly enjoyed it when Geoff massaged

that curvy bottom and pressed her forward so her pubis massaged his erection. He was stroking the delicate in-slope now, pushing the silk in towards her stickiness, not caring that he'd soil an expensive robe she'd bought especially to please him. She didn't care either, not when he was rubbing her swollen, sensitive folds and getting closer and closer to the core of her. Unaware that she was inciting the process, she began wriggling and shimmying against him.

'Come on, you little sex-pot,' he laughed into her ear, 'let's get you into bed before you come right here in the lounge.'

That sort of thing had also upset her at first. His almost mocking reaction to her sexuality: her easy readiness for him, and the way she couldn't resist even the slightest of his caresses. The way her body showed her arousal so clearly. The hardness of her nipples, the excessive wetness that flowed like sap between legs that slid open without resistance.

The cynic within her noted that he didn't even try to lift her up and carry her. She wasn't *that* heavy, but it would need someone who worked out a tad more than Geoff did to sweep her off her feet and whisk her into the bedroom – and still maintain his Mr Perfect look as he did so.

When he undressed, there was a distinct 'Chippendale' feel to the process. He was most definitely posing, but Rosie wasn't put off by it. His body was so attractive, and what he would soon be doing to hers with it was enough to excuse his airs and graces. She could already taste the smooth fresh warmth of that high-gloss golden-tanned skin; feel those muscles pressed against her softer, feminine body; feel the push of that penis as it forged its way inside her. Oh dear God, the man was so lovely to be loved by he was almost edible!

'This is going to be so good, Rosie,' he said confidently, stepping out of his boxer shorts.

Oh yes, it is! she echoed silently, watching his cock swing up and slap against his flat, sexy belly. Her body rippled involuntarily, already feeling him inside her, and though she should have been used to it by now, her own wantonness still managed to astound her. She licked her lips as her man took himself in hand and began to work the loose suedey skin of his sex over the strong hard core at its centre. He was stiffening himself and readying himself, and she felt a momentary pang, a disappointment that he was planning to penetrate her immediately and forgo the delicious preparations: the strokings and lickings that made her whimper and moan with pleasure, and the chance, and the time, to do some stroking and licking of her own.

'Don't worry, kid.' He grinned his film star grin at her. 'I'm going to come quickly . . . then I'll last longer for the second round.'

It made good sense, but somehow the moment was spoiled. As she watched him rubbing his penis, there were two Rosie Howards observing the phenomenon; and while one, the newborn sensualist, thought the sight was extraordinarily beautiful, the other, the cynical Yorkshirewoman, decided that the more desirable a man became, the more his ego inflated.

Stop it, you! she told the hard-eyed realist inside her, and through an effort of will that person was banished. Okay, so Geoff was a bit self-centred, but he was also gorgeous, a wonderful lover, and here with her when he could have been chasing one of the rake-thin achiever-girls from his office. All of whom lusted after him, by his account.

He was building quickly to his climax now, one knee braced on the edge of the bed, hips thrusting forward, his cock hard and reddened in his fingers. She pulled open her robe, baring her pale, waiting body in a mute plea that his semen spurt upon her.

'Please,' she whispered as the cynic turned her back in disgust and walked away.

'Yes, baby, yes!' cried Geoff, his handsome face contorted, his eyes closed. Rosie sensed him to be elsewhere, somehow in a different world, as he pumped his own male flesh and brought himself right to the pinnacle. His slim hips were a blur for a moment, and as her sigh underpinned his groans, his pure white semen shot out of the eye of his penis, arced high, and landed with an unstudied accuracy on the palpitating plain of her belly.

Without conscious thought, she pressed her fingers to her own curved body, paddled in his essence and smoothed it into her skin. It was as if he'd annointed her, and that his erotic white ejaculate contained an aphrodisiac that inflamed her even further. She slid her hot, sticky fingers through the tangle of her pubis and opened up her vulva to caress it.

Geoff was lying down beside her now, edging her across the bed, interrupting the very beginnings of her pleasure to make himself a space to lie down in. Rosie felt a momentary flash of annoyance, then forgot it as he propped himself up on his elbow and smiled down at her.

'Your turn now, my horny little Rosie,' he purred, nudging at her wrists to encourage her. 'Bring yourself off for me, darling. You know how I love to see you diddling.'

She wanted to do it. She wanted both the pleasure itself and to please him, but even so twenty-eight years of inhibition made her blush the same colour she was nicknamed. Hot and pink, she closed her eyes and let her fingertips find their own way between the thick puffed-out lips of her sex.

Embarrassed by her own extreme moistness, she parted herself, knowing that her pinkness would be almost crimson down there, slick and gleaming to Geoff's sharp, observant eyes. With a sigh of resignation, then a ragged gasp, she dipped a finger in the well of her juices and drew it up slowly across her clitoris.

'Oh! Mmmm,' she murmured, her thighs slowly moving as she fingered her tiny bud of pleasure. This considered touch, this deliberate self-stimulation, was still quite new to her, and the novelty added extra spice. She flicked herself, then circled, groaning as the flesh itself seemed to grow and re-sensitise in response. Her bottom was lifting from the bed now, her hips swaying, and she was dimly aware that she must be putting on quite a show for her lover. Even as that thought crossed her mind, she felt his fingers slide in next to hers, pushing and pressing to make hers work harder and the tender flesh beneath them leap.

She cried out long and loud, her orgasm flaring wildly, stoked by Geoff's rough touch. Her own fingers had been knocked away by his bigger, stronger ones and he was rubbing her more jerkily than he usually did, as if trying to squeeze her into climax by force alone. There was a faint strand of pain amongst the pleasure, but Rosie was beyond such differentiations now, her body incandescent with sensation.

'I want you, Rosie,' he growled into her ear, his fingers still scrubbing at her sex. 'I want to be in that lush, hot body of yours. I want to screw you so hard that you'll never forget what it feels like.'

In Rosie's more rational moments, an utterance like that would have fazed her, set her analytical mind a-pondering. But right now, she had Geoff's fingers between her thighs and analysis and reason wouldn't function. She wanted only what he wanted. To be made love to. To be taken.

With a soft, incoherent cry, she widened her thighs and pulled at him. She urged him to mount her and enjoy the body that was totally his.

'Patience, little sexy,' he taunted, his fingers still moving, still rubbing.

To her shame, Rosie heard herself whine with frustration. Rolling her pelvis, she pulled her legs open wider with her own hands, making her vulva accessible and available.

'Please,' she moaned again, her breath hissing wildly between her teeth as a finger plunged right inside her.

'Please what?'

'Please make love to me.'

'Come on, Rosie, you can do better than that. I want to hear you talk dirty, Miss Prim . . . Miss Librarian with fire in her knickers.'

'Please! I can't!'

'If you don't say it, I won't do it!'

She sobbed, hating herself for being helpless against his ultimate threat. 'Please, Geoff . . . Please will you screw me.'

She hated that word, and could only whisper it so faintly that it was barely audible – but it seemed to suffice.

'Alright, sexy, I'll screw you.'

But something was wrong. The finger stayed inside her and started pumping back and forth, surging in her juices and making a hideous and mortifying squelching sound.

'Geoff!'

'But I'm doing it.' His fingers plumbed her remorselessly, searching crudely for the heart of her shame.

'Please, Geoff. Use your . . . your . . .'

'Say it, Rosie.' His voice was suddenly quite cold. 'Ask me for what you want.'

'Use your cock,' she cried wildly, beside herself with need and frustration – and against her better judgement, with love. 'Put your cock in me, you bastard!' she screamed, almost coming again she felt so desperate.

'That's it, my sexy,' he answered, slipping away his hand as he moved between her quaking, stretched apart thighs. She was trapped by him, pinned by him, caught as much by her own desire as by his rigid body. The head of his cock touched her vulva and she keened like a hound when he wouldn't put it straight inside her. She heard him laughing softly and almost wanted to kill him; then she sighed and gulped in air with relief as he sank down upon her and into her.

And he'd been right. He did last longer. Longer than ever before. So long she lost count of her orgasms and felt revivified by the sheer excesses of pleasure.

In the precious moments afterwards, she'd felt both drained by the exhilarating climaxes and peculiarly dynamised too. She was good at this, she decided, and she liked it; she felt strong and confident, a confidence that she knew could spread out and filter through into the whole of her life.

Half-dreaming, she thought about striking out, trying different things. She'd already tentatively applied for a new job, but now she felt like trying a bit harder. Maybe getting the damn thing. She could be much more the sort of woman Geoff really wanted if she put her mind to it – and right then, flying high on the glow of good sex, she'd felt grateful to him for both the pleasure and the impetus to change.

Ah, but wasn't there always a sting?

And God, how that sting had stung, she thought now, after a week of pain and recrimination, and a fury that was directed far more at herself than at him.

As she'd torn up his photograph, it was herself she was cursing for gullibility, not the man in the image for his perfidy.

Even so, she didn't like to think of the details too much. He and she weren't going anywhere, he'd said. They weren't really compatible. He'd met someone else. Someone at his work. She was in PR, she was happening, and on her way to the top.

Rosie had shut off then, knowing that she was none of those things and too much the outsider in his world ever to be able to compete. To her great satisfaction she'd remained calm, composed and almost friendly – until the door had closed firmly behind him and she'd smashed half a dozen dishes in her sorrow and fury, then chastised herself soundly for giving in to it.

Sulking and moping achieved nothing. Weeping and wailing achieved nothing. Breaking things achieved nothing except the expense of buying new things!

The only way forward now was to learn, re-group, start again. And go out and show handsome, self-centred bastards like Geoff that they couldn't get the better of Rosie Howard!

2

Mister Hadey's 'Private Case'

If I was still with Geoff, I might not have come here,
Rosie reflected as she waited. Fiddling nervously with
the deeply revered neckline of her jacket, she surveyed
one of the most sumptuous rooms she'd ever seen,
and almost thanked her ex for his treachery. Foolishly
lost in her dreamworld of sex with 'golden boy', she'd
probably have ended up changing her mind after all,
backing out of the interview, and missing all this
magnificence.

A case-hardened realist now though, she still didn't
rate her chances of getting the job all that highly. It
was out of her league – well within her technical
abilities, granted, but so different from the world she'd
always inhabited that it might as well have been on
another planet. Nevertheless, a drastic change was
what she'd decided she needed. And if she got this
job it would mean a *really* drastic change.

Right from the time of getting her degree, Rosie
had always taken the safe jobs. The humdrum jobs.
The routine jobs. There'd never actually been much

excitement in library service anyway, but looking back, the posts she'd taken now seemed the dullest she could have chosen. A wind of change had to blow soon, she realised, or any illusions she'd ever had would disappear. She'd stagnate. She'd be a senior assistant librarian in a medium-sized municipal library forever. A week ago, she'd had only a vague post-orgasmic yen to be bolder for Geoff's sake; but now she needed that 'something new' as much as she needed air to breathe. It was survival now, a shot at self-redemption.

Hence this make-over. The radical re-vamp she still wasn't sure about. The hair, the make-up, the clothes.

Crossing her knees and smoothing down her skirt, she wondered what the girls behind the desk in 'adult loans' would think of her now. This certainly wasn't their Miss Howard with her neatly-bunned hair and her conservative Marks & Spencer outfits. This was a new being entirely, with hair worn loose and swingy right down to her waist, face skilfully made up, and body that was distinctly power-dressed. Rosie had always tried to look attractive – and succeeded, after her own fashion – but she knew that at this moment she looked more like one of those lip-glossed, corporate career-girls than a woman who catalogued books on geraniums and geography for a living. It was all a bit unnerving.

Her slim-skirted pin-stripe suit had cost a fortune, and its hemline was a good six inches shorter than the length she'd always favoured. She'd definitely had a brainstorm when she'd chosen it, she decided, and probably another when she'd bought black patent stiletto-heeled pumps to go with it; but at heart she knew it was simply a figurative thumbed-nose, or more aptly a vee sign, in the direction of Geoff and his betrayal. He'd implied she wasn't 'happening', that she was too parochial. He'd hinted that without him she wasn't sexy. This sharply feminine suit and the cool but challenging look that went with it were a way of telling him he was wrong, and that she didn't need him. What's more, the suit even made her look slim!

Well, not exactly slim, she admitted, primping discreetly at her skirt. What this sexy suit did was make her curves look fashionable, her full breasts fabulous, and her flaring, womanly hips not quite so flaring.

Still trying to adjust to being a brand new creature, Rosie stared around the beautiful, antique-strewn room and reviewed the peculiar advert that had brought her here.

Experienced young woman required to catalogue extensive collection of rare books. Pleasant work in amenable surroundings. Applicant will be expected to do a small amount of secretarial work in addition to library duties, and should be prepared to live in.

The word 'experienced' seemed ambiguous, and the last stipulation about living in had been off-putting to the Rosie of a fortnight ago.

The Rosie of today still felt dubious about being experienced but she kind of liked its hint of naughtiness. She was also aware that her own small flat held too many memories of ecstatic nights with Geoff, so living elsewhere would be a blessing. Especially if it was in this house. The place was a palace and its elegant opulence was a pure, sensual thrill. To work in such a haven as this, she was beginning to think she'd do anything! Well, almost anything.

As if wishes could motivate action, the tall beautifully polished double doors to the hall suddenly opened, and in walked a quite different kind of beauty.

Oh no, not another God's gift! thought Rosie in the few seconds it took to assimilate the newcomer's appearance. She was infinitely glad now that she'd decided on her suit, her shoes, and her seductive new hairstyle. Because Mister Julian Hadey – if this was the same person who'd placed the advertisement – looked like a man who could probably only relate to women as sexually all-confident as he was. He wasn't the same blond god type as Geoff, but his dark, menacing, almost middle-eastern looks had an immediate and similar effect.

'Rosalind Howard?' he enquired, his voice like melting caramel. His brown-eyed gaze was already panning over her body as he strode forward and reached for her hand.

'Rosie, actually,' she replied, leaping to her feet and letting him take her fingers in his, setting her inner parts shaking and shivering.

He answered with a narrow, assessing smile; a brief, telling twist of a mouth that was sinfully beautiful. 'Even better,' he murmured, squeezing the hand he still held and looking directly into her eyes. Directly and very, very probingly. 'And I'm Julian Hadey. Please,' he nodded to a long brocaded sofa some feet from the chair Rosie had previously chosen, 'take a seat and let's get to know each other.'

I can't cope! I can't cope! screamed the old, gauche version of Rosie, panicking silently in the face of such refined and unfiltered maleness.

Shut up! You can! the new look Rosie ordered from behind her armour of sleek suit, sleek make-up and a steel-clad determination to never again be bested by a glamorous, unprincipled man. A gut feeling already told her that this would be a job interview unlike any she'd ever had before; or dreamed of having. And even though she'd dazzled this Hadey with only two unimpressive words so far, she sensed an unaccountable rapport forming. A tension like fine wires stretched between them; as if she were face to face with a hot and sizzling new lover rather than a prospective employer.

Surprisingly, she felt quite poised. Matching his smile, she allowed herself to be led to the sofa, then sat down, wary of her slim, tight skirt. Hadey sank smoothly down next to her, his blue-jeaned knee just an inch or two from her gunmetal-stockinged one. He seemed to take note of her checking their proximity, and moved slightly closer on purpose.

'Please excuse me, Rosie, I don't usually dress so casually to interview.' The Arabian Nights grin widened, making his even teeth look white as ice in the olive-toned setting of his face. 'But at home I find a suit too restricting.'

There was a teasing note to his voice, something indefinably, yet appealingly suggestive – as if he'd just said he'd prefer to be naked and wouldn't she like to undress too?

You're going mad, Howard, Rosie told herself

frantically. He'd said nothing of the sort! It was her own interpretation. Her own ridiculous idea. Her own desire that instead of wearing those narrow jeans and that fluidly-styled creamy-beige shirt, Julian Hadey should be utterly and beautifully nude. For an instant she imagined him thus, and the picture almost threw her completely. Her well-planned résumé went flying out of the tall Regency windows, and she could think of nothing else but this handsome man and his elegant, unclothed body. His beautiful shirt and jeans were there before her, fitting snugly on his lean, muscular shape, but Rosie could no longer see them.

He was smiling again, a wolfish, dark-eyed smirk; but in Rosie's mind, the smile – and the man that went with it – had shifted to a different location. He was lying on a spacious bed somewhere, in a tangle of pale silk sheets, his bare brown skin damp and gleaming. His body was as swarthy and exotic as his dusky face and hands had indicated, and he was peppered with dark male hair: a thick, wiry mat at his chest, a soft fuzzy forest at his groin. He was slim of waist, broad of chest, and unequivocably solid of cock. And as the image of *that* reared up like a club to torment her, Rosie prayed that she hadn't started blushing.

Whether intentionally or not, this Julian Hadey seemed hell-bent on stirring her libido. His every move was both languid and graceful, and as he reached for a manilla file that lay on a small table beside him, then leaned back into the cushions of the sofa, his hard body flexed and shifted explicitly as he crossed his jeans-clad legs. It was almost as if he were aping the fantasy somehow, exhibiting himself, even though there was no way he could know what she was seeing. Without speaking, but still smiling, he settled the file on his lap and flipped it open.

For what felt like a millennium, Rosie watched him peruse various papers; amongst them, presumably, her letter of application and her photocopied diplomas. She was mesmerised by the length of his coal black eyelashes as they flicked and fluttered in the course of his reading. She imagined them tickling the skin of her belly as his roving lips discovered her.

'Very impressive,' he murmured, looking up.

Blood surged ominously through Rosie's body, as all her most inappropriate responses fired up at once. She felt warmth surge through her belly, a tightness in her breasts, a hypersensitive readiness throughout all the surface of her skin. On the face of it, Hadey's words were an observation on her genuinely excellent qualifications, but his eyes said they were nothing whatsoever to do with certificates and references.

He was studying *her* now. Everything about her, and in blatant, indecent detail. This was the archetypal male 'undressing the female' look and this time, to her fascinated horror, Rosie basked in it.

She thought of how she'd seen this look so often recently, and how, when it had come from Geoff, she'd felt demeaned. But this time, here, she felt better for it, not worse. No matter how smoothly and suavely he projected himself, she sensed that Julian Hadey was a fundamentally straightforward man; an honest man who really was impressed with what he saw. With her, with her body, and even with her shaky façade of sexual *savoir-faire*.

'Tell me about yourself,' he said, facing her with the interviewee's perennial nightmare question.

'Well,' she began, wishing for just a second that the man was as ugly as sin, and that she wasn't so strongly attracted to him. At least that way she could have thought and answered coherently instead of sliding head over heels back into fantasy. 'Well, since I left University I've worked mainly in public libraries. Mostly doing reader enquiry work, but recently I've been doing more cat –'

'No, Rosie, tell me about *yourself*,' he interrupted. The emphasis on 'yourself' was silky and intimate, and she felt as if he'd asked her, straight out, what she liked to do best in bed. Insanely, she imagined telling him, but at the very last second, bit her tongue.

Not long ago, Rosie had attended a yoga course and learned the principles of bio-feedback. Now, under the intense, almost spot-lit scrutiny of Julian Hadey, she fought hard to remember those techniques, and to remain in control. Through sheer power of will, she suppressed the beetroot-red blushes she'd always been prone to, and managed to keep her breathing and her voice quite steady. There was nothing she could do about her arousal; it was running riot. She could only give in and enjoy it.

'Well, Mister Hadey,' she began, astonished by how together she suddenly sounded. 'I'm Rosie Howard, I'm twenty-eight, and I come from a small town in Yorkshire. I'm a chartered librarian. I love books and love being around books. But recently, something happened . . . and now I want a complete change. I want to work somewhere different. Somewhere quite unlike the sort of libraries I've always worked in . . . I . . .'

She faltered there, and felt her heart bound madly as Hadey's brown eyes thinned, and his attention visibly sharpened. This was a minefield, and she knew it. She braced herself for the inevitable questions, and when he didn't immediately ask them, she took a chance and plunged ever onwards.

'When I saw your advertisement, I decided I'd found just the change I wanted. I'm good at "cat & class", it's my speciality, but I'm fed up of dealing with romantic novels and books about knitting all day. Rare books in a private collection sound much more interesting. I also have no particular fondness for the flat I live in – and I'm a free agent in general – so living in wouldn't be a problem. Especially not here!' She waved in the vague direction of all the beauty and comfort around her.

She stopped for a moment then, wondering if she'd said too much. Hadey was still watching her closely, his dark eyes unwavering, his body motionless, his long brown fingers resting lightly on the papers before him. To her increasing embarrassment, he said nothing, but just continued to look her straight in the eye.

He was challenging her to explain herself, to expand on her free agent notion. To admit she'd been ditched and sexually humiliated. Her heart speeding faster, she rushed on. 'I think I'd be perfect for your job, Mister Hadey. You'll have to go a long way to find someone with my qualifications who's available.'

The minute it was out, she realised she'd just blown all her personal PR clean out of the water. Available, indeed? What an air-head thing to say!

Julian Hadey smiled. Not the thin, judging smile of before, but a soft, mischievous grin that bordered closely on an out-and-out chuckle.

In that moment, he looked even sexier than ever, and if possible, both older and younger at the same time. His obvious amusement was as natural and unaffected as a boy's, but simultaneously, Rosie noticed the distinguished flashes of grey in his thick dark hair, the tiny crinkles of his laughter lines – and the almost palpable air of 'this man has lived' that seemed to overlay his entire persona. As she waited, breath on hold, he put her file aside and rose lithely to his feet.

'The name's Julian,' he said, reaching out for her hand to pull her to her feet. 'And I'm absolutely delighted you're "available". Because *I* think you're perfect for the job too.' His lips quirked slightly on the word 'job', as if that was a further source of entertainment, and somehow not quite what it seemed. But his brown eyes were so bright and compelling, and his smile such a welcome relief that Rosie dismissed her faint shiver of alarm.

'Come on, Rosie.' He drew her forward after him, 'I'll show you some of my books.'

As they made their way to the library, Rosie was struggling. Struggling to understand that suddenly, and without the interview really starting, she seemed to have acquired herself a job; struggling to cope with the presence of this Hadey – this Julian – and all the powerful effects he was having on her.

A lot of them seemed to stem from his penchant for touching. It wasn't offensive or gratuitous though; every time he laid hands on her, there was a relevance. He touched her to urge her to her feet. He touched her to guide her to the correct door amongst what seemed like a dozen in the huge spacious hall. He touched her very courteously to propel her into the library before him. All these small actions required that his fingertips rest somewhere on her body for a moment – and that he brand her skin with his heat through the finely woven cloth of her suit, and even, in some cases, through the fragile silk underwear beneath. When he touched her on the waist to lead her towards one of the tall, mahogany bookcases, she almost squealed aloud with unexpected pleasure. The intensity of the miniscule contact was so sensual that she felt it through the whole of her body: her flanks, her fingertips, her toes – and deep in the very centre of her sex.

As they stood before the serried ranks of books, ostensibly discussing their future disposal, it was all Rosie could do to stop herself from swaying towards him across the scant few inches that divided them.

The library around them was a wonder. A haven of words and paper; of rich, old carpeting; of angled light and the fragrance of leather upholstery. Under any other circumstances Rosie would soon have been lost in it, totally absorbed, but now, to concentrate, she had to fight the influence of its owner.

Julian Hadey possessed many thousands of books on dozens of topics, a great number of them rare first editions. Someone, at sometime, had begun to group

them in a vague sort of sequence, but it was fairly
haphazard. There was a lot of work to be done, but
basically, Rosie didn't think anything more elaborate
than the classic Dewey Decimal Classification would
be called for.

That was until Julian touched her again, quite
casually, and led her towards a set of four crammed
book-cases which, unlike the others, were protected by
leaded-glass fronts. As he turned towards her, his
expression had altered slightly, all the subtle sensuality
rising up from within him and shining unchecked in
his eyes.

'This is the most important part of my library,
Rosie,' he said, his cultured voice infinitesimally
thickened. Reaching into the pocket of his tight
blue jeans, he drew out a key, and unlocked the
first case. 'These are the books I want you to take
special care of. The books I want you to cherish,
and to read and understand.'

Running a finger along the bottom shelf, he
pulled out a volume, a large leather-bound tome, then
opened it, slowly and carefully.

Rosie was puzzled by the way he held the book at
an angle so she couldn't see the contents. She was
puzzled by the way his eyes seemed to widen and flare
with heat as he flicked the precious pages; and by the
way he unconsciously ran his tongue – his soft and
very red tongue – across his lower lip, then smiled
with an obvious enjoyment.

'This . . . and these,' he gestured elegantly from
the open book to its companions still brooding on the
shelves, 'are the very heart of my collection, Rosie.

The books I've gathered for myself.' Staring at her from under strangely lowered lashes, he passed the open book to her.

'Oh my God!'

The priceless volume nearly fell, but Julian neatly supported it, his fingertips brushing Rosie's in the process, and lingering.

Mounted in the centre of a recto page was one of the earliest photographs Rosie had ever seen. Its sepia tones were a delicate, washed-out amber against the pure white backing sheet, but otherwise it was star-tlingly clear and beautifully composed.

It was also unrelievedly pornographic.

A moustached Victorian gentleman was reclining sideways across a tumbled bed, wearing a frilly dress shirt unfastened to show his open combinations beneath. His penis, photographed with astonishing clarity given the times, was being sucked by a buxom young woman who knelt between his legs, her own clothing in similar disarray to that of the gentleman she was pleasuring. Her pose was carefully arranged so that her ample breasts were shown to dangle between the gentleman's legs; and her bottom, which was artfully on display through a slit in her elaborate lacy bloomers, was being kissed by another girl – this one clad only in some sort of short, embroidered chemise and with her completely shaven sex on show for all to see. The faces of the man and the sucking woman were strangely mask-like and emotionless, but the bottom-kisser's bore the faintest ghost of an impish smile.

'Oh my God,' murmured Rosie again. Julian was

supporting the book fully by now, and without thinking she touched her fingertip reverently to the photo. The title of the scene, hand-inscribed on the white paper beneath it, was 'The Pleasures of Mister Delaney.'

'So . . . What do you think of it?'

'I . . . I . . .'

Well, what did she think of it? The knee-jerk reaction, her old self's reaction, would be the meta-phorical hands-thrown-up-in-horror. But after a deep breath, and a mental-shapeshifting into the new personality she was now supposed to be, Rosie dis-covered that she liked the photograph. That she more than liked it.

To her surprise, and in a way, with wonder, it suddenly dawned on her that the bawdy old picture excited her. Aroused her intensely. Aroused her phys-ically. She wanted to be *in* the photograph. To be the girl in the middle; sucking that handsome man's penis and being sucked, obscenely, in return. The looks of that Victorian dandy were dark, and faintly exotic. He could easily have been Julian Hadey.

'It's wonderful,' she said finally, knowing in some deep and unfathomable way that she'd sealed her fate, passed a test, and confirmed that the job of cataloguing these outrageous books was truly hers. 'Are they all like this?' she enquired, looking up from the old-fashioned but incendiary image to the rows upon rows of similarly leather-bound books.

'I'm afraid so,' said Julian, grinning as he put the book he was holding aside and reaching into the case for another. He looked ever-so-slightly shamefaced for a second, but Rosie found this extraordinarily appealing.

It made her wonder what he'd been like in his youth, when he'd been an innocent just discovering this breathtaking new world.

She shrugged. Julian Hadey could never be that way now; he was quite obviously steeped in worldliness, profoundly experienced and probably familiar with nearly every practice described in his sexual library. But the image of the untutored young man seemed to stick in her mind somehow, lingering in her thoughts to excite her as Julian laid a second open book before her.

This one was Japanese: a pillow book of outlandishly coloured woodcuts showing copulating couples entwined in bone-cracking positions. It was as much a curiosity as it was a work of erotica, but nevertheless there was much that was stimulating.

'I collect "mucky books", as they say where you come from,' Julian admitted frankly, in a fair approximation of a Yorkshire accent.

Without thinking, Rosie flashed him a sharp, disapproving look. It was nothing to do with his salacious choice in literature – she'd already admitted that she liked his erotic books. His gentle gibe at her origins however, had hit on her rawest raw nerve. She saw Geoff's laughing face in her mind, and heard him mocking her pronounced northern accent and her occasional provincial naïvety.

'I'm sorry. I didn't mean that to be in any way disparaging,' said Julian contritely, her fierce look obviously noted and logged for future reference. 'Your accent's charming, Rosie. Quite sexy in fact. And it'll be useful to have a Yorkshirewoman in the house just now. My wife's cousin is staying with us and he comes from Yorkshire. He's . . . Well, he's a bit of a shy young thing, and I'm sure he'll feel more at home with a familiar sounding voice around.'

Rosie was momentarily intrigued at the thought of a fellow 'Yorkie' to keep her company, but soon forgot the unknown house-guest as Julian pulled out more books.

The collection was a repository for what had to be some of the most exotic prose and images in the country. In addition to the illustrated volumes they'd started with, Julian's private case contained every imaginable classic of sexual writing available.

De Sade, Boccaccio, Restif de la Bretonne. The great and the notorious from all ages jostled with each other on shelves that were packed with books.

Nabokov, Anaïs Nin, Sacher-Masoch. The list of names was endless, and interspersed at regular inter-vals with that most prolific sexual scribe of all: 'Anonymous'. There were even, in the fourth case, a set of novels by contemporary writers; names that probably wouldn't go down in history, but who still seemed to be producing hot and blood-stirring fiction. Julian had no prejudice against these latter-day pornographers with modern names – the books were obviously mass-market in content, but even so, his copies were privately printed on superior paper and bound in leather just like their more literary counterparts.

'Here. Take these with you when you leave,' he said enthusiastically, taking three books down together from a high shelf. As he reached up, Rosie caught a subtle waft of fragrance from his armpit: a sophisticated perfume, his deodorant no doubt, and beneath it, just a tang of male sweat. For a second she felt dizzy, intoxicated by the images she'd seen and the snippets of raunchy prose she'd read, but even more so by the primal odour of Julian's lean, dark body. As he passed her the books she almost dropped them.

'Dip into them tonight.' His bitter-chocolate eyes twinkled wickedly. 'Get acclimatised.'

'Er, yes . . . Thanks, I will,' muttered Rosie, still disorientated, as she stared down at the three slim books, each embossed on the spine and front cover with the design of a domino. Acclimatised to what? she pondered, fingering the indented leather.

'Okay. That's enough porn for now, eh?' he went on pleasantly. 'Why don't we go back to the sitting room, have a glass of sherry and discuss all the strictly practical details?'

She's right. She *is* perfect for the job, he thought, and took a sip of the exquisite bone-dry sherry that Rosie had earlier refused in favour of a sweeter, more feminine variety.

The woman he'd just employed had left now, clutching her dark and educational books, and looking faintly bemused. Julian Hadey recalled her presence with some satisfaction, both applauding his own split second decision, and feeling a fresh wave of sexual excitement over the lovely young body he'd selected.

He smiled as he imagined her. A pretty, northern

lass. Rosie. Well-named, because she did have a bloom
about her. A sexy, innocent lushness that would be so
useful for what lay ahead.

Good for me too, he reflected. Technically, he
hadn't intended her for himself; but if she was willing
– and he was perfectly certain she was – there was no
reason why he shouldn't enjoy her as well.

He was back in his library now, and as he shifted
his hips in the deep, leather armchair in an attempt
to ease his erection, he pictured how she'd looked
here earlier. The body that'd inspired his hardness.
Specifically, he saw again the sight that had plagued
him throughout the whole of the interview: that truly
gorgeous cleavage between those long, charcoal
pinstriped lapels. A deep and succulent cleft that was
designed for the male mouth to forage in. And not
just the mouth.

He wondered what she'd thought of his scrutiny.
Julian had never hidden his abiding interest in women
and their bodies; he felt it dishonest, somehow, to
snatch furtive peeks and stolen leers. If he admired a
woman, he told her with his eyes; and thus far his
frankness had always been rewarded.

Putting aside his sherry, he laid his hand across his
groin and considered Rosie Howard.

She was an intriguing and mouthwatering girl, and
quite obviously not what she'd tried so hard to project
herself as. Her performance had been good, granted,
but he sensed that her smooth, sleek style had been
a one-off act, or a persona that was still quite new to
her. The idea that she'd been trying to deceive him
– just as much as he had her – both aroused and

amused him. There was much entertainment ahead, he decided, his smile widening. For both of them.

Beneath his fingers his cock was like iron. Had she noticed it? he pondered. Had she seen it pushing at the fly of his jeans? He'd felt her studying him as they'd talked – at least as intently as he'd studied her. What would she have done if he'd calmly unzipped and taken himself in hand, as he wanted to do now. He rather thought she'd be alarmed at first, her blue eyes wide with outrage. After a moment though, her look would soften and grow smoky, and she'd move forward and touch him. Stroke his silky stiffness, then fall down gracefully to her knees and take it deep in her scarlet-painted mouth.

'Oh yes,' he whispered aloud, aware that he'd pushed himself too far in his fantasy to back out now, in reality. Relief was essential. He saw no reason to suffer further. Sighing, he unbuckled his belt, drew down his zip, and pushing down his snug-fitting underpants, drew his penis out into the open.

After a moment of simply enjoying the air on his flesh, he began to adjust his position for further comfort. The people who worked for him were aware of his sensual nature, and never disturbed him un-necessarily. He had all the total privacy he needed to masturbate to orgasm, here in his own library; yet the fact that it was broad daylight, and others were moving efficiently about their duties not far away, only added to the piquancy of the act.

Pushing both jeans and briefs down to his knees, he pressed his naked bottom to the leather, and felt its cool surface kiss his inner cheeks. He wriggled slightly, enjoying the smooth hide rubbing against his balls and the slow majestic wave of his heavily rampant cock. He didn't touch himself directly just yet though. He was free for the rest of the day, so time had no meaning. He could extend his pleasure as much as he wanted. Or as long as his body would allow.

Leaning back, closing his eyes, he saw Rosie Howard spread before him on a bed. On her bed, the one that was prepared for her upstairs at his behest. The sheets were crisp cotton in the deepest pink – as if he'd known, uncannily, what her chosen name would be – and her white body looked paler than ever against them. Her delicious white body that seemed to cry out in silence for his dark one.

Because she was new to him, he'd made her nude. Tantalising clothing would come later, to add spice once the first fine madness was gone. Now he needed to see her rounded, bulging breasts, see their very fullness pull them sideways. He needed to see her lush limbs, her soft belly. She wasn't what he considered overweight, not by a long shot, yet there was a delicate ampleness about her that suddenly almost drove him to violence. His fingers tingled, dying to grab at his penis, but he refrained – tempering his need momentarily with a picture of a different, but equally desirable woman.

'Forgive me, Celeste,' he murmured to his absent wife. He knew that his lust for Rosie Howard was no threat to the happiness of his marriage, but he felt bound to acknowledge Celeste anyway. He always did as he took a new woman. Always afforded his spouse one moment of his attention, even as he enjoyed other flesh. It seemed particularly significant now, because this almost Amazonian Rosie was so different.

Celeste, bless her beautiful heart, had the body of a goddess. Every line, every toned and splendid curve, was aesthetically perfect. When he was with her, possessing her, inside her, she satisfied him utterly; and yet sometimes, he knew, it was just *because* she was such a paragon of perfection that he had a yen for someone who was flawed.

Like voluptuous Rosie, whose body was so delightfully more than svelte. In his increasingly vivid fantasy, he loomed above her now, on her bed. He'd made her naked, but he wore a robe. A favourite of his, a short happi-coat in a fine, but vivid turquoise cotton lawn that looked good against his deeply olive skin.

Returning his attention to his 'prize', he felt a moment of mischief, then saw her wrists fastened to the shining brass bed-rails by soft silken cords. He chided himself for such an easy, chauvinistic ploy, but accepted his predilection. Right now, he felt dominant. He felt the need to gently and kindly master her – and with her hands tied, she was perfectly displayed for his whims.

Behind his eyelids, her squirming body entranced him. Her breasts swayed and her long thighs scissored, giving him momentary glimpses of her soft, pink quim. She was glistening, already needing him madly. She wasn't struggling to get away from him, she was struggling to entice him to her sex.

'No, no, no! You pretty young thing!' he said aloud, regaining control of his own hot dream. He'd known what he wanted the instant he'd set eyes on Rosie Howard, and he'd have it now. Even if it was only in his mind.

Moving his dream-self over her, he straddled her belly, supporting his weight on his strong, lean thighs. He imagined the caress of her smooth skin against his testicles, the tickling sensation as she wriggled beneath him. Her blue eyes were like midnight now – the intense deep colour of the very edge of space – and she was imploring him for something. For anything. Begging that he continue his pleasures so that she might soon attain hers.

With a soft triumphant growl, he cupped her large, firm breasts in his hands and created the channel he'd been longing for. Settling lower, he laid his penis in its velvety containment, holding her flesh around him, careful not to hurt her, but quite set on the sensations he wanted.

Even as he moved and slid, and quietly groaned, he could still admire the physical composition before him. Rosie's pretty blushing face and her long wheat-coloured hair spread out across the pillow. Her white teeth snagging at her moist lower lip. Her pale, plump breasts distorted by his grip, his own long, darkly-livid cock, shining with pre-come, slipping and thrusting in its niche.

He'd wanted this to last, he'd planned for so much more; but suddenly, in the real world, his stimulated loins betrayed him. Barely aware of his actions, he'd been pumping his cock like a madman, and now, crying out, he felt the familiar tell-tale fire come roaring like a train through his guts. As his hips lifted high above the leather, he cupped his glans in his palm to contain his copious spurts.

But his semen escaped him, forcing its way through his fingers, oozing across his wrist, and dripping down onto his thighs, his jeans and the chair as he writhed in his self-induced ecstasy.

'Thank you, Rosie Howard, thank you,' he gasped as he fell back, his cock deflated, at peace, and temporarily eased from its aching. 'But next time, we do it for real.'

3

The Wages of Success

'Oh God, I've really done it now!' said Rosie aloud as she settled the receiver in its cradle.

All through this odd, dreamy day, she'd had the comforting feeling that she could still change her mind, ring Julian Hadey and say 'thanks but no thanks'. But after hearing his suave, creamy voice just now on the phone, and realising how far things had progressed, it was obvious that a U-turn was impossible.

Strings had been pulled, wheels set in motion. There was no notice to work out because Julian had had a quiet word with someone on the library committee. He'd had a similar word with her landlord, it seemed, and she suspected that money had changed hands over that one; although Julian himself had refrained from mentioning anything so sordid.

All in all, her transition to his household would be both soon and trouble free. The only thing that remained for her to do was pack up her clothes and personal belongings. And even these would be collected by his chauffeur, when she herself was collected. Such luxury for a lowly librarian!

Hearing Julian's voice again had unnerved her. He sounded so close, so intimate; as if they'd known each other for ages, and been lovers for almost as long. How on earth was she going to cope with that on a day to day basis? It sounded as if he took an active interest in his library, and spent time amongst his books. How the devil would she be able to concentrate on her cataloguing with his gorgeous dark body in the room? He'd played havoc with her judgement today, and they'd only been together an hour or so!

She'd walked down the steps of 17 Amberlake Gardens with a cushion of air beneath her feet, on a massive high from getting the job so easily and meeting a man, a truly sensual man who made no bones about finding her attractive.

His eyes, his voice, his occasional feather-light touches. All these had told her what he'd felt, and shown an admiration that was neither patronising nor glib. Unlike Geoff, Julian Hadey didn't make her feel he was doing her any favours by ever so gently and elegantly leering at her.

Yes, she'd really done it now.

The intoxication of the interview had spilled over into the rest of the day too. Rosie was usually quite a thrifty person, but half way along the Gardens, she'd hailed a cab and had herself transported to the West End – and the shops. For some reason best known to himself, Julian had assured her that a sum of money in advance of wages would be paid into her bank account. To cover her moving expenses, had been his explanation, but Rosie was dubious. It was as if he'd anticipated her qualms, and was trying to sweeten the pot even more to make sure she took his job.

She'd had precious few qualms in Bond Street though. And none in South Molton Street or the Burlington Arcade either. Buoyed up by success, and the lingering scent of her new employer's cologne, she'd spent and splurged in shops she'd never been in before, and flashed her plastic in fine style on the strength of his generous cheque.

It had started fairly innocently. She'd made her first purchase solely to get a carrier bag to put Julian's books in. They were so obviously treasured collector's items, and she didn't want to drop them or have them snatched. Treating herself had felt so satisfying though, and the prospect of using the scented body lotion she'd bought was so wicked and self-pampering that one thing had led to another. And another and another and another in a long, delicious orgy of unaccustomed and liberating spending.

Clothes, perfume, accessories. All sorts of notional knick-knacks. She was starting a new life, so she needed all the trappings of one. Julian had seen her in her one and only 'power' outfit, but she had no intention of disappointing him on Day One of the job by going back to her library mouse ways. He'd said she was perfectly at liberty to dress as casually as she liked while she was working; but there was casual, and there was casual. Whilst ever she was around Mister Hadey and his outrageous and indecent books, she decided she was going to look the part. Or at least as much the part as years of conditioning would allow.

But that didn't account for the lingerie, did it?

In a small, specialist shop she wouldn't have dreamed of entering a week ago, Rosie's groaning credit card had taken its hardest hammering of all. Pretty, curvy under-wired bras had, naturally, to be worn with cobweb-fine matching panties. And that meant, automatically, a matching suspender belt for each set, and a few dozen pairs of sheer stockings. And with it being almost summer now, and the weather delightfully warm, some broderie anglaise camisoles with French knickers to match seemed like a good idea too. Thinking of such soft, unstructured fripperies, Rosie blessed all the toning exercises she'd always persevered with. Her bosom was big, admittedly, but it was also perfectly firm. She could easily get away without a bra.

And the nightwear had been out of this world. Touching the slinky, strappy creation she was wearing now, she thought of several other similar beauties that were still nestled in their tissue paper wrapping. Just waiting to be worn for her dark and dangerous Julian.

'Rosalind Howard! You bloody idiot!' she hissed at herself. It was one thing daydreaming about going to bed with your employer, but buying lingerie on the strength of it? Good grief, by all accounts the man was happily married anyway. If Julian Hadey had a wife as beautiful as the woman in the portrait in his drawing room, he was hardly likely to dally with his fat Yorkshire librarian, was he?

But as she looked at herself in the mirror now, she started to wonder. She wasn't fat. She wasn't even chubby really. It was only Geoff and his cruelly svelte friends that had made her *think* she was.

The woman who stood before her was attractive. Pretty even. She was most definitely sexy. Her body looked tempting and voluptuous in a deep rose-pink nightdress that clung lovingly to her firm, high breasts; and though her hips were generous, at least her waist was small, and her legs long and shapely. Drawing her fingers across her belly, then her midriff, then her bosom, Rosie started to smile.

'You look damn good, kid,' she told herself huskily, then reached for her celebration glass of wine and made a toast. 'To new beginnings, Rosie Howard! No surrender and no way back!'

The wine was sweet and cheerful: Asti Spumante, her rather unsophisticated favourite. Alcohol always made her randy, she acknowledged, drinking deeply; and tonight was no exception. For a moment, she felt a sad, masochistic yearning for Geoff. Then she remembered her toast, and her hopes, and banished him severely from her mind. The only way now was forward: towards a man named Julian Hadey.

A man who was truly the stuff of fantasy.

Topping up her glass, and giggling at how much of the wine she'd drunk, she sat down on the squashy old sofa in her flat and thought of the luxurious surroundings and superior furniture she'd soon be living with. She imagined the room that awaited her, and taking a few liberties, made it an exotic eastern boudoir – the ideal setting in which to wait for an exotic eastern lover. For Julian, who'd revealed in the course of their conversation that he'd had a Sudanese grandmother; a princess no less, stolen away in her childhood and saved from arranged marriage and a life of domestic repression.

Closing her eyes, she imagined that she too had been stolen away. Rescued from tedious servitude at the Reader's Enquiry Desk, by Sheik Julian of Arabian Wonderland. She took another sip of her wine, put the glass aside, then dimmed the light, lay down and closed her eyes.

'I await you, my Lord,' she whispered, grinning at her own fancifulness as she arranged her arms and legs in what she imagined was an odalisque's pose. It was all very silly, she told herself, but suddenly, it was exhilarating too.

He'd look fabulous in a djellabah, she thought, trying to imagine the picture. Julian, in a long, snow white robe, with its neckline slashed to show his muscular brown chest and the curls of his crisp, dark body hair. It was a sublime image, and sinfully easy to embellish. Julian's romantic looks were clear and seductive in her mind, and his aura so powerful and male it seemed to sweep out across the city and engulf her.

It would be a thin robe too, she decided, mentally sketching in the silhouette of his hips and torso, and the hazy, but threatening shadow at the juncture of his long tawny thighs. He'd be erect already, his sex alive with his craving to possess her.

This is such tosh! said the cynic inside her; while the woman who was hungry for sex and magic and mystery said 'More! More! More!'

He was beside her now, his hand gently cruising her body. Sighing, she created the touch herself, placing her hands on her thighs and sliding the ruby coloured silk across her skin. It was a subtle caress, a gentle, courteous caress, but she knew it was correct. Julian would be a skilled lover, a considerate lover, building his mate's pleasure slowly, knowing in the final analysis that the better she felt, the better he'd feel himself.

The lighting in her dream was low and evocative, but even so she could clearly see his face above her; his eyes smouldering, his lips infinitesimally curved, his expression intense and thoughtful as if he were selecting exactly the move that would please her. She could smell his minty breath on her face, and both within and around that, a heady, dizzying perfume, the scent of his body, a body steeped in flowers and spices and musk. Her waking mind knew this was the expensive new fragrance she'd wallowed in, smoothed on – and generally gone over the top with – but her fantasy transferred it to him. He was a man who loved luxury and sensual refinement; when he came to a woman with love on his mind, he'd have perfumed his hair, his skin, his armpits, his every last hollow and niche.

In the fantasy, he kissed her, for the first time, his warm lips meltingly soft. It was exactly how she wanted it. A slow, gradually building experience; no hard-plunging tongue, no jaw-cracking force. Her dream-lips opened of their own accord, tempting him in, luring him, hinting at the parallel entering he'd enjoy in the heat between her legs.

But in this leisurely, fragrant dreamscape, there was still a long way to go. A whole night of simmering pleasure before the moment of ultimate joining.

Writhing involuntarily on her elderly and ordinary

couch, Rosie sank deeper into a new and extraordinary dream. As she eased up the full skirt of her nightdress, Julian, miraculously, was nude in her mind. How easy it all was when you didn't have to struggle with clothing.

His body was strong and sturdy; lean, but almost buzzing with power. His penis was large, long and purple-tipped. She wondered for a second whether he'd be circumcised. In this dream he was supposed to be a sheik, so he was most likely Moslem. Did that mean he'd be cut? Not certain, and for purposes of now, not really worrying too much, she decided that he had been shorn of his foreskin, and that his glans was a neat round bulb, fat and shining and already running with liquid.

As she observed the sheen of his juices, she became keenly aware of her own, and the way her labia slid against each other as she moved uneasily on the couch. She felt swollen and puffed between her legs, all her intimate feminine flesh in a tingling state of readiness.

Unlike Geoff, her dreamy idealised Julian did not taunt her with his body. He didn't tease and make her wait and struggle and plead. Instead, he gently eased down the top of her gown and began kissing her breasts and licking them. His tongue was faintly rough, like a cat's, and its gossamer friction was heavenly. As he moistened her skin and caressed her, she felt a hot need stir in her sex. She moaned in her throat as long fingers stole between her labia: light as feathers yet deadly and accurate in their search. Within seconds the sweetest spot, her unsheathed clitoris, was being manipulated with fabulous delicacy.

He wasn't rough. He wasn't too fast. And neither was he too slow. His fingertip swirled on her flesh in a rhythm that was almost celestial, a clever little circular beat that synchronised sweetly with his tongue, as it slid round and round on her breast.

In the real world, Rosie was performing her own manipulations. Two fingers of one hand running rings around a nipple, while a singleton, from the other, palpated her aching clitoris.

She'd never been much of a one for masturbation until now, but suddenly she'd found a rare and special skill. It was as if Julian, or some powerful fantasy djinni, had taken control of her swiftly moving fingers and was guiding her surely to orgasm. She felt the loveliest of tensions building. A huge need to come, swelling in her quim like a crystal balloon that quivered on the edge of bursting.

Then it did burst, and she cried out hoarsely, her loins aflame, her heels drumming wildly on the sofa.

'Julian Hadey, you bastard! You bastard!' she shouted, more in thanks than in insult as his dark presence slowly faded.

Was he really like that? she wondered, waiting for her heartbeat and breathing to steady. Was he really so courteous, so kind and so deliciously and erotically magnanimous? Somehow she didn't think so. A man as handsome, successful and confident as Julian was far more likely to be a patronising chauvinist like Geoff.

There was no harm in dreaming, though, was there? Dreaming of being wooed, not exploited. Pleasured to extremes, not used.

But the problem was, it had to *remain* a dream. Anything else and she could wave goodbye to her job. It was going to be difficult, very difficult. She couldn't avoid Julian while she lived in his house – and if she couldn't avoid him, what chance did she stand of resisting him?

On her first morning, however, resistance had been easy. There was nobody there to resist!

When she'd settled in and gotten over how luxurious her room was, she couldn't even find her employer, much less succumb to a seduction. The staff of the house were helpful, and thankfully, very friendly, but apart from them no-one else was home. Mrs Hadey – or Mrs Brent-Hadey, as Rosie discovered she preferred to be called – was in Paris for a few days with her cousin, and Julian himself was at a business conference and not expected home until late.

It was both a relief and a disappointment. A chance for Rosie to find her way round at her own speed, yet a huge anti-climax too.

Face it, Howard, she admonished herself, you actually wanted him to try something on. You wanted everything in one day. Mousy librarian to adorable, irresistible seductress with no stops on the way. You idiot, you're just dying to give in to him!

'You should write all this down, Rosie,' she murmured wryly as she entered the deserted library. The fantasies she'd been having for the last few nights were as steamy as anything in the private case, she was sure. And some of them had even taken place right here, in this sunlit, leather-scented room. It was easy to believe she'd been taken on the opulent chesterfield, or been molested like a she-bitch on heat on the priceless Aubusson carpet.

And it wasn't only in the library. She was also starting to believe she'd had sex in a perfumed Arab tent, on a slatted wooden bench in a steam room, and in the back of a black limousine. She was going to have to disabuse herself of these rare notions soon though, she decided – or Mister Julian Hadey was going to get some awfully strange reactions from the newest member of his staff.

Looking around, she let the serenity of the books make her feel calm, like 'Rosie the Sensible Librarian' again.

It was such a beautiful room, and the contents of its shelves were priceless. It was hard to believe that this was only half of the collection, she reflected, studying the tall ranks of books. There was another hoard – at least the equal of this – stored at Julian's house in Norfolk. It was part of her job to catalogue that too. In situ.

Standing in the corner of the room, caught in a shaft of filtered sunlight, was an item Rosie hadn't noticed on her last visit: a black and gold lacquered chinoiserie screen. Curious, she walked across and looked behind it, only to smile and sigh with relief.

On a fine Regency library table was a device without which her labours would be decidedly tedious; a state of the art and obviously brand-new computer terminal, complete with printer and modem. She'd been wondering how she was going to create an integrated catalogue for the two libraries – and now she knew.

Here was the modern technology she needed, masked by an antique object of beauty; just as the darkest realms of sleazy perversion were hidden amongst this treasured wealth of learning.

Reminded of perversion, she glanced down at the books she was returning, the three choice volumes that Julian had already lent her. She'd expected them to be a spicy read, but what lay between these tooled leather covers was a domain of total eroticism. A world that was dark, bizarre and extreme. A realm of pain and its transformation into exquisite, unimaginable pleasures. A lifestyle that was entirely unlike Rosie's; yet which had some disturbingly familiar facets.

A disillusioned heroine who sought an escape from oppressive mediocrity. A woman in search of purpose, understanding and control. A woman going through changes. Like herself, after the débâcle of Geoff.

But in the novels those answers were only to be found in the world of fetishistic spanking. In exotic clothing; in whipping and beating. Stroking the strangely warm covers, Rosie wondered if their contents were a pure fabrication, conjured from the air; or some wild and deviant reality with which her old, dull life had never intersected. She couldn't see herself finding salvation in the rod – she found pain to be just that, pain – but even so the cleverly paced prose had stirred her. Her body had physically roused as she'd read: her sex had engorged and moistened, her nipples had swollen, and her pale throat had turned pink with the blood of excitement.

As she returned the books to their places – the private cases were unlocked now – she imagined

the man who owned them enacting their principal
scenarios. She imagined Julian spanking her, right here
in the library.

He had that air about him of knowing everything,
having done it all, and being adept. He'd take hold
of her with strength, bend her bare-bottomed over
his knee. He'd inflict pain with his hand, then soothe
it, stroking her pale, shuddering body. For stimulation,
there'd be nothing to choose between the two.

Rosie knew she shouldn't be thinking such thoughts.
Fantasy was therapeutic and harmless, and the more
she indulged in it, the better she liked it. But she was
astounded that she dreamed of being dominated. It
ran counter to her new internal politics, her vow not
to be done down by men.

But no matter how incorrect they seemed to her,
she still saw her wild, sexy visions. A spanking from
Julian would demean her, yes, but in a sense it would
also uplift her. Her new boss wasn't Geoff; he was a
giver not a taker. He was a teacher and a tutor, not
a person who mocked her and subtly sneered.

Oh my, this is all very heavy, thought Rosie, lining
up the books with their neighbours and giving herself
a strong mental shake. Julian Hadey was her employer.
He'd flirted with her – extremely lightly – whilst
interviewing her, and here she was now, considering
kinky sex with him. It was absurd! Especially with his
wife due home from France tomorrow.

And that was another thing, she thought, switching
on the computer and finding, to her relief, a familiar
operating system. Celeste was bringing this 'David'
with her – the cousin that Julian had mentioned so

pointedly. Rosie had a strong suspicion that being company for the lad was as good as on her job description. Julian had stressed repeatedly how helpful David would be. Apparently the boy was both an avid reader and an intellectual – albeit a more or less self-taught one – and he was also strong enough to hump books around when the library was assembled in its elegant new sequence.

Rosie was still dubious though. Goddamnit, the kid was supposed to have just had a nervous breakdown! He was hardly likely to be a scintillating conversationalist!

Almost immediately, she felt ashamed. She'd learnt hard lessons herself about being an outsider – most of them from Geoff – so she owed it to the boy to be nice to him. Keep him busy with interesting jobs; bring him out of himself; let him know she understood his problems.

She was still worried though. Julian had described his cousin-by-marriage as a shy young thing – and Rosie only hoped for both their sakes that this didn't equate with nerd, wimp or stuttering, anoracked oddball.

'Okay, Howard, let's get organised,' she told herself sternly, opening a file, 'and we'll worry about David when we meet him, shall we?'

Day one in the library passed quickly. Rosie soon found her way around the computer, and in the notepad, found that her helpful-as-well-as-handsome employer had left the electronic address of a well-known software house, plus *carte blanche* to order whatever she needed. Such largesse was intoxicating after the privations of local government budgeting, and by the time Rosie logged off at five o'clock, she'd spent several hundred pounds of Julian's money!

Of the man himself, there was still no sign; just a message passed on by his housekeeper, Mrs Russell, when she brought in Rosie's afternoon tea. Mister Hadey had phoned, he'd be late, but he'd try and make it home for dinner. Rosie, however, was not to wait. He didn't want his librarian going hungry on her very first night in his house.

Hungry for what? mused Rosie as she made her way slowly to her room. Dinner wasn't until eight and she felt quite weary. She'd barely left the library all day, apart from a stroll in the garden at lunchtime, but she must have been up and down that step-ladder at least a hundred times. Her thighs and shoulders were aching, and her eyes were tired from poring over small print and the monitor. A short rest, to recharge her batteries, was what she needed; followed by a long, hot bath. But it was worth being tired, just to enjoy such a luxury.

Just over a week ago, she would have had an irritating stop-start bus journey after work, followed by a trudge round the local supermarket, and then more aggravation while she waited for an ancient immersion heater to heat up six inches of water.

Here, everything was done for her: laundry, meals, even the meticulous tidying of her room, which looked, incidentally, more like a courtesan's boudoir than staff quarters. Just to add icing to the cake, Mrs Russell had promised to pop up with a relaxing glass of sherry whilst Rosie was dressing for dinner.

This is the life! she thought dreamily as – having decided to bathe first, then rest – she sank into rose-scented water. She'd brought all her own cosmetics and toiletries with her, but the row of exotic looking potions in her private bathroom had been far too tempting to resist. Half-dizzy from sniffing most of them, she'd chosen Cosmetics to Go's 'Rose-tinted Spectacle'. 'Roses for a rose,' she'd whispered as she'd sloshed it in, aware of a certain irony, but too content at that moment to fret.

As she lay in the water, she let her hands move lightly on her body. She felt extraordinarily relaxed and sensual, and put it down to the sumptuous comfort of her setting. She considered indulging in her favourite new pleasure, masturbation, but couldn't seem to summon the energy. Just lying in the water was erotic enough for the moment. Her body was suffused with a delicate low-key excitement; a kind of soft, vague arousal that was so nice a state to be in that it simply didn't need changing.

The water cooled. She topped it up. It cooled again. Time seemed to melt and flow.

Finally, almost purring with self-indulgence, she hauled herself out of the bath, dried herself with leisurely thoroughness and moisturised both her face and her body. Letting her hair down from its knot, she wandered naked into her bedroom and noticed, by the small ormolu clock on her mantlepiece, that there was still a good hour to kill before dinner was served.

Outside, the edge of summer twilight was falling, but during the day, the sun had shone strongly into the room and warmed it. Cautiously ascertaining that she couldn't be seen, Rosie opened a window, drew the curtains, then lay down on the bed, still nude. It seemed distinctly decadent to be lolling around in the buff all of a sudden, but this was a new life, she reminded herself as a trance-like drowsiness overwhelmed her.

It's a new world, she thought, drifting. A new freedom. I can do anything now. Any damn thing I want.

She awoke with a furious start, aware of a presence in the room even before she'd opened her eyes. For a micro-second she reassured herself it was Mrs Russell with her sherry; then every nerve-end in her body started dancing and every instinct in her brain screamed danger.

'Sherry?' enquired a voice so silky and amused she seemed to feel it poured across her skin. With her eyes still tightly shut, she recognised a certain inevitability. This scenario had been in her mind from the very first moment she'd met her visitor; she just hadn't imagined it happening so soon. Intensely aware of her naked breasts and the soft patch of hair between her legs, she sat up and faced him.

'Yes, I'd love some!' It came out sounding almost blasé, but the heat in Julian's eyes made her quiver.

The way he was sitting on the edge of her bed, shirt-sleeved and tieless, seemed to suggest that the first thing he'd done on getting home was rush up here with *her* sherry. There were two glasses on a silver tray on her bedside table and as she answered, he took the one with darker, sweeter contents and handed it to her.

He was testing her; that was obvious. There was purpose in his look; a slow, assessing scrutiny, as well as just plain old desire. It was almost as if he were waiting for her to lose her cool and cover herself.

'You don't mind this, do you?' he enquired with a smile, leaving it to her to deduce that 'this' referred to her nakedness.

'Er . . . No! Not really,' she answered cautiously, shifting her position on the bed then cringing within as her breasts swayed visibly. She took a deep sip from her glass and found the rich warm flavour revivifying. She'd been naked for a man before, but never so casually, or in a strange way, so comfortably. It was weird, but as she thought back to his question, it dawned on her that in her heart she *didn't* mind. At all. Julian was studying her bare body closely, but his luminous brown eyes weren't a threat.

There was no criticism in his look either. A fact which made Rosie's spirits soar giddily, and her confidence with them. Her lushness – her full, firm shape – seemed to please him not disgust him. There was none of the implied criticism she'd always sensed in Geoff: the unspoken but ever-present suggestion that she diet.

'Good!' he said crisply after a long long pause, 'because we tend to have a fairly relaxed attitude to nudity in this house.' He paused and sipped his own paler, clearly dryer sherry. 'A relaxed attitude to everything really.'

What was he telling her? That he expected sex? That his wife wouldn't mind?

'What's that supposed to mean?' she enquired,

astounded at her own leading question. She took a last long hit of her sherry, then hurtled on. 'That sex is part of the job?'

Julian laughed and laughed, putting aside his sherry glass and reaching for her hand. 'No, Rosie, having sex with me isn't a part of your duties. Although if you want it, I'd be delighted to oblige.' He drew her fingers to his lips and kissed them lightly, his tongue flicking out at the very last second to tease her skin with its moisture. 'Just let me unwind. Have a shower . . . then we'll eat. And after that, who knows?'

'I didn't mean that,' she said quickly, snatching back her hand and fighting the urge to retreat, to drag the sheet over her body and cover herself. She'd just made the most enormous gaffe. She'd boldly gone and opened her mouth, and in a backwards about way, almost offered herself.

'Pity,' murmured Julian, reaching out again, and trailing the back of his hand against her breast. 'You're a beautiful woman, Rosie. I'd enjoy making love to you.' With a flip of his wrist, his fingers were pad-down against her skin, his hand curving slightly to cup her, his thumb settling neatly on her nipple.

To Rosie's horror, her nipple erected instantly, and seemed to burn. He was simply holding, not caressing her, but the contact was electric. Clenching her own hands into fists, she fought an almost unbearable yearning to sway into his grip, and moan out aloud with desire.

Julian said nothing more, but just regarded her steadily, his hand warm and still on her breast. Rosie felt blood pulsing wildly through her body, making her skin turn pink and her sex start to quiver and engorge. It was terrible. In the space of a few seconds, she wanted him desperately. She imagined his lips on her skin, as well as his fingers, then his cock sliding slowly into her softness.

'Damn! This is unfair of me, isn't it?' he said suddenly, then before she could stop him, or protest, he leaned over and kissed her breast – exactly where his fingers had been.

This time, Rosie couldn't contain herself. She leaned towards him, almost presenting him with the curve. But Julian withdrew.

'I'm moving too fast.' He was on his feet now, smiling almost shamefacedly. 'There's something we've got to discuss first.'

'What something?' Rosie demanded. She was angry now, furious with her own arousal, furious that she'd revealed it and furious with Julian for rejecting what she'd offered.

'A proposition,' he said evasively, moving away from her. 'Something you could help with. But I won't go into it now. It'll wait 'til after dinner.'

Before she could dispute this, he was gone, and the room felt empty without him.

Rosie's thoughts whirled. Proposition? What proposition? He'd said he didn't expect sex, but he'd clearly wanted it. Was that what they had to discuss? The ground-rules for a clandestine affair?

The idea appalled but thrilled her, and she turned it over and over as she envisioned herself locked in Julian's arms. His after-image was strong in her mind, and it was easy to imagine his body. And how he'd use it. She could smell his cologne too, his insidious man-smell. And see that dark skin, those smouldering eyes, and that broad shouldered, slim-hipped male body.

She really didn't want to say no.

Dinner was delightful, but uncomfortable. Delightful in that the food was superb – a light meal, skilfully prepared from the finest ingredients. Uncomfortable in that the company was even more tempting.

Julian made no reference to the scene in her bedroom, although his look when she entered the dining room was patently admiring. She'd chosen a soft, cotton jersey dress in a deep shade of blue; a flattering thing that embraced her full breasts closely yet flared out from the waist into a full circular skirt. The neckline was low but not plunging, and to lengthen the line of her neck, she'd put up her hair in a cleverly coiled twist and left a few tendrils dangling alluringly so it wouldn't look too workaday. She'd considered dressing safely, but had abandoned the idea. Caution seemed pointless at this stage; she just prayed she could carry off the image.

It wasn't too difficult, though, because Julian's presence felt strangely unthreatening. He complimented her, but with no salacious overtones. He touched her as he guided her to her seat; and though Rosie trembled slightly, he didn't capitalise on it. Instead, he seemed intent on putting her at her ease: discussing his books and enquiring on her progress in the library. It was all territory she knew, and she guessed he'd chosen it deliberately. To put off the proposition.

But Rosie couldn't put it off, at least not in her mind. All through dressing and making-up, she'd mulled it over. She kept coming to the same conclusion. The proposition was sex – as a novelty for him, perhaps? A change from his beautiful wife.

And she was still battling with what her answer might be. Still fighting the urge to succumb.

When he'd left her room, Julian had left her unsatisfied. He'd touched her, with both his fingers and his glamorous male aura, then abandoned her. Her libido had been primed and made ready. Her juices had flowed shamingly, and were still flowing. Her breasts ached, her vulva felt heavy, and her whole body felt twitchy and restless. She was bathed and perfumed and deodorised, yet she still felt like a bitch on heat, surrounded by odours and pheromones.

Could Julian be aware of all this? Rosie took another sip of wine, and studied him covertly.

He looked gorgeous, but that was obviously normal for him. He was dressed elegantly yet casually, in chinos with a darker-coloured polo-neck sweater in just the same chocolate brown as his eyes.

Oh God, he's just edible! she thought, then blushed. She saw herself eating this edible man; kneeling between his legs, sucking obediently on his penis as he stroked her face, her hair and her throat.

'Are you alright?' Julian's soft voice brought Rosie rudely back to reality.

'Yes, I'm fine. Just a bit warm.' She fanned herself with her napkin in an attempt to distract him. She felt so visibly ready for sex that there was no way his sharp eyes could miss it.

'Yes, it's a lovely evening,' he answered easily. 'I'd offer to take you for a walk in the moonlight, but I'm afraid I've some paperwork to attend to.'

Rosie was flabbergasted. What about the proposition? What had happened to the man who was going too fast? Wasn't he interested any more?

'Oh,' she said, keeping her voice bland and trying to suppress her confusion.

'Don't worry, sweet Rosie. We'll get our chat.' A long, brown hand snaked out across the tablecloth and took hold of her pale, tensed fingers. 'And believe me . . . You won't be disappointed.'

4

The Proposition

Beast! thought Rosie later, as she lay on her bed still waiting, and still fuming.

Sitting up, she looked across at the ormolu clock. It was just after midnight and there was still no sign of Julian. Rosie couldn't bear the edgy sensations that consumed her. She got out of bed and went to the window, letting the moonlit calm soothe her soul.

The whole situation was mad. She'd applied for a job to get over one man, and was now hung up about another. How stupid could you get?

And yet she knew that if Julian did disappoint her, it wouldn't be quite in the way that Geoff had. In spite of his arrogant, intimate touch, right here in this room, there was still something detached about Julian, something that would always belong elsewhere. He loved his wife, she presumed. His beautiful, sexy wife. Celeste's portrait was breathtaking; she was one of the most genuinely lovely women Rosie had ever seen. And one of the slimmest, she thought, gritting her teeth with envy.

Thoroughly unsettled, she returned to her bed, but as she did so, she noticed that the drawer in the bedside table was open very slightly. She'd put a box of tissues in there earlier, and distinctly remembered pushing it closed.

Flipping on the bedside light, she pulled open the drawer, then caught her breath. Someone had left her a present.

There, tucked innocuously in her tissue box, was a red plastic vibrator, and beside it a tiny glass pot containing a clear gel-like substance that looked suspiciously like lubricant. Rosie hardly dare reach in and touch either, but curiosity overcame her.

The vibrator was a surprisingly substantial little toy, and to her untutored eye, seemed well constructed. She'd seen pictures of such things in magazines, and though she'd never plucked up the nerve to send for one, she'd often wondered if she ought to – so she could think of herself as liberated.

So, Howard, you wanted to try a vibrator? Well, now's your chance. Courtesy of Mister Julian Hadey, one presumes, she observed wryly. Had he suspected his paperwork was going to over-run and left this rude approximation of his penis to keep her occupied? He could easily have secreted it here while she'd been drinking coffee in the library.

Hefting the slim plastic cylinder in her hand, she couldn't bring herself to turn it on.

'Come on, it won't bite!' she muttered, then twisted the bevelled end in her fingers until the small device started to purr. She wasn't quite sure what was normal for such things, but the vibrations were smooth and consistent, and instinct told her that this was a Rolls Royce amongst love toys. She twirled the control around a bit, experimenting with different speeds, while her conscious mind avoided the issue.

Was she going to try it?

She imagined Julian lying in his bed right now – or maybe still sitting at his desk – and picturing her with this lewd red monster inside her.

To ignore it would be to resist him; but on the other hand, did she want to resist him? Even now, when he was so clearly playing games? Almost breathless with trepidation, she decided to try his gift.

But how did one go about it? Uncertain, she lay back on the bed and spun the toy's bevelled end again. It buzzed cheerfully, and she pulled up the pink silk skirt of her nightdress, then slowly, very slowly lowered the finely trembling plastic to her sex.

The intensity of sensation made her squeal aloud. The vibrator's smooth, pristine tip seemed to shoot pure lightning through her innards as she pressed it unwarily to her clitoris.

'Oh God! Oh God!' she groaned, her frustrated body orgasming hugely under its first electronic kiss. She jerked her hips, she couldn't help it, then scrabbled frantically between her legs, desperate not to lose contact with her toy. Her vagina pulsed and squelched like a wet, marine mouth, and her juices were so copious she could actually hear the sound of her climax.

Instantly addicted, she soared again and again and again. She was just going for her fifth brilliant orgasm when a knock at the door broke the spell.

Julian! The bastard! He must have been planning to catch her all along.

This time, mercifully, he didn't walk straight in, and Rosie had time to stuff the vibrator back in its hiding place and shut the drawer on the evidence of her sins. She wondered, frantically, how thick the door was, and how long Julian had been just outside. The vibrator was far from silent; what if he'd been listening for it, purposefully?

Still panting slightly, she went to the door, glancing down at her body as she did so. A hot, rosy flush was making her chest almost the same colour as her gown, and when she looked in the mirror, she saw the same pink blotches across her throat and cheeks: lurid and impossible to hide.

'I didn't mean to be this late,' said Julian as she let him in and felt his eyes dart quickly over her. He was noting her pinkness, she just knew it. The blush felt so intense to her that she could almost imagine him feeling it too, before he'd even touched her. His gaze was molten in the dim, shaded light, cruising her breasts unashamedly through the thin, shiny satin of her gown.

Rosie herself had plenty to look at. Julian's short, cotton happi-coat was a brilliant, singing turquoise, and open to the waist showing chest-hair rampant, just as she'd imagined. Beneath its mid-thigh hem his muscular legs were bare. As were his feet.

Nervous, Rosie backed away from him, retreating to the bed and sitting down abruptly on its edge.

'Still warm, Rosie?' he enquired, settling himself elegantly beside her and reaching out to touch her glowing, reddened throat. She felt sweat beads start to form at her brow, beneath her arms, and in the creases of her groin. Why on earth did she feel so hot, when Julian – goddamn him – looked so cool?

'Yes, a little,' she answered, wanting to pull away, but pinned by the delicate caress of a fingertip that slid slowly down towards her breast. She hardly dare breathe, for fear it slide beneath her lacy bodice, touch her nipple, and sample its puckered hardness. Controlling her quivering, she looked him boldly in the eye. 'What is it you want from me, Julian? What's the proposition? An affair? Casual sex? My fair, fat body in return for that fabulous salary you're paying me?'

'Fair, but not fat,' he whispered, flipping down the thin silk ribbon of her shoulder strap, then exposing a single breast. Cupping the milky-pale orb, he held it for a moment, staring as if mesmerised at the arrangement of brown on white. As he squeezed slightly, and Rosie gasped, he looked up again, his eyes heavy-lidded, almost sleepy. 'It is sex I want you for, Rosie. But not casual. And not – primarily – for me.'

'What do you mean?' she asked, her voice wavering as a light clicked on in her mind. She didn't need an answer. She wasn't slow or stupid. The hints had been there almost since the beginning.

'It's your cousin, isn't it? You want me for this precious David of yours.'

'He's my wife's cousin,' he corrected, smiling. 'And yes, I do want you to have sex with David.'

'You're insane!' she cried, shuddering as his thumb

moved slowly on her nipple. 'That's outrageous! I'm a librarian, not a prostitute.'

'You're a gentle, beautiful girl, and David is an innocent young man who needs you.' The thumb flicked, then was joined, in a delicate pincer, by his forefinger. 'You'll be perfect for him. Sensual but not intimidating. Experienced but not jaded.'

'But I'm not experienced,' she blurted out, wriggling as he pulled, gently. 'At least, not very.'

From very close, Julian eyed her, his expression full of knowledge. 'It doesn't matter, Rosie,' he said kindly, touching her face with his free hand. 'In this case, the tutor doesn't have to be too learned. Too much technique would be frightening. The two of you can learn together.'

'But –'

'And you do have the experience that David needs.' He paused, slid his hand around the back of her head, and kissed her once on the mouth. 'You've been hurt recently . . . so you won't hurt him.'

How does he know? she thought as his lips returned to hers. She felt his strong, mobile tongue prise her open like a clam, then the kiss began in earnest. While he tasted and explored and sucked her, his fingers palpated her breast, squeezing gently and circling the flesh.

'Quite lovely,' he whispered, releasing both mouth and breast, only to tweak away her other strap and let her bodice slither down to her waist. With his prize uncovered, he shuffled a little way back from her, his smile narrow and triumphant.

Rosie felt even her breasts blushing now, especially

the one he'd fondled. She remembered the portrait of Celeste, and how slim she was, how perfect and delicate her shape was.

'Not as lovely as your wife,' she said firmly, trying desperately to put him off-stride.

'Different, Rosie,' he replied, unfazed. 'Celeste has a magnificent body, but there're many different kinds of magnificent. And I suspect that David will like *your* kind.'

While Julian had been moving, his thin robe had been slipping, and as he reached towards her again – drawing her arms clear of the straps of her nightie – it seemed to slither like a wave and fall open, exposing his darkly-furred body.

Helpless, Rosie stared at his penis. It was risen and fully erect; a solid bar of ruby-toned flesh that reared up from his groin, its tip circumcised, just as she'd imagined.

When she lifted her eyes to his face, he was smiling again. Her fascination with his genitals seemed to amuse him and he made no attempt to hide either his feelings or his sex.

'See how you please me,' he said quietly, reaching for her hand and placing it on him. 'Think how you'll please David.'

'He mightn't like me,' she said shakily. His penis was hot and smooth and seemed to pulse in the palm of her hand. She felt a great urge to squeeze him as he'd squeezed her, to rub and caress him; to affect him as he'd affected her.

'He might think I'm too chubby!' she persisted, panicked into a simplistic objection.

'But you aren't,' he countered. He was really close now and their thighs were pressed together, his burning hers through the skirt of her gown. He put his arm around her shoulder and held her against him, his free hand settling on her belly, then beginning to snake beneath the bunched up silk at her waist.

'Your skin's so soft and your body's firm – a perfect combination.' His fingers continued to creep and search, creep and search, and she bit back a moan when he reached his ultimate target. 'And your sex is lush and wet. No man could resist you. I certainly can't.'

As if to validate his words, his cock leapt slightly in her hand, the tiny eye at its tip weeping slowly with a thin, clear moisture.

Julian's touch was gentle and clever. He nudged her clitoris to and fro in a delicate, measured rhythm that obliterated all thought and reason. It seemed like a year since she'd parted from Geoff, and her frustration was enormous. She'd made her own pleasure, and it'd been good, very good, but she'd missed being touched by a man.

'But what if I'm no good?' she whispered, still doubting, while at the same time cursing herself. 'What if I don't know enough to teach him?'

'Let me be the judge of that.' There was a smile in Julian's voice, a kind smile that he pressed against her neck, just under her ear. 'And if I find anything you need to know more about, I'll tutor you in it myself.' He kissed her neck, his mouth wet and hungry, his tongue sliding and darting with a beat that matched his deft fingering. 'Now, hush! And let me make love to you!'

Rosie hushed. Words were becoming difficult anyway as she succumbed to Julian's sure hands. She sighed as he eased her back onto the bed, still stroking her clitoris, but with his thumb now because his fingers – one, two, oh God, three! – were inside her. Trapped by the satin of her gown, his wrist was pressed tight to her belly, and she could feel his pulse against her skin, its thud thud, thud thud, fast but perfectly even. Somewhere in their manoeuvre, she'd lost her grip on his cock and she searched around blindly to retrieve it.

'Don't worry about that. You're what matters now,' he breathed in her ear as he rotated his tormenting thumb. Her hips lifting crazily, she scrabbled still, desperate to touch any part of him; desperate to touch his smooth, fragrant skin, and convince herself this was real and not some disturbed dream brought on by an unfamiliar bed.

But Julian was not a man to be shaken off easily. Even as Rosie squirmed and wriggled, her body falling deep and hard into orgasm, he held her close, turning her in his arms until they lay on the bed spoon-style, her back nestled up against his front.

Rosie cried out hoarsely, her flailing legs hampered by her skirt, her heels beating Julian's shins. Around his fingers, her vagina pumped steadily, sucking and grabbing and contracting as her clitoris throbbed beneath his thumb.

'Oh God! Oh yes!' she howled, pressing back with her bottom to caress him in return. He was good. He was kind. Outrageous but, in his own way, caring. She wanted him to have pleasure now too. He made a low, throaty sound and pushed against her, his juicy tip wetting her nightie.

'Do you want me, Rosie,' he asked, his dark voice gruff and broken; and for an instant, she remembered Geoff asking the same sort of question, his attitude gloating and confident. Julian Hadey did not sound like that. His questions were genuine, as if he honestly wanted to be welcomed.

'Yes,' she gasped, coming again as his thumb dove and swirled.

'Good!'

As he spoke, Rosie felt him pull away and withdraw his caressing fingers with a last, affectionate pat on the tip of her clitoris. She started to turn towards him, reaching for her gown to get rid of it, but he placed a hand on her shoulder and said, 'Stay still, sweet Rosie.'

Lying motionless on her side, she watched their shadows shifting on the wall while Julian wiggled her nightdress down over her hips and thighs, and then tossed it away across the bed. After that, he shook off his own flimsy robe, and laid himself down behind her, his body pressed to her back and his hard cock poking at her buttocks.

Trembling and sweating, she felt him rubbing himself up and down the groove. Bizarre ideas flashed insanely through her mind, followed by an even weirder sense of acceptance. She'd never given anything other than her vagina and her mouth to a man – even though Geoff had hinted and wheedled – but with Julian things could be different. And he had promised to teach her what she didn't know already.

She felt his moisture pooling warmly at her anus, and felt the smooth acorn-shape of his glans. Flexing her inner muscles, she tried to catch him and tempt him, but as she did so, he adjusted her position.

'Not tonight, gentle Rosie,' he whispered, rubbing his face in the silken mass of her hair and reaching down with his fingers to guide his own stiff flesh to its goal. 'It'd be a beautiful thing to do, but we're not ready.' As the tip of his penis found her, he made a little shuffling movement and lodged it there – then took a firm, assured hold on her hips and tilted her body to receive him.

'Relax . . . Relax . . .' he purred in her ear, his grip unyielding but careful. She felt him pushing, pushing, pushing, and her own tightness yielding with a slow, delicious ease. Then in one smooth glide he was inside her – not deeply, because of the angle – but touching all her zones of pleasure completely.

Rosie sighed contentedly. The position was comfortable, and comforting. She felt cherished, treasured – something she'd never felt once with Geoff – and the sensation was so novel and longed for that it was almost a climax in itself.

Almost.

Her vagina rippled nervously around Julian as he shifted their bodies against each other, adjusting the fit of their flesh so she could get the best from him, and he from her. His cock slipped out as she moved too, but his fingers moved quickly to reinstate it. He laughed softly and Rosie found herself joining in. He was laughing with her, not at her, and somehow that seemed strangely erotic. Entranced, she wriggled her back against his front, feeling the tickle of his wiry male hair as it rubbed against the skin of her bottom.

She was almost lying on him now, cradled in the curve of his body, her hips angled so their sexes could mesh together snugly. His arms came around her: one hand cupping a breast, while the other slid down between her thighs, seeking what he'd sought out before. Burrowing in her fleece, he found her clitoris with ease, then made her groan as he unsheathed it and pressed it. Without conscious thought, she put her fingers over his, guiding and encouraging them, as her other hand slid back, across his hip, and cupped his buttock.

'Lovely girl,' he whispered, his mouth seeking her ear through her thick, shiny hair as his fingers worked wonders down below. 'Your quim feels like heaven.'

Rosie had never heard that word spoken aloud, and it had a powerful effect on her. Her clitoris leapt and she had a small soft orgasm that made both of them gasp.

'God, you're wonderful,' he growled, bucking his hips and stabbing upwards into the white-burning heart of her. She was held tight against him, assaulted by splendid sensations from without and within, his cock pushing into her in short, hard thrusts, his fingertip dancing and rocking. She grunted, her voice uncontrolled and guttural, wishing she could kiss him on the mouth to thank him.

As quickly as he'd started moving, Julian stopped, holding his penis quite still inside her, at the deepest point of his stroke. She sensed him containing a mighty force – checking himself for her sake – and even as this registered through her rapture, she resolved to remember it. It was a wisdom, and it could be passed on. Taught to one less experienced.

Filled already, she accepted more of his bounty. His kisses on her neck, her ear, her jaw. His swirling fingers, ceaselessly pleasuring her clitoris. His pure animal warmth like a blanket of tenderness around her. Never in her short sexual life had Rosie had a lover so giving. Geoff had been grasping, a chauvinistic taker, and the very few others had been fumbling incompetents when set beside Julian.

What will David be like? she wondered suddenly, then moaned and forgot the boy completely as Julian and his magic claimed her body.

'Will you do it then?' a creamy voice murmured in her ear.

'Do what?' Rosie queried, her faculties blurred by sleep and sex. Bodyheat had been replaced by a thick, soft quilt that felt cool and fresh against skin that was sweaty and sticky. As she stirred, and bunched the covers around her ears, she sensed that the source of the voice was outside the bedclothes, that Julian was no longer lying beside her.

'Will you help him, Rosie?' he asked again, almost whispering. 'Will you teach David about sex?'

It seemed wild, peculiar, a request beyond her experience. Yet, she reasoned muzzily, isn't that just what I want? A wilder life, something different?

'Yeah, alright. I'll do it,' she mumbled into the pillow, her mind still drifting.

'Lovely girl, I knew you would.' Gentle lips kissed

her exposed temple and she caught a waft of a now familiar cologne, then felt the brush of an ever so slightly stubbled chin against her cheek. 'He's damned lucky, you know.'

She wanted to roll onto her back, pull him down to her, reach again for his penis. But something told her their interlude was over: that he had to leave her now. Even as she realised it, she realised too that the idea didn't bother her. She'd had him, it'd been wonderful, but now she must sleep. Alone.

'Sweet dreams, Rosie,' Julian whispered, placing one last kiss on her passion-mussed hair. 'Sleep well. It all begins tomorrow.'

The last thing she heard was the pad pad pad of bare feet moving away across her carpet.

'Lovely girl,' Julian murmured again, to himself, back in his room.

He'd received precisely the answer he'd wanted. The one he'd known he'd get. What surprised him was that Rosie was so much more than he'd hoped for. He'd expected an average performance from a pretty girl; but what he'd received was an orgasm of dazzling clarity and intense pleasure from a full, fresh and deliciously responsive body. Rosie had come alive to him the instant he'd touched her, her moans and writhings luxurious and unstifled.

He smiled. She'd called herself inexperienced, and her history – as he'd discovered from various sources – seemed to confirm that.

Yet, when they'd coupled, her reactions had been wholly positive. And in a strange way, quite sophisticated.

His penis twitched now as he thought of her hand closing over his, instinctively directing its movement. Once the dance of love had begun, Rosie Howard had chosen the steps. His and her own.

He knew he was right when he told her David was lucky. She herself was a jewel, a true rose; a hot, full-blooded flower who could reach into a young man's soul and bring his libido to life.

Suddenly Julian wanted to share his discovery, his elation. He wanted to tell Celeste that her worries for her cousin would soon be over; and as much as anything, he just wanted to hear her voice and let her share his delight in Rosie.

His bedside clock registered an unholy hour of the morning, but even so he picked up the phone and started dialling the number of a Paris hotel.

As he waited for the connection, he couldn't stop grinning. There was every likelihood that Celeste was occupied right now, indulging her voracious appetites just as he'd been satisfying his. He pictured her in their usual suite – her sleek thighs wide as some bell-boy or gigolo pounded and toiled between them. He saw a tight male bottom bouncing; heard Celeste's triumphant screams as her dark head tossed on the pillow, and her painted nails scratched and gouged at the back and buttocks of the convenient young man who was in her.

Or maybe it was a woman? His spouse had shown a marked interest in female lovers recently, mostly of the mild and submissive type. He imagined her riding some poor girl's head, mashing her sex against the tongue of a chit she'd enslaved with a single glance.

When a familiar, smoky voice said 'hello' at the other end of the line, he almost couldn't speak. His mouth was swimming with saliva and the imaginary taste of his wife's sweet nectar.

'I've tested her,' he said without further ado, reaching down to take hold of his penis. It was semi-hard and blushingly warm, still glowing with the heat of recent activities, yet already anticipating more.

'And?' prompted Celeste huskily, as if she'd spent the few hours since their last phone-call just waiting for a bulletin on his progress.

'She's ideal, my love, just right.' He heard Celeste gasp and wondered whether it was a response to his words, or to some other, unknown stimulus. He half-hoped it was both.

'Yes,' he went on, working himself firmly. 'She's definitely the one for David. And I'm quite excited by the fact,' he enunciated carefully.

The key word was 'excited' – his signal to Celeste that he was masturbating and that he'd like her to do the same. If she was at liberty to do so, that was. If there was no finger, tongue or penis already on the move in her service.

'Yes, I find it exciting too.'

His wife's voice had deepened now, fallen almost to a modulated groan. 'Most stirring,' she continued, indicating that she was indeed stroking herself. He tried to picture her, imagine what she was wearing. Celeste was not one for nakedness in bed, and even when she was set on a long night of sex, she would always wear something. He thought of the nightgowns he'd seen her packing. One in black silk-gauze with panels of filigree lace; another in forest green, a mini-nightshirt that barely covered her bottom; a bias-cut forties-style tube in heavy flesh-coloured satin.

As he pictured her in each of these outfits, his cock ached furiously. She'd know he was speculating; she'd be waiting for him to ask. To tell him herself what she was wearing would be giving in, and beautiful Celeste had a habit of always, always making him the supplicant.

'So, what did you do to her?' she asked, panting slightly.

Before Julian had a chance to reply, there was a subtle click which indicated 'hands-free' operation at the Parisian end of the line. Reaching out – one-handed – he pressed a button on his own machine, then returned the receiver to its cradle. For an instant, he released his cock and stripped off his robe. Unlike Celeste, he *did* want to be naked, so he could submit his bare body to her whims.

'I went to her room after midnight. She looked very flushed and warm. I think she'd been touching herself. Or using the vibrator I left her.'

'Oh Ju! You wicked man! Was it one of mine?' Julian smiled and returned his fingers to his penis. Would he be punished for misuse of her toys?

'Yes, a red one. I found it in your secretaire . . .'

'A good choice,' gurgled Celeste, her sexy voice suddenly rough – as if she too was using a vibrator. 'And what was she wearing when you went to her?'

This was a prompt, a tease. She knew he was still dying to know what *she* was wearing.

'A nightdress. Low cut, satiny, the colour of cherries.

It was very thin – I could see her nipples straight through it. And the hair between her legs.'

He could see it now – Rosie's soft, pale, fawnish fluff. Then the vision phased and the hair darkened to shiny ebony black – an elegant, heart shape – Celeste's precious, perfectly-clipped motte.

'Are you thinking of her now? Her body? How she felt when you took her?'

'Yes,' he murmured, squeezing the tip of his cock, his head full of lust, his loins full of fire and his heart full of love for his wife. He felt all these, and affection for a naïve yet strangely knowledgeable new bedmate. 'Yes!' he reiterated, squirming naked on his sheets, 'but I'm thinking of you too, my love. Imagining how you are now. Wanting you . . .'

Hard and quivering, and he rose, through pleasure, towards orgasm. And behind his closed eyelids, his beautiful spouse moved towards him, her divine, sexual mastery erasing all other fantasies. Even those about feisty girls from the north with big, blue eyes and large, curvaceous breasts.

'Celeste,' he groaned, his soul in another country: in Paris with a beautiful, masturbating woman in a nightdress as sheer as black vapour.

'Celeste!'

At the sound of her husband's tortured voice, Celeste Brent-Hadey groaned too – but contained the sound inside her by biting her left thumb, hard. The fingers of her right hand were moving firmly but delicately on her clitoris, sliding in her own heavy dew. Her fragile, misty-black nightgown was crumpled around her waist.

She loved her husband so much tonight. She felt so lucky to have him. He'd come through for her so wonderfully over this dilemma with David, and she was filled with gratitude and fondness. Emotions that turned easily to sexual desire.

As she listened to his broken voice, and his gasps and grunts, she imagined him at home in their bedroom, and wished him the greatest of pleasure in his own magnificent body.

Ju was such a handsome bastard! With his brown, sexy skin, and eyes that were even browner and so often sultry with passion. She loved *all* of her husband, relished every part of him. He was strong and muscular, graceful and light on his feet. She loved his sparkling white teeth, and his crisp black hair that was curly on his head, fuzzy on his chest, and thick and tickly round his cock. She adored the way that hair meshed with her own black curls when their bodies ground together in sex. She loved the way he was sometimes arrogant and sometimes so wryly self-mocking. She loved his boyish expression, his cheeky grin. It was hard to believe he was a 'forty something'. Her serious David, her quiet, bookish cousin, sometimes seemed older by far than her husband; and David was only nineteen.

And as she listened, and touched her own body, she began to consider David, and what a strange conundrum he was.

She'd almost wondered whether to educate the boy herself. The idea had a real appeal to it. A lover so unschooled would be quite a novelty, and in his own offbeat way, David was almost as handsome as Julian.

It would be no hardship to go to bed with David, to sample that lean, creamy-skinned body and teach those long, flexible fingers what it meant to give pleasure to a woman. She'd been very tempted, but the simple truth of it was that they were cousins. Their relationship was several times removed, true, but even so, Celeste still felt a little uncomfortable with the idea of sex with her own kith and kin.

'Celeste!'

Ju's voice sounded frantic now, and Celeste imagined his lordly brown hand sliding and slipping on his cock. The skin on his member was fine and satiny, stretched tight, when he was erect, over a core as hard as bone. She pictured him spreading his own slickness as a lubricant; it was a sight she would never tire of, no matter how many times she saw it. She saw her beautiful, sensual husband, desperate to orgasm, rubbing himself like a callow young boy, yet afraid to come without leave.

'Are you naked, Ju my love?' she enquired archly, her own fingers working and moving. Her body was totally open now, her thighs rudely and lewdly spread. She had two hands pressed between them, caressing both without and within. She thought longingly of that stubby red vibrator, and how good it would feel in her channel as a surrogate for Ju's stiff flesh.

'Yes,' he said, perfecting her picture.

'I'm not,' she whispered, wondering if he'd hear. 'I'm wearing that black silk nightdress that you like so much. The one we bought together in Circe . . . Do you remember?'

'Oh God, yes!' His voice degraded into broken

moaning, and Celeste wondered if the fight was lost already, and he was coming. The memory she'd referred to was enough to stir a saint!

Slowly manipulating her clitoris, she slid off her heap of supporting pillows and lay splay-legged across the bed, her mind a maelstrom of images.

Not long after their marriage, when they'd been as silly and insatiable as teenagers, Julian had taken her to Circe, a fabulously exclusive lingerie boutique, and insisted on spending an obscene sum of money on lace and silk and satin. With a twinkle in his eye, and a huge and very visible hard-on, he'd insisted that she try on this particular gown – the wisp-like garment that so inadequately covered her now. And with the management of Circe so eager to pander to customers, no-one had turned a hair when Mister Hadey had followed his wife into the changing cubicle.

Inside, he'd made her stroke her own body as she disrobed, conveying his wishes by gesture alone because only a bolt of thinly-lined velvet divided them from the sales staff and fellow shoppers. When she was stripped to her high heels and hold-up stockings, he'd made her rest her foot on the seat of the velvet-padded reproduction chair, then finger her opened-out vulva until she reached silent and body-wracking orgasm.

The thought of that clandestine climax nearly made the same thing happen now. She felt her intimate tissues flutter as her juices flowed out across her buttocks, coating their glassy inner slopes. She pushed her finger in deeper, then gasped and writhed as her mind spooled quickly through her Circe memory.

Unable to stay on her feet, she'd let Julian grab her by the waist and drape her face down across the back of the chair. She'd lain there, mute and burning, while he'd mounded and fondled her bottom. She'd almost screamed with incredulous glee when she'd heard the distinctive whir of his zip.

She remembered muttering some muffled reply when the assistant had called out 'Is everything alright?', then almost biting the lush upholstery as Ju placed his cock between her buttocks. She'd been prepared for him taking her – in fact she'd been aching for him – but when he'd started pushing his way into her bottom, she'd almost lost her nerve.

Just the thought of it triggered her now. She came violently, here in Paris, while she remembered what had happened in that high-class London knicker shop. With potential discovery just a heartbeat away, her husband had sodomised her vigorously, his virtually fully-clothed body jerking hard against her vulnerable near-nakedness. She touched her anus now and climaxed again, imagining that tiny sensitive portal stretched wide around his marvellous male girth. She'd had five distinct orgasms as she'd hung by her bottom from his shaft, and now she had at least as many more as she remembered her delicious humbling.

'Thank you, Ju,' she said at last, wondering if her breathy tones could be heard across the aether.

'Thank *you*, my love.' The words were filled with that beautiful smile of his, the most gorgeous of all his smiles – the relaxed, sated grin of a happy man who'd just climbed the highest peak of pleasure and was ever-so-slowly drifting downwards. For a moment,

Celeste wished she was there to really see him; there, so she could kiss his mouth, his eyes, and his soft and satisfied cock.

She wondered if Rosie the librarian had sucked him, and found the vision intriguing. Julian had described his marvellous find in a previous phone call, and Celeste found herself looking forward to meeting her. Though slim herself, she had a penchant for curves in her female partners, and this lush northern girl sounded perfectly toothsome.

'So,' she purred, touching her breasts through sheer black lace and imagining them bigger, rounder and quite virgin to the hand of a woman. 'Will *I* like this Rosie of yours?'

Julian laughed richly. 'You'll love her, my dear,' he said softly. 'But I'd advise you to approach her with caution. She's bright and sensual . . . and very willing.' He paused, obviously remembering just how willing. 'But our games might seem a little sophisticated as yet.'

'We'll see,' replied Celeste, easing down the bodice of her nightgown and thinking longingly of a shy girl's kisses.

5

Enter the Lion Cub

'Look, woman, this is a sophisticated household . . .
Try and act sophisticated, will you?' Rosie braced
herself with yet another little homily as she put the
final touches to her hairstyle. She'd heard the breakfast
gong a while ago, but somehow it had been difficult
to respond.

How should she behave this morning? As an
employee? A lover? A woman employed to be a lover?
She slicked on a little more lipstick and wondered if
she looked like either.

Julian's proposition was so bizarre it was almost
sensible. Almost. And she'd agreed to it, she seemed
to remember. She was going to teach sex to a nineteen
year old boy she'd never met. What's more she'd even
taken a 'practical' for the post!

Ah, but did I pass? she pondered on the way to the
dining room, her heart beating wildly.

Her throat tightened as she hovered in the hall,
thinking of last night in her room. She seemed to feel
a warm body pressed against her back again, and knew

that beyond the dining room door was a man who'd promised he wouldn't disappoint her. A man who *hadn't* disappointed her.

Taking a huge breath, she smoothed at her soft, pink angora sweater and touched the hairstyle she knew to be perfect. It was now or never. She reached for the door-handle, turned it and went in.

'Good morning, Rosie,' said Julian, his voice smoothly pleasant as he rose to his feet, the perfect gentleman. There were only two places set for breakfast – intimately close – and Rosie wanted to panic and run. Even in his dark business suit Julian looked poised for sex, and the combination of brown skin and white shirt made visions flare and bubble. She scarcely dare approach him. If she got one whiff of that cologne of his, she was finished. She was half dizzy with lust already.

'Good morning, Mister Hadey,' she said, flipping out her napkin as she sat, and wishing it was good form to tuck it into her neckline. Her nipples were hardening already and showed clearly through her thin, cuddly sweater. Even to her eyes, her cleavage appeared deeper somehow, far more of a plunge than it had looked in her bedroom mirror.

'Mister Hadey?' he queried, his eyes flashing sparks. 'Isn't that a little formal?'

'Er . . . Yes, I suppose it is,' she said, reaching for the coffee he'd poured as she settled herself. What had he expected? she asked herself, sipping gratefully. An endearment? Some reference to last night? A kiss?

Studying Julian over her cup, Rosie realised her feelings were hard to quantify. He smiled at her, and as his mouth formed that beautiful curve; she *did* feel fond of him – not so much for the pleasure, which had been considerable, but for his kindness too. What she didn't feel was besotted. There was no shivery emotional mushiness, no fear of losing him, as there had been with Geoff. And surprisingly, as the coffee cleared her thoughts, she felt the welcome return of control. She desired Julian, even now, but to her relief, her heart was her own.

There was a bond between them, yes, but it was more like friendship than anything. A delicious sense of complicity. They were in a sexual conspiracy together. Something risqué, but positive; and as Julian reached over and patted her hand, she knew she could do what he'd asked – always providing that David wasn't too much of a dork!

'I wouldn't worry about the library today, Rosie. I've something else I want you to do.'

Hot blood flared her cheeks as the night returned to her mind. She thought of things she would have liked to have done, that there hadn't been time or energy left for.

Julian laughed gently. 'No, no! Not this morning, alas.' He gave her hand a quick squeeze, then reached for his coffee.

As she watched this simple but elegant action, she saw Julian's plate was empty. He'd obviously finished his breakfast some time ago.

'I'd like to, Rosie, believe me.' He nipped at his lower lip with his teeth, and Rosie's loins warmed and wept. 'But I've some heavy meetings this morning and I can't put them off,' he continued, regretfully.

'What I want *you* to do is go to the airport in the limousine and meet Celeste and David. I'd go myself – she likes me to – but under the circumstances, I'm sure she'll be happy with you.' A slight lift of his head made Rosie meet his eyes – and she felt a fresh pang of lust as he winked. 'And the sooner you meet David the better, eh?'

In theory it was a good idea, but as she sat in the long, black car, Rosie had the jitters again. She'd hoped to meet these two separately, and ideally in the library where the aura of the books would empower her. But now she had to face them both at once, stone-cold, without even the questionable support of Julian. The wife she'd wronged and the boy she was going to have to teach – what a combination. She felt sweat break out under her arms, and prayed that her deodorant could cope.

The chauffeur, Stephen, wasn't helping matters either. He was a tall, black guy with an impressive, muscular physique, and a dazzling smile. Yesterday, when he'd collected her from her flat, she'd enjoyed his frank male scrutiny; but now it just made her nervous. She'd sensed his eyes on her as he'd held open the car door, felt him studying her breasts in the thin, soft sweater, and the shape of her hips and thighs in her tailored linen trousers. There was nothing she could say to him really though, because his surveillance was too subtle to object to.

At the airport, Rosie tried bio-feedback: calming her nerves by sheer force of will, and suppressing the threat of blushes. Breathing deeply, she expanded her diaphragm and stood tall, projecting a sham of cool poise while her heart leapt wildly in her chest.

When the flight arrival was announced, she started counting silently and trained her eyes on the area where the passengers would emerge. At two hundred, the butterflies in her stomach turned to humming-birds, flapping up a storm. Two figures – one male, one female – had appeared in the entrance, and every instinct she had said, 'They're here!'

The woman was unmistakably the one in the portrait at Amberlake Gardens: an exquisite sylph with a lovely face, a slender, perfect body, and thick, straight, shiny-black hair worn in an immaculate Cleopatra bob. She was clothed in scarlet lycra ski-pants and a matching form-fitting top that made everyone around her look drab. She wore boots and had a fringed, suede jacket draped around her shoulders. Her eyes were hidden by aviator shades and her lips were the reddest and glossiest Rosie had ever seen.

Beside her was David. The enigma.

Oh God, he's peculiar! thought Rosie, her spirits plunging. I can't do this, she wailed inside. I just can't!

But as the couple drew closer, something very weird happened. Rosie's perceptions did a sudden flip, and 'peculiar' and 'strange' seemed wrong. 'Different' took their place. And so did 'special', 'unique' and 'potentially wonderful'.

Celeste's companion was tall, lean and graceful, his long body clad in black denim and a mustard coloured turtle-neck sweater. His skin appeared quite pale for a man's, and his features were sharply defined and startlingly symmetrical. His light pink mouth was

firmly sculpted, and his nose noble, almost roman.
His eyes were large, long-lashed, and a shade of brown
so light and lustrous it was almost gold. As if to highlight this, he'd brushed his brown hair straight back
from his brow in a style that was neat, yet vaguely
leonine.

Rosie stood stock still for several long, countable
seconds. The young man's gaze was intent and unwavering, and seemed to root her to the spot. She could
almost believe that he already knew her, and her
purpose; although common sense said that he was
only staring at her because she was staring at him!

'Er . . . Hello,' she said finally, hating herself for
being so dull in her choice of greeting. 'I'm –'

'Rosie, of course,' said a husky, feminine voice.
Rosie jumped. Unlikely as it seemed, she'd almost
forgotten about Celeste.

'I'm Celeste Brent-Hadey,' the dark-haired woman
continued, her voice unexpectedly intimate, 'and this
is my cousin, David Brent.' As she said this, the boy
– man? young god? – stepped another pace forward
and solemnly held out his hand.

'How do you do?' he said quietly, his soft voice
surprisingly deep. It was only the shortest of speeches,
but Rosie instantly warmed to his accent.

'A fellow Yorkie, eh?' she said, smiling to cover her
shock. His hand was deliciously cool, the contact
almost electrical. His long fingers seemed to fold
around hers.

'Yes . . . Yes, I am.' His reply was hesitant, and his
mouth quirked slightly as if he were afraid to smile
outright. She sensed wariness, and if not suspicion, at

least a certain confusion, yet he withdrew his hand slowly, as if he too relished their contact.

'Well, let's get to that car, shall we?' said Celeste briskly, diffusing the odd little moment. 'I'm about to die for a large gin and tonic in the comfort of my own home, and I'm sure you two must be keen to get into that library and start rummaging through all those books.' She turned to David with an innocuous smile, 'Rosie's the new librarian, David. I can't remember if I told you about her or not . . .'

Rosie felt grateful for Celeste. She was a natural hostess, and without overt manipulation, she filled in the spaces between them, her conversation soothing and fluid. Rosie found it easy to chat and answer questions, and while David didn't say much, he didn't seem unduly nervous either.

He was watchful though. Rosie sensed him observing her, and when she turned away from Celeste for a moment, she found his eyes on her, his look direct and fiery. He was sitting opposite her, in the jump seat, and in the car's tinted glass gloom, his great golden eyes were like beacons of scrutinising light. When he looked away it seemed more out of politeness than discomfitude, and Rosie felt both rattled and exhilarated. He wasn't at all what she'd expected.

While Celeste chatted idly of Paris, Rosie allowed her attention to wander. Towards David. Towards his differentness, and his possibilities.

He'd had a mild nervous breakdown, Julian had said, yet there seemed no outward sign of it. He was quiet, but it was the quietness of thought, not nerves. His body was still, his long legs stretched out in front of him, relaxed but somehow not casually so. There was a sense of feline readiness in him, but for what, Rosie couldn't discern. She could only be impressed.

More than ever now, she felt excited by the task ahead. Her pupil was quite beautiful in a silent, self-contained sort of way, and though she couldn't see much of his body, she sensed it would be as fascinating and fine as his face. She imagined hairlessness, quiet strength, wiry limbs, and a penis that was slender but long. Without thinking, she glanced towards his groin.

Her heart thudded. His black jeans were snug and well-cut, and there was marked fullness behind their neat double-stitched fly. Did he have an erection already? Because of her? Suddenly, she wanted to believe it.

Once again, she felt his focused attention, and when she looked up, something lurched in the pit of her belly. The pale boy was no longer quite so pale, she realised; there was a faint haze of a blush along the high, bright lines of his cheekbones, and as their eyes met, his skittered instantly away.

Good grief! Oh God! It *had* happened already. Before it was supposed to. He was aroused right in front of her, and she sensed it was against his will. She felt as if she'd drunk a dozen of Celeste's gin and tonics, and her body surged in response, its secret, female reaction concealed beneath the layers of her clothing.

It was all hidden, but it was as exciting as being thrown on a bed, stripped naked, then caressed until she moaned uncontrollably. She felt her breasts swell in the lace of her bra and the flesh between her legs start to tickle.

She imagined telling David what was happening to her, quietly describing the condition of her body and her sex. It would be his first instruction, and she'd place his hand between her legs and watch that faint veil of pink spread out across his face and throat. His fingers would move slowly in her moisture, examining it by touch. He'd make a sound of surprise, a soft, rough cry. She wished suddenly that they were alone in the car, so she could make her fancies real, take off her jumper and show him her hard crumpled nipples, thick and dark beneath her thin, silk bra. She pictured herself reaching out to him across this opulent, leather-scented space, then drawing his perfect young face to her bosom and stroking his sleek brown hair.

'It's alright,' she'd say when he trembled. 'It's alright, you're a man, it's your birthright. You can have me, David. Don't worry . . .'

How would it feel to lie there beside him? she wondered. To guide him on top of her, and into her? He'd be hasty, desperate. She'd have to steer his stiff, young penis to the right place, then steady his charge towards orgasm. Tempering her own need, she'd have to show him where to touch her. How much and how hard. Her vagina fluttered and she felt wetness in her panties, her body already smoothing his path. They were sitting several feet apart in a car, in the late morning London traffic, but in her mind, they were already making love.

'Are you okay? You look a bit dazed.'

Celeste's voice shattered Rosie's fantasies. Julian's

wife was regarding her with mischievous interest, her violet eyes twinkling as if she'd seen the same visions herself.

'Yes. Thanks. I'm fine,' Rosie stammered, losing control now, blushing vividly pink and hot. 'I didn't sleep very well last night –' Her pulse pumped faster as she remembered part of the reason. 'A new bed and all . . . But don't worry, I'm sure I'll get used to it.'

'I'm sure you will.' Celeste's voice was strangely loaded, and for a moment Rosie was convinced the woman knew everything. 'But if there's anything I can do, just let me know, won't you?'

On any normal level it was a simple offer of help, but suddenly Rosie sensed more. As she turned to Celeste, she saw the same heat in those lavender eyes that she'd seen in David's golden ones; and the sight of it shocked her. She felt a deep, hard jolt of something that she wanted to ignore, but couldn't.

She's a lesbian! thought Rosie wildly. A bisexual. She wants me just as much as Julian did. As David does. Oh God, what have I got into?

Mercifully, the car soon slid to a halt before the front door at Amberlake Gardens. Patently delighted to be home, Celeste entered the house like a whirl-wind, all sighs and melodramatic gestures, and smiles of greeting for her staff. David held back politely and let Rosie precede him, while somewhere behind them, Stephen dealt quietly with the luggage.

Rosie felt dazed and befuddled by Celeste and her vibrancy, and by the strange feeling that on some deep, instinctive level, she'd already got through to David. They'd exchanged virtually no conversation, but it didn't matter. He'd looked. She'd looked. He'd seen her look. He wasn't yet conscious of her dual role in the household, she was sure, but he was certainly aware of her body. So aware that he was forced to escape, pleading tiredness, to his room.

'*He* hasn't been sleeping well either,' observed Celeste, looking at Rosie over her shoulder as she led the way into the sitting room. Rosie followed, then wondered whether she should.

Aren't I supposed to be working? she thought as she dithered on the threshold. Celeste seemed to be assuming her company, but when all was said and done, she – Rosie – was only paid help.

'Oh don't worry about the books!' Celeste twirled around, smiling, and her lovely hair fanned out like a glossy black bell. 'They'll keep a while. Have a drink with me. Let's get to know each other.' Without asking, she poured for both of them – and Rosie felt a frisson of alarm when she was handed a sweet sherry, the very one she'd told Julian she liked so much. As she sat down where Celeste indicated – next to her on the sofa – she wondered just how that knowledge had been imparted.

Up close, Julian's wife was extraordinary, her face as flawless as a jewel in the smooth, black frame of her distinctive Egyptian hairstyle. Her delicate features had a soft, sweet bloom that made Rosie wonder how old she was. Celeste looked young in years, but seemed old in confidence. And when she turned, Rosie almost flinched – those huge violet eyes were far too candid.

'So what do you think of David?' Celeste asked.

Rosie took a calming sip of sherry. What she said

depended on what Celeste knew. 'He seems very nice,' she offered after a moment. 'A bit shy, but nowhere near as shy as I'd expected. Is his insomnia due to his . . . his illness?'

'No, not really,' replied Celeste with a slow, arch smile. 'He's more or less over his breakdown now . . . It was fairly mild anyway.' There was an impish glint in her eyes now, a mischief that was almost dizzying. 'No,' she continued, 'I think his sleeplessness is the sort that afflicts most young men of his age. He's horny, Rosie. He's desperate for sex and lies awake half the night faking it with his own right hand!'

Without thinking Rosie drained her glass, and Celeste laughed.

'It's true!' she said blithely, taking Rosie's glass, then getting up to refill it. Her hips swayed sinuously as she walked across the room on her high, spike-shaped heels.

'He's ready, Rosie. It's as if he's just woken up from a sleep and his hormones are driving him crazy. He's had a sexually repressed upbringing so far and he needs to catch up. Soon!'

Celeste spoke quietly and sincerely now. She handed Rosie her drink and seemed to watch her intently as she sipped it.

She knows! thought Rosie, hardly tasting the sweetness in her mouth at all. She's in on it!

Rosie resisted the urge to drain her glass again. She'd have to think fast now, and clearly, because her job, at the least, might depend on it.

But Celeste began to talk about her cousin.

David had lost his parents at an early age, as had

Celeste herself. But while she'd been wilful and head-strong, and come to live in London as soon as she was legally able, David had stayed put.

Being younger, he'd lived with his grandparents in the wilds of the Yorkshire Dales; and though the old couple had been kind to him, their smallholding home had been miles from anywhere, and the life isolated. After his grandmother's death, David had been left to care for his grandfather alone and his existence had become even more solitary. A natural genius, he'd more or less educated himself, devouring every scrap of knowledge he could find from books: both at home and in every library he could get to from his remote moorland locale.

'He's almost *lived* in our library since he came here,' Celeste said, nodding her gleaming head in the library's general direction. 'He's reading everything! Which was all very fine until he discovered Julian's special collection . . .' she let her voice fade delicately and looked Rosie straight in the eye. 'You can imagine the effect *that* had on him can't you? An impression-able boy just beginning to understand his own body . . .' She took a sip from her glass, and her slim throat rippled sensuously. 'It was like dynamite, Rosie. Pure dynamite. And now *we've* to do something about it.'

'We?' Rosie put down her sherry, carefully. She could see her fingers shaking.

'Oh come on, Rosie, you know why you're here.' Celeste's voice was silky and cajoling, a feminine echo of her husband's – as it had sounded last night.

'But I'm a librarian,' Rosie said firmly. 'What can *I* do?' Her innards were trembling and her heart pounding, and in her panic she clung to the safe, old Rosie.

'Yes, I know,' said Celeste with a laugh, 'and by all accounts a very accomplished one. But what about your other duties? The ones my husband outlined to you last night. When you were in bed with him.'

It was like being thrown into a river; a river of ice-water. What could she do, or say? She opened her mouth and nothing came out. She couldn't look at Celeste at all.

After a moment, gentle fingers settled on her cheek and made her look up. At the same time, a surprisingly forceful arm slid around her shoulders and cradled her, just as a lover would. 'It's alright, Rosie, I know everything,' said Celeste like a zephyr of sweetness, her face all smiles. 'Last night was my suggestion. I thought you'd feel lonely in a strange house, and Julian agreed to help.'

Rosie gaped at her.

'It was a nice welcome though, wasn't it?'

Rosie nodded. She felt off balance, numb, shocked: by both Celeste's words and her scented closeness. The heat in that red-clad shape was astounding, and Rosie could feel it warming her. She wanted to get closer, but she was frightened. She'd never responded to a woman before, never been held like this by one. She couldn't believe the way her own body felt.

'Julian and I have never had a conventional marriage.' Celeste's voice was even, clear, untroubled. Rosie was quivering, but her companion seemed to think nothing of stroking her and squeezing her with a touch that was far more than friendly. 'I love him and he loves me, but we've both always had other lovers . . . Other men and women for sex.'

The emphasis was unmistakable, and it suddenly occurred to Rosie that men and women might apply to Julian also. Her fuddled mind boggled at the thought, but her body found it thrilling.

Celeste was speaking again, breathily, coaxingly. 'I would've . . . I would've dealt with David myself, but he's my cousin. Third cousin, maybe more, but it bothers me.' She shrugged, her beautiful curves shuddering in their tight red shell. 'It's a shame because I think he's exquisite . . .' She pulled away, her lilac eyes still asking the question.

'Yes, he is,' whispered Rosie. It was true, after that first sudden revelation at the airport, she couldn't deny it. He was as beautiful in his own way as his cousin: pure, erotic, and stunning.

Celeste seemed to pick up the thought.

'Imagine what you could do with him. A perfect, innocent boy with a fresh young body.' Her eyes sparkled. 'I've seen him naked, Rosie, and he's a gem! Don't let that pale face fool you, he's no wimp. His chest, his legs, his sex . . . Everything about him is superb. Just think of it . . .'

Think of it? She could hardly stop thinking of it. She saw David in her mind; his smooth body, his long, yearning penis. She saw his solemn face reddened with lust and contorted with pleasure. In her imagination, she gazed down at him from the heights of experience; riding his impetuous flesh, bearing down as he thrust upwards. She was dimly aware that her eyes must be glazed, and that Celeste could see it. But there was nothing she could do about her fantasies, they were out of her hands. Uncontrolled. The coming task obsessed her, and made her body stir and prepare itself. She was wet in her silky panties, and she wished she was days or weeks advanced in it all, so she could go up to David's room now. And make love to him.

'Hey, wake up!'

Focusing slowly, Rosie saw knowledge in Celeste's brilliant eyes. Wicked knowledge. It was as if she really could see Rosie's thoughts.

'I'm sorry,' Rosie whispered. 'It's all so new. I want to help David. Really I do. But . . .' She hesitated, searching for the words. 'Until last week I had a tedious job in dull surroundings. A steady, monogamous relationship. We'd gone through all the normal stages. I was just . . . conventional. Then I came here –' She waved her hand in a small sweep. 'It's like being on another planet!' She paused again, thought, then smiled. 'It's a planet I like though. I think I could like it a lot. But it'll take some getting used to.'

'I'm glad,' said Celeste gently. 'I'm glad you like it here. I know it sounds corny, but I want you to feel like part of the family. I think it'll help with your . . . your objective. Make it easier for him to accept you.'

Rosie's head was spinning, but it wasn't from the sherry. Her mind was filled with strange pictures: images of a slim, pale boy with golden, almost cat-like eyes. A lion cub waiting to be blooded.

And she found Celeste befuddling too. Her beauty and her perfume, and the intimate nearness that should have seemed simply companionable, but which held the promise of more, much more.

'I . . . I . . .' she stuttered, at a loss to know what to think and feel, much less to say.

'I know, it's all a bit much, isn't it?' said Celeste kindly, compounding Rosie's confusion by closing the last gap between them and kissing her, just once, on the cheek. 'Why don't you take a lie down before lunch. Just relax, think things over. You'll see it all more clearly when you're rested.'

Rosie realised she must have looked alarmed, because Celeste kissed her again, then squeezed her hand reassuringly. 'Go on, off you go. I promise you there'll be no visitors.' She winked and urged Rosie to her feet. 'Well, not this afternoon!'

But as she ascended the stairs to her bedroom, then lay down, bemused, hot and bothered, Rosie realised she would have welcomed a visitor.

When a visitor did come, it was a dream.

In it, she was being led along a wide panelled corridor by a tall, black servant. He was silent and smiling and quite naked, but that seemed alright because she wasn't wearing much herself, just a beautiful slippy kind of underskirt made of pale pink silk, and high-heeled slippers in the rich red colour of roses. The tiny chemise was so short that her bottom was almost visible, and a warm, naughty breeze was tickling at her thighs and sex.

At the end of the corridor stood two tall doors that opened as they approached. The black servant entered first, then stood to one side to let her pass.

'The Dauphin's tutor!' he called out loudly, by way of announcement, and she walked past him into the magnificent chamber beyond.

Two high thrones stood at the far end of the room, and to one side was a cushioned and gilded stool. The thrones were occupied by the King and the Queen, smiling benignly, and on the stool sat the Dauphin, his oval face solemn and watchful.

'Approach,' said the King, augustly. He was a dark and beautiful man; exotic, a Moor from the Atlas mountains. His face was brown, his eyes were bright, and his fine strong body was clad in a turquoise robe. As he spoke he was fondling his penis, which was protruding boldly from the silken folds at his groin.

'Yes, please do approach,' echoed the Queen softly from beside him, her purple eyes darting from her husband's long, swarthy shaft to the shy girl standing before her.

The Queen was beautiful too, from the same continent as the King, but from a region more easterly, the vale of the fertile Nile river. Her hair was black as a raven's wing, and her face a vision of perfection. Her lips were brilliant crimson, the same bright colour as the long, shiny gown that clothed her fabulous body.

'And who are you, my dear?' the lovely monarch enquired.

'I am the English Rose, Ma'am, come to serve the Dauphin.' She could not help but look at him as she spoke his name. This boy, to whom she owed her body, was the most beautiful of the three, and his demeanor was calm and quiet. A torch burnt in a stanchion behind him, and its light seemed to glint like a diadem on his smooth, brown, brushed-back hair. His skin was the colour of cream and his lips were as pink as sugared almonds. A half grown lion cub was lolling on his lap, and its eyes, and his, had the selfsame yellow-gold gleam.

'Then serve him,' said the King, his voice heavy with lust and his bare legs shifting with pleasure. His dark eyes closed as the Queen replaced his grasping hand with her own.

The English Rose did as she was bidden, falling to her knees before the Dauphin's stool, her body stirred by the sight of him. As she crouched on the carpet, she felt her nipples ache and the nectar flow between her legs. Defying the wrath of the regal family, she lifted her slip and touched herself. Her core was hot and puffed and molten, and as she groaned, she saw the Dauphin's eyes flare with passion. Pressing a kiss to his pet's soft fur, he urged the cub gently up off his lap, then crushed his gloved fingers to his groin in a gesture of utmost torment.

'Hurry, girl! Give him your mouth,' cried the Queen, her fingers on her husband's red penis, while her other hand caressed her own breast.

Her mouth? But where? On his soft pink lips? His long pale hand beneath its gauntlet? His naked chest, between the folds of his white silk shirt?

No, no, none of these! As she came up on her knees, the Dauphin reached forward and pulled her face against his loins. With trembling fingers, she unfastened his garment – a pair of black velvet breeches – and reached inside to seek out his treasure.

And when it sprang out, proud and free, it was a greater treasure than the English Rose had imagined – a stiff, rosy branch of flesh that wept silken juice from its rounded tip in anticipation of the delights to come. With a long sigh of content, the hungry, besotted Rose leant forward and absorbed him, sucking on his beautiful penis as daintily and cleverly as she could.

There were gasps from close by, small sounds of approval and of satisfaction. Even as they pleasured themselves, the Royal couple looked on, and the English Rose was glad of it. She licked rapidly at the fine warm staff in her mouth, and heard the Dauphin's voice join the others, groaning softly and brokenly in time to the swirls of her tongue.

In another chamber of the palace, a piano began to play, and as she reached between her thighs, to her damp and swollen-hot place, the beautiful music seemed to set the seal on the bliss of all of them. She heard the King and Queen sob out each other's names, and at that very moment the Dauphin whimpered loudly, caressed her hair, and graced her with his hot, sweet semen. And while her own sex throbbed hard beneath her fingertips, rippling like a wave in the sea, the piano played on and on and on . . .

Rosie woke up having an orgasm: her sweating face pressed into her pillow, her hips rocking, and her fingers jammed hard between her thighs. The cotton beneath her face was damp because she'd been crying with pleasure in her sleep; and in another part of the house, in a room somewhere below her, she could hear someone playing the piano.

6

Early Learning

For several minutes, Rosie just lay there. Listening to the music. Thinking about her dream. Touching her sex and riding her receding orgasm. She'd taken off her trousers to lie down and her silky knickers were soaked where she'd rubbed herself through them.

She recalled seeing the Steinway piano in the corner of the library, and wishing, not for the first time, that she could play – not as a virtuoso, she didn't really aspire to that, but it would have been nice to be able to play like the person who was playing now. The melodies had begun tentatively, with pauses for repetition of fluffed notes interspersed with outbreaks of keyboard doodling, but gradually the pianist seemed to grow in power and confidence, and the playing became more accomplished, the tunes more recognisable. Rosie's knowledge of the classics was slight, but all the same the muted sounds were soothing.

Was David the unseen musician? In his secluded life until now, there must have been plenty of time to practice, and the hesitancy of the early bars seemed to mesh with his shy, quiet reticence.

He hadn't seemed so reticent in her dream though. The Dauphin had been quite certain of what he wanted, and his eyes had been hot with lust.

It had been a vivid dream, textured and realistic, and needed little in the way of symbolic interpretation. It had just been Julian and Celeste, dominant and sexy, and their plans for David and herself. The lion cub? Well, that came from David's eyes, she supposed. And the way he wore his hair. And his light, cat-like grace. Nothing more sinister than that. Or was it?

As the piano finally fell silent, Rosie thought about getting up. The quality of the light that streamed in through her window looked strangely slanted, as if she'd slept longer than she'd planned.

The clock astounded her. It showed well past five. She'd spent the whole afternoon dreaming and playing with herself. She wrinkled her nose as she sniffed her fingers. They were pungent with her scent and the gusset of her panties felt sticky. As dinner was at eight, it hardly seemed worth changing twice, so she slipped into her thin silk robe.

When she looked around, Rosie found that some kind soul had brought her something to eat. There was a tray on the table at the end of her bed, with a plate of neatly cut sandwiches and a glass of milk. Her mouth watered, but just as she was about to wash her hands, an ominous thought occurred.

When, exactly, had the snack been delivered? Had someone watched her toss in her sleep with her hands rubbing hard between her legs? She reached out to the tray, then saw a small piece of paper tucked beneath the plate. It was a sheet from her own notepad, the one she used for jottings. The one that still lay on the table, along with a pencil.

Almost reluctantly, she picked up the note.

Dear Rosie, it said, *I didn't want to disturb you, your dream looked far more delicious than this sandwich! Please tell me about it later! Love, Celeste.* Below a long row of 'x's was a postscript. *Your bottom is beautiful. I nearly kissed it but I didn't want to wake you!*

Rosie's stomach felt tight and knotted, and she suddenly couldn't face her sandwich. Celeste had come into her room and seen her masturbating. Seen her bottom in only a thin pair of panties with the crotch ridden up in her groove. The idea was as hideous as it was exciting, and she wondered what would have happened if she'd woken. Would she have had her first taste of loving a woman? Or would she have resisted? Somehow she didn't think so.

With an age to go before dinner, Rosie took her time getting ready. First she washed and conditioned her hair, then she wound it in a towel while she took a leisurely bath, filling the tub as deep as was safe and slopping in nearly a cupful of scented bubbling essence from the vast selection on her shelf.

The room smelt like a herbalist's, and the perfume, as she sank into the water, made Rosie feel dizzy. The scents of frankincense and patchouli seemed to unlock something wild inside her, releasing a circuit between her loins and her brain that had been blocked until now. She'd had an orgasm in her sleep. Probably several. But she still wanted to play with herself, to touch her breasts, her belly and her clitoris beneath the veil of the heavy, silken water.

She brought lovers into her mind to share her sensuous stroking. Julian. Celeste. More than ever, David. She made herself focus on him, thinking about what she should tell him, and how to begin. What he might feel like when he used his lessons.

'There. Touch me just there,' she whispered, picturing him sitting on the side of the bath and reaching down into the water. She could almost feel his cool fingers. Feel them – guided by hers – slipping in through the grove of her pubis and finding her quivering core. Sliding deep into the water, she set her gaze inwards, and saw only a pair of hot, golden eyes with pupils darkened by pleasure.

Rubbing slowly, very slowly, she brought herself to a long, steamy orgasm, murmuring David's name as a mantra while she writhed, imprinting him on her brain and her senses. Making him what *she* wanted, so her task would be easier. Or not even a task at all.

The bathwater was much cooler when she got out, and the bubbles all gone. Her skin felt very smooth and slightly oily; sensitised and ready to be touched. As she dried off, it almost seemed to glow beneath the towel, and she began thinking about the evening ahead.

It was impossible to predict really. She'd spoken only a few sentences to David, so nothing much could happen just yet. Even so, she decided to dress optimistically. Standing naked before her wardrobe, she dithered over various outfits: both old ones, from her previous life, and new clothes she'd bought with Julian's moving in allowance.

Nothing too obvious, she decided. She had a few things that both plunged and clung, but she wanted to hold them back for now. Instead she chose a light, smoked-pastel chiffon two piece that achieved quite a lot by mere suggestion. The colours were blended and smeared – peaches, lemons, muted oranges and tans – all softly floating across a smock-like top and a full swirling handkerchief skirt. Beneath this she wore a camisole and French knickers in oyster satin, with matching suspender belt and sheer oatmeal coloured stockings. She felt almost like a bride in all her finery, and it was only when she stepped into her sandals – which were beige, strappy, and deliciously comfortable in spite of their height – that she felt a pang of disquiet. She remembered being with Geoff the last time she'd worn them, and suddenly realised it was the first time she'd thought of him all day.

Only a week or so ago he'd meant the world to her, and she'd have done anything to please him. Now, strangely, she could hardly bring his face into focus. He seemed blurred to her, indistinct. He was part of another world now, only significant as a negative ex-perience. Someone who'd exploited her. The pain was still there, but it was dimmer now, like a nearly-healed sprain that only nagged occasionally. It would be gone soon, she realised. Would she then completely forget what he'd looked like?

Purging her mind of such unknowables, she turned her attention to her hair. It was almost dry, and combing it smoothly away from her face, she secured it with two mock-ivory slides in a simple, but sophisticated style. And she made up the same way. Smudged taupe eyes, lots of mascara, and a deep but lasting lipstain. Crushed cranberry that would endure and endure. If it needed to.

There was a knock on the door, and Rosie's heart leapt, but it was only Mrs Russell. Would she like an aperatif brought to her room? Or would she join the others in the library?

Downstairs, in the library, Rosie wondered if she'd strayed into a fairytale. Julian was in perfect, devastating evening dress, and Celeste wore a black, ankle-skimming tube-like dress covered entirely in sequins, with black silk gloves that sheathed her completely from fingertip to upper arm. Her black suede court shoes had heels that looked about four inches high, and her hair was sleeked back from her face and gelled, accentuating a flawless maquillage that was even more Cleo-like than ever.

'We've decided to go out,' she said as she undulated elegantly across the room towards Rosie, her deportment faultless despite her tricky shoes and her narrow dress, 'to an artshow. It'll give you and David a chance to get acquainted.'

'Er . . . Yes. Okay. Good idea,' replied Rosie, struggling to stay calm. She'd been banking on company tonight, with the Hadeys on hand to help her.

Julian's brown eyes flashed as he put down his glass and walked towards her, a girl's wet-dream in suave tailoring and a pure white shirt. Rosie felt a pang of pure lust at the sight of him. Her body remembered his, recreating the warmth of his skin against it. She glanced at Celeste, fearful of betraying herself, but the other woman's eyes were as vivid as her husband's, and aglow with expectation.

'Don't worry, Rosie,' said Julian softly as he pressed his lips against her cheek. 'He's a lucky boy. I almost wish *I* could start again.'

Rosie gasped as his hands settled knowledgeably on her body, exploring her breasts and her bottom through the malleable film of the chiffon. She felt her nipples respond immediately, and her cleft grow soft and moist, excited as much by Celeste's bright gaze as by Julian's long, roving fingers.

'You're beautiful,' he whispered, kissing her throat and moving his groin against her hip. His penis was semi-erect already, and hardening fast, and his kiss was wet and thorough. Rosie felt herself drowning, slipping deep beneath the high waves of need as his caress settled firmly on her mound, and he massaged her sex through her skirt.

'Julian, please,' she moaned. Celeste was grinning at her, over his shoulder, her violet eyes glittering like black-lined stars, and her slender silk-gloved hand at her own groin as if she found the sight of her husband groping another woman arousing.

The fondling seemed to go on forever, and Rosie's knees went weak. He was rubbing her insistently now, stroking her bottom through her paper-thin skirt. Without thinking she closed her eyes and put her arms around his shoulders, and as she did so, a pair of soft, feminine hands settled lightly on her shoulders.

'Relax, Rosie. Enjoy him,' whispered Celeste, her voice rough and compelling as her fingers slid and explored. Rosie felt them on her back, then sliding around her ribs to her breasts.

Rosie shook violently as they roused her, and made her respond to the touch of four hands. She locked her fingers around Julian's neck, swaying because her legs wouldn't hold her, and felt him rock her on her own hot vulva.

'Relax, Rosie. Give it up,' murmured Julian against her neck, swirling his hold, and making her come.

'Oh no! No! No!' she whimpered, her body betraying her. Her legs seemed to buckle and her strength leeched away. Only seconds later, she was being settled on the sleek leather sofa, still panting while her quim leapt and rippled.

'Why did you do that?' she gasped, as first one, then the other sat down beside her. Celeste produced a drink for her, the sherry that Rosie was oh-so ready for. As she drank most of it down, she felt a hand – Celeste's – settle gently, almost possessively on her thigh.

'To prime you, sweetheart,' the other woman said softly. 'To set you thinking of sex. So that David will too. With your eyes so sparkling, he'll know something's happened. And he'll want something to happen for him too.'

Rosie could feel heat in her cheeks and smell her own perfume swirling around her. She could well believe her eyes were glowing.

'You're very lovely, Rosie. Very sensual. He'll find you irresistible,' said Julian, giving her shoulders a squeeze as if what they'd just done was quite normal.

Maybe it is? thought Rosie suddenly, sipping her

last drop of sherry, then letting Celeste take the glass and refill it. What had he said? *We're pretty relaxed about things here.* Maybe he and his wife shared women all the time? Lots of them? Men too? Maybe they had orgies a plenty, and needed to hurry up and get David eroticised so he could join in?

'We have to go now,' said Celeste, passing the glass back to Rosie. 'But don't worry. Nothing *has* to happen tonight. Although if it did . . .'

'David will be down in a minute, Rosie,' Julian interrupted, his voice ineffably kind. 'Just take a deep breath, be yourself, and I'm sure it'll all go well.'

Rosie watched, dumbstruck, as he rose, took his wife's arm and escorted her across the room. At the doorway, they turned – as one – blew Rosie a kiss, then left, their voices echoing softly in the passage.

Oh God, I don't know if I can do this! she thought, sipping quickly from her newly filled glass. The time of reckoning had come, and here she was still dizzy with pleasure from the weirdest, most unexpected kind of sex.

It wasn't a rape because she hadn't been penetrated, or forced. Nevertheless, she *had* been railroaded. By a man, and his wife. Working as a team! Julian's fingers, and Celeste's eyes; it had taken both of these to make her come.

Pull yourself together, Howard! she told herself sternly, running her hands over her top and skirt, checking for any sign of what had happened. Everything seemed okay, but there wasn't time to make sure; even as she patted at her hair, then touched her fingers to her burning throat, the door handle turned, the door itself slowly opened, and David appeared on the threshold.

Oh dear Lord, he's amazing! thought Rosie, stunned anew by the boy's fresh, pure beauty. He'd clearly dressed-up tonight, whether in her honour or not, she'd no way of telling. She only knew he looked wonderful, and that his clothes were elegant and well-chosen: a pair of stylishly baggy black linen trousers and a rather Italian-looking maroon silk shirt.

'Hi!' he said in his softly accented voice. 'Have the others gone?' The bright, golden eyes looked wary, but to Rosie's relief, not unfriendly.

'Yes,' replied Rosie, sensing his nervousness, and feeling a strange surge of kinship. They were both in this: both strangers, both not quite sure of themselves. Apart from sexual experiences, they were more or less equals, and she felt instinctively that David could probably help her just as much as she could help him.

'They've gone to some exhibition or other,' she continued, finding it suddenly easier to smile. 'So it's just you and me . . . Would you like a drink?'

As soon as she'd said that she wondered if she'd slipped up. What if he was on medication or some-thing? 'Do you drink?' she added, cautiously.

'Yes. Yes, I do,' he answered, with a small tentative smile. 'Not a lot . . . But I'm working on it.' The smile widened, and Rosie felt a slow, luscious softening of her innards. For a second, she wondered if she knew any jokes; because that tiny hint of what his smiling face might look like was more intoxicating than any amount of alcohol. And she was mad for more of it.

Trying desperately to pull herself together, she did

her best nonchalant walk towards the silver tray, and its extensive cache of drinks. 'Sherry?' Her fingers hovered over the various decanters.

'Er . . . Yes, please.' He sounded hesitant again.

'Sweet or dry?'

'Oh, sweet, please. I know it isn't very sophisticated, but it's the only kind I like.' He shrugged his shoulders helplessly, and flashed just an instant of that smile again.

'Well, thank God for that!' Rosie said with feeling. 'I'm fed up with people who think I'm an uncivilised oik because I only like drinks that are sweet!' She had a split second vision of Geoff's disapproving face when she'd requested something that didn't suit his image. 'Try this!' she went on, pouring a glass of the same sherry she was drinking.

He took the glass very carefully from her, but still their fingers touched. She sensed that he was wanting to flinch, but controlling it.

Then he smiled.

Rosie had never seen a transformation like it. She could almost imagine the sun had come up, or the moon risen. The shy, edgy boy had gone and in his place stood a sexy young man with magic in his brilliant, golden eyes. It only lasted a second but the afterglow left Rosie dazzled.

After a moment or two, she realised he was holding out his glass towards her, offering a toast. Half-numbed, she topped up her own and chinked it to his.

'To being uncivilised,' offered David after slight hesitation.

'To being unsophisticated,' answered Rosie, fighting

for self control as the smile appeared again, briefly but tellingly.

The ice was broken now, or at least dented, and as they sat down together, Rosie felt able to start a conversation. 'That's a beautiful shirt,' she ventured, with meaning. The rich, dark colour really suited him; accentuating the distinct red tint in his smooth brown hair, and making his pale skin look paler than ever, and twice as dramatic and unusual. She wondered if the effect was intentional, and by extension, marvelled at how someone who'd lived in seclusion could manage to choose such good clothes.

'I got it in Paris,' he replied, smoothing his finger-tips along his sleeves, the action measured and sensuous as if the texture of the cloth gave him pleasure.

Rosie felt a cool sharp frisson as she watched him. His fingers were long and narrow: very tapered and elegant. Without stopping to think, Rosie imagined them running slowly over female skin, caressing it thoroughly, comparing its consistency with that of the inanimate silk.

'Celeste took me around all the shops and boutiques.' He paused, then shrugged again. 'Or at least it *felt* like all of them!' His smile sent her composure sliding. 'I've never had so many new clothes in my life, and . . . Well, it's weird, I actually enjoyed it once we got started. Choosing. Trying on. Buying. It's the last thing I'd ever have thought I'd be interested in, but there you are. There's always something round the corner to surprise you, isn't there?'

This was the longest speech Rosie had yet heard him make, and the most mature. His soft, even voice seemed to play across her nerve-ends; its richness, its slight northern lilt, affecting her strangely and powerfully. She wondered what it would sound like when he was whispering endearments, or gasping in ecstasy. She wondered how he'd react, and what he'd say, if she reached out and touched him right now.

'Too true,' she replied after a couple of seconds, belatedly responding to his philosophical observation. She'd had her own share of surprises in the last few days, and she was sure there were still many ahead. Probably from David himself.

As a speculative silence fell, the dinner gong rang out cheerfully.

'Shall we?' said David, rising. He held out his hand like a courtier, helping her up and onto her feet as if she were a visiting princess, rather than a member of his cousin's household staff.

'Love to,' she replied, taking the offered hand and trying not to tremble. David's fingertips were warm now, and his grip, for a moment, was surprisingly firm and confident. It seemed as if he was going to hold onto her hand, and keep holding it as they walked to the dining room. But, almost immediately, Rosie sensed he was unsure of her again. Unsure of how to act. Unsure, perhaps, of what he was feeling.

But what was he feeling? she thought as they sat down to their starter. She'd seen him react in the car, and instinct told her his disappearance afterward had been linked to it. So was the same chemistry at work now?

He seemed calm, and as they ate their beautifully prepared meal, he chatted quietly about books and about the time he'd spent in Paris. He even asked questions about Rosie's previous jobs, and where she'd lived and studied. But somehow, beneath the still exterior, she sensed an inner agitation. He was like a hurricane in reverse, she realised. More or less unruffled on the surface, but underneath, in a violent emotional turmoil.

Instinct – and wishful thinking – told her that this ferment was sexual. It could be due to his recent emotional upheavals, but something told her these had been transient, because basically his underlying persona was strong and stable. He was most likely reacting to her womanhood and her femininity because she was the first female he'd met since coming here who he could think of as a viable partner. His cousin – and presumably her female friends – were too experienced and sophisticated to approach, and there was no-one else around of quite the right age. He was too new to the City to go out seeking companionship – so that only left Rosie Howard. Rosie wasn't a member of the glitter set; she was older than he was, but only slightly; and she was around in the house, and seemed perfectly placed to befriend him.

Good grief, it's no wonder he's nervy! she thought, trying not to watch him and make him feel worse.

But it was difficult not to watch him. It was almost impossible not to feel attracted to him, or to respond to his youth and his maleness – especially as his presence here tonight had been engineered for her just as much as hers had been contrived for him. The very artificiality of their pairing was a subtle but potent aphrodisiac.

Rosie couldn't eat much, but she was glad that

David's appetite seemed normal. He ate moderately, yet appeared to quietly appreciate his food and the single glass of wine he took with it. The movements of his slender hands as he handled the cutlery were strangely erotic. His fingers were long and flexible, and his actions neat and deft. She wondered what those hands would feel like on her, and now being almost certain that David was the phantom pianist, she began to speculate how long it might take him to transfer his artistry at the keyboard onto the flesh of a living woman; like herself.

Surely if he could play music so expressively, he could understand the beauty and delicacy of lovemaking. He clearly had a poetic soul, which meant he was halfway to being a lover already.

'Are you the one I've been hearing playing the piano?' she asked, taking a sip of wine.

'Yes. It's me. I play a bit.' He smiled modestly and shrugged his shoulders. 'I've never had any proper tuition, but I've had a lot of time to myself to practice. I hope there weren't too many duff notes!'

'You play beautifully,' said Rosie, knowing it was the truth. A feeling for the music meant so much more than sterile technical skill, especially for her purposes. 'Would you play again for me,' she asked, 'when we've finished our dinner?'

David looked doubtful, and bit his lip, snagging its full, pink softness with his strong, and very even white teeth.

'Please,' she pleaded, aware that the wine and the sherry she'd drunk were making her dangerously forward. She'd have to be careful not to push too hard.

David was far more confident than she'd expected, but she sensed his self-worth was still fragile.

'Alright,' he agreed, smiling his amazing smile again. 'But don't say I didn't warn you.'

The rest of the meal passed smoothly, in spite of Rosie's growing excitement. David described how he'd more or less taught himself to play the piano by listening to recordings of the classical masters, and also learnt to read music from a book. It seemed a peculiar way to go about things, but Rosie was impressed. David was obviously determined and resourceful, and would work hard to get what he wanted, no matter how daunting the task. It filled her with a strange kind of awe.

When they returned to the library, someone had been there before them. A small fire had been lit to take the edge off the early summer evening chill, and a bottle of sparkling wine stood cooling on ice, with two tall crystal flutes beside it.

How clichéd, Julian, thought Rosie wryly, but she smiled when she saw that it wasn't champagne in the cooler, but the sweet Italian spumante she preferred.

'Would you like some of this?' she asked David, who was already perched on the piano stool, flexing his fingers and looking mildly apprehensive.

'I'll have some afterwards, if that's alright,' he said, then bit his lip again, the gesture small but innocently sexy. 'I'm bad enough when I'm sober!'

'Get away!' said Rosie, with a laugh, knowing she wasn't quite sober herself.

David didn't reply, but began a few hesitant practice phrases.

Half-entranced already, Rosie took a seat where she could discreetly watch him play without making him feel too nervous.

After a few minutes he launched into a fully fledged melody, although not one Rosie could name. It sounded vaguely familiar, as if she'd heard it in the background of a television programme or a film. Her knowledge of classical music and piano technique was negligible, but within moments she knew one thing. As she'd suspected this afternoon, David really could play. Play well – and entirely without music.

There was something exquisitely sensuous about the delicate flow of the notes. Rosie suppressed a sigh, her whole body alive and quivering as David unknowingly played magical tunes on it. The sweet wine helped, of course, but it wasn't only that. Rosie felt as if she could drift away, floating on a mist of relaxed and delicious languor. She forgot all her qualms about her task, and surrendered to fate itself. What would happen would happen; whether tonight or another night. All that mattered was a beautiful young man playing the piano for her.

Suddenly, Rosie recognised a piece she could put a name to: Beethoven's *Fur Elise*, a melody she'd always found disturbingly erotic. The rolling, rippling phrases seemed to synchronise perfectly in her mind with little forays of foreplay, rushes towards pleasure, then teasing moments of stillness and anticipation. The notes seemed to hover on the brink of being played, like a lover's fingers circling, approaching, but not quite touching a particularly sensitive zone.

Putting aside her glass, she sank back into the chair

and closed her eyes, letting the music paint a picture of herself and David. Making love.

He'd undressed her cautiously and reverently, pausing as each garment was removed to admire what his hands had revealed. She could almost feel those elegant, pianist's fingers exploring the contours of a breast, a thigh, the slope of a hip. She could imagine those firm pink lips pressed gently to her belly, and the tantalising swipe of his inquisitive young tongue as it dipped into her navel, swirled around, then cruised downwards to areas more sacred.

She shifted her body on the shiny leather sofa, restless as she wondered what David's naked body might look like.

He'd be pale certainly, but attractive. Lithe but strong, his limbs fresh and limber, his sex eager and untested. He'd be a natural gentleman, she sensed. Anxious to please her as much as himself. He'd push into her slowly, very slowly, the strain contorting his face. He'd cry out softly as he plumbed her waiting body, and she would too, enraptured by the stretching of her channel around the bulk of his warm, thick member.

With a start, she realised that she'd actually sighed aloud. And that the music had stopped, probably some time ago. She flicked open her eyes, and looked across at David.

He was watching her, intently, and almost fearfully; as if he'd seen her dreams and was screwing up his courage to ask if they could ever be real. She could almost taste his confusion and the way he was being torn by urges he didn't understand.

'That was wonderful, David,' she said, keeping her voice low as she would have done to an inquisitive but timid wild animal. He was so close, so close to being ready, but commonsense whispered 'beware'. A false move now and he'd be crushed.

'Shall I play something else?' he asked, his voice not quite steady.

'Yes, that'd be lovely.'

He still needed a breathing space, she realised, just as she needed a chance to cool off; to channel her desire, and regain control of the situation and herself.

With a slight nod, he began to play another tune she knew. Debussy's *Clair de Lune*, a piece so haunting and lovely that she recognised straight away that she'd made a mistake. Vivid images assailed her, more tempestuous and sexual than ever. In her mind, her young lover was playful, confident and virile. His timing was perfect and his hot, gleaming penis had a rhythm and purpose of movement that touched her right to the core.

Rosie felt a compelling urge to masturbate. To assuage the unbearable hunger that the music, and the musician had triggered. She looked across at David again, and the sight was incredible. His beautiful face was a picture of concentration, and he was clearly as enraptured by his music as she was. He seemed so lost in the notes that flowed from his fingers that he barely seemed to have to look at the keyboard. His lips were parted, and his cheeks slightly flushed, and she could almost believe he was aroused. As he played a long, sparkling run, up and down the octaves, he sighed imperceptibly, and in that moment Rosie could have sprung to her feet, run across the room and kissed him.

Oh God, I wish I dare kiss her! thought David as he played almost without conscious control.

He'd always been able to do this; set half of his mind to a task, while the other ran free with something else. But tonight it wasn't just his mind running wild, it was his body too. His glands, his hormones, and the stiff wayward thing between his legs that was aching and as hard as a bone.

As his fingers danced smoothly on the keys, he could think of nothing but the beautiful woman who sat just a few feet away from him. Rosie Howard, the librarian, who perfectly embodied everything he longed for. Everything his confused libido had been craving for these past few terrifying weeks.

Sex. It had hit him all of a sudden, and rushed through his senses like a runaway train. No longer abstract as it had always been before – on television, and in books and films – sex had become real and irresistible and urgent.

It was right at the centre of things now, plaguing his every waking thought and his rampant, undisciplined body.

David had known the rudimentary technical details of sex for many years now. He'd read the entry on human reproduction in his encyclopaedia when he was ten, scanning the description with a strange sense of detachment, finding it hard to believe that his own genitalia could join with those of a woman. The word 'pleasure' had been just that, a word.

Things had begun to change in his teens. His body had responded occasionally to the prettier girls at school, and he'd blushed furiously, terrified that someone would notice his penis swelling in his trousers. He'd felt befuddled by what he knew was an erection – confused that it could feel so good and so bad at the same time. He'd started finding himself stirred by unexpected thoughts – and he'd been shocked at the sublime sensations that stroking his own flesh could produce. He'd dreamed luridly and often woken up clutching his penis, with his own sticky semen splattered all over the sheets and his body. For a while he'd felt guilty, then commonsense had prevailed. It didn't seem to do him any harm and afterwards he always felt glowing.

His interest in sex had waned when he'd left school at sixteen; swamped, he now realised, by his responsibilities to his grandparents. He'd sought solace in books, in the piano, and in solitary study; barely thinking of his body at all, except for the basic tasks of maintaining his health and hygiene.

He remembered little of the dark days after his grandfather's funeral, and it seemed now that he'd consciously blanked it out, living in a zombie-like state until he'd woken up one day, and suddenly felt alive again. Since then, he'd been constantly ravenous for knowledge and experience, his imagination going crazy, and his penis always ready to rise. Just the thought of a woman could do it, and the reality drove him to distraction.

Girls in the street. Girls in shops. His cousin's friends. Even Celeste herself, sometimes, although this troubled him. They were fairly distantly related; but even so, her kindness, and the way she'd taken him under her wing when there was nobody else seemed to exclude her from the list of women he could lust over. She was also married, and to a man she so obviously adored.

He'd been very attracted to Celeste's personal fitness trainer – the quaintly nicknamed 'Ladybird' – a stunning red-haired sylph who came to the house almost daily to organise Celeste and Julian's exercises. She was a friendly and sociable woman, but despite this, David decided she was far too sleek and glamorous. And also probably far too sexually accomplished to have time for a nineteen year old virgin. Like all the other women he'd come into contact with in London, and more recently, in Paris, she simply seemed too experienced for him. He'd been forced to resort to masturbation again, using either vague images of women he'd met or seen, or the books that he'd clandestinely borrowed from Julian's library. Every night he'd pick something from the special case and take to his room to study.

But now, as he swept into the final romantic phrase of *Clair de Lune*, he knew he'd found a better inspiration: Rosie Howard, the custodian of both the chaste books and the rude ones.

Julian's new librarian was as good to look at, if not better, than any women he'd encountered so far – and also terrifyingly approachable. As his penis kicked hard inside his trousers, his fingers shook on the keys and the resulting discordant clatter made the object of his dreams look towards him.

'Are you okay?' she asked softly.

'Yes ... I ... I just lost my concentration for a second,' he answered, inwardly cursing the blush that was colouring his cheeks. When he looked too closely at her, her gorgeousness made him weak and unco-ordinated, and the lovely rounded curves of her body made *his* body throb and disobey him.

'Why don't you take a break? You've played so well you deserve a rest. Come and have a glass of wine.' She patted the settee beside her and nodded to the bottle in its cooler.

David felt a hot surge of nervousness. He'd managed pretty well so far, at a safe distance, with pianos and tables between them, but now she was inviting him closer. He'd have to sit next to that warm, soft body, and be near enough to touch it. Would he be able to control his erection? It felt as if it was standing out in front of him like a signpost, even though – after the way he'd reacted in the car – he'd chosen his underwear carefully, to try and keep his unruliness in check.

As calmly as he could, he sat down and accepted some wine. When he took his first sip, the sweet effer-vescence made him feel a bit more settled, so he drank half a glassful then put it back down on the tray.

'I love this room, don't you?' Rosie said, gesturing at the shiny polished woods, the thick carpet, and the great mass of books all around them.

'Yes, it's wonderful,' he whispered, agreeing but really more interested in the way her slight, graceful movement had made her top pull tight against her, the thin, gauzy stuff outlining the lushness of her shape.

She had the most beautiful breasts. He'd admitted to himself, and to his shame, that they were almost the first thing he'd noticed about her. This morning she'd been wearing a soft, tight sweater that had moulded to her curves and made his fingers tingle with the unbearable desire to touch her. He'd imagined how he might actually hold her breasts, cup them in his hands, and discover their weight and consistency. The floaty garment she wore tonight didn't cling in the way the sweater had done, but its slight almost ghostly consistency hid very little of her marvellous silhouette. The misty multicoloured fabric lay closely against the long, firm lines of her thighs, and even hinted at the vee-shape between them, the greatest female mystery of all. David had seen topless women in newspapers, and even on television, but what lay between a woman's thighs was rarely so easily seen. He'd glimpsed the odd magazine, circulated secretly at school; but it wasn't until he'd had the run of this library that he'd finally seen the sight that so intrigued him.

Oh God, what a revelation! Unable to tear his eyes from the chiffon shrouded contours of Rosie's soft belly, he imagined what the body beneath the cloth must look like. The delicate creases of the groin. The deep, dark dent of the navel. The shadowy triangle of hair that he imagined would be the softest and prettiest on earth. He wondered what colour Rosie's pubic grove would be. The hair on her head was thick and glossy, a long heavy fall, perfectly straight, and a subtle ashy-blonde colour. He tried to transfer the same shade and texture to the hair that protected her sex, then decided it was probably curlier, like that of the women in the pictures.

When at last he managed to look up again, Rosie was looking intently at him, her blue eyes as vivid as cornflowers and bright with a strange excitement. He shifted uncomfortably on the sofa, willing her not to repay the compliment and glance down at his crotch. *His* state would be no mystery at all!

'So what are your favourite books then?' she asked smoothly, her calm voice at odds with the brilliance of her eyes. He sensed that she was nervous too, and it comforted him.

'The Conan Doyle first editions,' he said after a moment's thought. It was an acceptable lie; he had read most of them, before he'd discovered the erotic books and lost interest in everything else. 'I've always been a bit of a Sherlock Holmes fan, and those books are so rare it's a privilege to handle them.' And so it had been – until the sex books had become an obsession, and he'd spent hour after hour handling both the books themselves, *and* the effect they had on him.

'And what about the other books?' she asked, sipping her wine, a faint sexy slyness on her face that both troubled and thrilled him. 'Have you looked at any of those?' She nodded in the direction of the glass-fronted cases that housed the erotica.

He was blushing again, he could feel it, and he was sure Rosie could see it. For an instant he considered denying all knowledge of Julian's spicy literature, but his pink face had already answered.

Rosie smiled, stood up, then walked across the

room, her back view as entrancing as the front. She had a finely-shaped bottom that swayed and lifted as she walked, the firm lobes moving freely as if her underwear was as filmy as her skirt. David longed to be able to touch her, and hold that sweet, rounded rump as he made love to her. His penis twitched and ached, and he thought of how superior it must feel to be held by a woman's body, instead of his own sweating fist. What would it be like to kiss her while he was in her, and feel her soft breasts pressed against his chest?

The dream was almost but not quite agony, his desire exacerbated by the elegant, assured way she reached into the cabinet and took out books, one after another, stacking them in her arms and holding them to her bosom to carry them, just as he longed to be held there and cradled.

When she brought the books back with her, and placed them on the table, he saw they were all large format illustrated volumes, the sort that were filled with the very pictures that had inflamed him the most – and begun his sexual education.

'What an incredible treasury this is,' she murmured, running her fingers over first one shiny cover then another. There was something intensely sensuous in the action, as if it were a succession of lovers she was caressing, not inanimate sheaves of bound paper.

'Look at this, isn't it beautiful?' she opened the top book on the heap, a collection of photographs by a contemporary French luminary, all devoted to the joys of the kiss. *Les Baisers Erotiques* it was called, naturally enough, and from a previous investigation,

David knew that some of the kisses were extremely hot indeed!

Nothing in his experience or reading had prepared him for such arrangements of mouths and skin. He'd trembled when he'd first seen them, and he trembled again as Rosie flipped quickly through the introduction.

The first kiss in itself was quite pure; a man and a woman with their lips delicately pressed together, the man's fingers cradling the chin of his partner with a tenderness that touched the heart. There was no other contact between their bodies at all, but the photograph's piquancy arose from the fact that these considerate and courtly lovers were naked on a black silk bedsheet. The man's penis was erect and yearned towards his partner, its swollen tip resting just an inch from her gleaming white belly.

It was so easy to imagine himself in that picture. His own penis was yearning too. It felt tense and feverish, harder than ever now, and even though it was contained inside his underpants there was a sensation of it stretching and reaching. It felt as if it no longer really belonged to him and was gravitating towards Rosie of its own accord.

What would it feel like to touch her with his penis? Have her warm, flawless skin against the most sensitive part of his body? To press himself, stiff and burgeoning, into the hollow between her thighs, while he kissed her mouth and held her.

And he did want to kiss her. He wanted to taste her mouth and touch her face. He'd be happy, in a way, with just that; and would probably have an orgasm if that was *all* that happened. He'd had them recently from much much less. He'd come just from thoughts and fantasy images.

It almost happened now, from shock, when Rosie turned the page, her perfume drifting out from her body as she inclined herself forward in front of him.

He could see the shape of her breasts with perfect clarity now. They were large and rounded and looked seductively firm. He longed to cup them in his fingers, to gently squeeze her. He'd never seen a living woman naked in his presence, but the idea of her bare body was a sudden, burning talisman. He wanted to see her, see the texture of her skin, then feel it and put his mouth against it.

He imagined sampling her skin again and again, putting his lips here and there, licking at her throat, her bosom, and even – oh God! – her sex.

That in itself would be enough for him, he realised. More than enough. His own body was so excited, so enraptured, that his crisis would come long before he ever made love to her; or tried to, he admitted realistically, aware of his paucity of experience. One disastrous, momentary fumble in the equipment store at his school didn't qualify a man as a lover. Especially as he had as little real idea of what to do now as he'd had back then.

Rosie turned the page.

The next image was the reverse of the first. The kiss it portrayed was savage, blatantly sexual, a reciprocal rape of the mouth. The participants were fully clothed, cumbersomely clad in the elaborate garments of the reign of Queen Elizabeth the First, yet somehow the man had his hand up the voluminous froth of the woman's layered petticoats, and from the splay of her legs, and the grimace on her face, it was clear he was caressing her vulva.

David moved uncomfortably on the settee. The pain in his penis and testicles was terrible now, but also marvellous beyond imagining. He felt like sobbing out loud, throwing himself on Rosie's mercy, forgetting his embarrassment and begging her to touch him. She was sitting quite still, yet obviously expecting something. It was as if she were waiting for a breakthrough. His breakthrough. She was staring down at the erotic kiss, but at the same time challenging him. Daring him. When she swayed slightly, then turned her head just the merest fraction, he gave in with a great sigh of relief.

Neither of them spoke, but Rosie's blue eyes told him volumes. Shaking violently, he leaned forward towards her, and tentatively put his lips against hers.

At first they just sat there with their mouths just touching. David was afraid to move a muscle. His penis was like a column of electricity, rigid and explosive, and even the slightest stimulation would trigger it. He felt as if it was wired to every single cell of his body, and he whimpered as Rosie's tongue stroked along his lips with a flicker and a dart, then pushed in a soft plea for entrance. He could feel the pressure of it, and its moist burning heat, right on the tip of his cock. He wanted to scream and cry and rub himself wildly, but instead he just opened his mouth and let her tongue slide in and explore him.

'Hold me, David,' she said against his lips, the

words breathing right into his soul. 'Put your arms around me. It's easy.'

It wasn't. It was the hardest, most dangerous thing he'd ever done. He knew it was crazy – because she had a full, strong, finely curved body – but she felt like eggshells in his arms. Any false or crass move would break her, and destroy this incredible moment.

And yet when he dared to do it, she purred with pleasure and pushed herself against him. Those breasts that looked so beautiful, now *felt* beautiful; rubbing against his chest, their heat and firmness barely shielded by the thin, silk layers of their clothing. Her nipples were like pebbles, like the stones of some perfectly ripe fruit. His fingers itched to seek them out and squeeze them, but constrained by fear and emotion, he could only lay his hands cautiously on her back.

For a while Rosie kept her hands cradled around his head, holding his face to hers so she could taste the interior of his mouth. He felt her licking at his tongue, his teeth, his palate. He felt her challenge him again, and goad his tongue into a duel with hers. She lapped and sipped at him, opening her own mouth so wide that he could feel the tension in her throat and jaw just as clearly as he felt it in his.

It was sensory overload. Her scent, her taste, the pointy tips of her breasts against his chest. The line of her back, trembling finely beneath his hot searching fingers.

I'm going to come, he thought fatalistically. Any second now. It's going to burst out of me. It's going to spurt inside my underwear, and I'm going to shake and jerk, and she'll know exactly what's happening. With a jolt of delicious terror, he felt her right hand slide away from his head, dip down and tuck itself in between them, cruising his midriff and his belly.

'Oh God, please . . .' he gasped into her mouth, not sure if he was begging her to touch him – or *not* to touch him. Whichever it was, she responded, her gentle hands closing on his groin, her fingers at the hub of his torment.

His trousers and briefs might as well not have existed. Her touch was infinitesimal, exquisitely light, yet he felt it as if he were naked. In some ways he was naked. He was raw and vulnerable and inexperienced, and she was holding him intimately, the first woman ever to handle his genitals with intent to arouse and excite him.

And how exciting it was. All-encompassing. As wild and thrilling as a wealth of complex, protracted lovemaking. Her careful, almost imperceptible hold was more stimulating than an hour of his own hand's rubbing. Tears filled his eyes, and he gurgled incoherently as his penis leapt and lurched, then turned to fire along the whole of its length. The same hot sweetness seemed to run like a flame up his spine, and he cried out harshly, his hips jerking uncontrollably as he came in the crucible of her fingers. He found himself falling against her, sobbing, his cock still twitching. Then he felt her sure, safe body take his weight.

It was like floating. His thoughts were hazy with pleasure, drifting free in a no-consequence place where only her warmth, and her sweet, fragrant flesh existed.

His groin was awash with heat and stickiness, and he was astounded when he realised he was smiling to himself, still euphoric with the aftershocks of orgasm. Orgasm with a woman. With a lover for the very first time.

Slowly, the enormity of what had happened began to dawn. What a wimp she must think him. She'd hardly touched him and he'd ejaculated helplessly. He felt like an abject idiot. He was a callow untutored boy, but shouldn't he at least have tried to be a little more than that?

Suddenly he felt weak and utterly ashamed, and he tried to pull away. Rosie seemed to want to hold onto him, but he shook himself free, keeping his gaze fixed stubbornly on the table before them. He couldn't let her see the humiliation in his eyes, the failure. He thought of the other men she must know. Men who could make love to her for hours on end, attending to her pleasure. Suave, experienced men like Julian who had sexual skill, and who didn't come in their trousers after just one caress. He wanted to look down and see if there was a stain, but he couldn't bear to.

'What's wrong?' Rosie asked, her soft voice making him jump.

'I'm . . . I'm sorry,' he muttered. He felt disgusted by his body and by his soft penis, bathed in accusing wetness and still tingling inside his underwear.

'Sorry for what?' she persisted.

David wished for the proverbial opening of the earth. It was clear that this was not going to be ignored. Rosie knew what had happened to him, but she still seemed to want him to tell her about it. Every shameful detail.

'I . . . I . . . Oh God Almighty, you know what happened to me!'

He was surprised by the fieriness of his voice, and as he sprang to his feet, fighting the fact that his knees almost buckled beneath his weight, he was furious that he hadn't felt this energy a little earlier.

'You had an orgasm,' Rosie said calmly. Irritatingly calmly. She sounded too much like a teacher, too understanding. David suddenly felt irrationally angry at her, just for being older and wiser. And so beautiful that it made him want to come all over again.

'Yes! Yes, I did! When you'd hardly even touched me!' He strode away, shakily but keeping his body as straight and unyielding as he could, and sat down on the piano stool. Out of the danger zone, his subconscious told him slyly.

'And I'm sorry,' he went on, running a finger agitatedly along the edge of the keyboard and still trying to avoid looking at her. 'I'm hopeless. I've never had sex. I don't know what to do with a woman and I can't control myself. There, are you satisfied?'

The irony of that final statement hit him like a blow in the gut. 'No!' he cried almost immediately. 'Of course you're not! How could you be? It takes a real man to satisfy a woman, not a gormless, over-excitable idiot like me!' He pressed his face into his hands as fresh tears began to fill his eyes; tears of frustration and disappointment. He suddenly wanted more than anything on earth to be able to pleasure her, no matter how much her beauty laid him low.

Rosie was light on her feet, that was obvious. After a few moments, David felt her sit down beside him, even though he'd never heard her cross the room. He flinched when she put her arm around his shoulders, but almost instantly, he began to feel better.

'If you've never had sex, David, what do you expect?'

He couldn't reply, but her arm tightened reassuringly around him.

'Everyone has to start somewhere. It's not all that long since . . .' She paused as if about to reveal something that embarrassed *her*. 'Well, it's not all that long ago since I started myself.' Her pretty face pinkened slightly, and David felt a sudden rush of something quite divorced from sex, but in its own way, just as breathtaking. 'Would it help,' she asked, 'if I told you that I often feel gormless and over-excitable too?'

7

A Room with a View

Now why on earth did I say that? thought Rosie a little while later, in her room.

Instinct. That was why. Her own impressions concurring automatically with Julian's. He'd said that David would never respond to her if she behaved like a worldly sexual superwoman, and he'd been right. Her honest 'I'm clueless too' approach had been the right one.

Even so, David had beaten another of his hasty retreats not long after they'd shared their kiss. Rosie supposed it was for the best, and that to rush now would be disastrous, but her hormones were completely at odds with her reason. David was beautiful and intriguing, a physical turn-on despite his naïveté, and he'd been quite right about her being unsatisfied. She *was* unsatisfied. Profoundly so.

She was so excited that her poor frustrated body was paining her. Her breasts were swollen and her vulva ached; her flesh had been primed to have an orgasm, and it hadn't happened. And she knew now that she'd have to bow to the inevitable.

The urge to masturbate was all-consuming, but she managed to resist while she undressed for bed. There seemed something so sordid about just lifting her skirt and rubbing herself. Something dirty and delicious. It was a huge temptation, but she had to control herself, if only to help David. Somebody had to be operating on a higher, more channelled level. Somebody had to rise above blind lust so they could guide, command and instruct. And that somebody had to be her.

Finally though, after completing her toilette with some difficulty, Rosie lay down on her bed, her tingling body clad lightly in a soft, white cotton nightshirt. It was a pretty thing, lace trimmed, and very short – reaching only to the middle of her thighs. She wore no panties with it, and the bedspread felt comfortingly cool against the uncovered backs of her legs.

Squirming slightly, she enjoyed the freedom and comfort of her surroundings: the temperate, well-ventilated room where she could do whatsoever she wanted in private. Julian Hadey's beautiful house suddenly felt more of a home to her than anywhere she'd ever lived, and its walls were solid and reassuring. Sound wouldn't travel far, she was sure; so she could scream out her delight in her own body and no-one would hear her. And even if they did, they wouldn't turn a hair. In this house the erotic was the norm.

Pushing her nightshirt up over her belly, she considered whether to reach for the vibrator. It was tempting, because its action was powerful and satisfying, but somehow she didn't think power was what she needed. Her sex felt puffy and expectant; almost in climax already. She was as excited and aroused as poor befuddled David had been, and she'd only need the barest of touches.

Closing her eyes, she brought his handsome image into focus, loving the fact he was so different, and so unconventionally attractive. She got the clearest picture of his pale, pale skin, and those eyes like two golden pennies. And yet in other ways he had all the standard male attributes. Beneath his elegant silk shirt, she'd felt shoulders that were strong and a chest that was hard and muscular. His legs were long and athletic, and between them she'd felt a mass so imposing it had shocked her. Stroking her outer labia very lightly, she smiled at herself for being so predictable. Intellectually she knew size didn't matter – but even so, she couldn't help but be pleased that David had a big, thick penis.

What would it feel like, she wondered. In here. She put a fingertip to her vagina and felt the opening pulsate like a tiny, oceanic mouth. A hot, starry sensation began to build further in, spreading out rapidly to encompass the whole of her sex. Her clitoris was on fire, and she hardly dare touch it. She imagined David lying above her, pushing in, full and stiff and glowing with heat. No longer able to wait, she drew her finger up the length of her groove, then pressed hard on her clitoris, screaming at the intensity of a climax she'd been needing for what seemed like days. Her quim leapt and fluttered beneath her touch, and she came – deeply and powerfully – as if it were the first time in this house, and not something that had happened many times already.

And she couldn't believe it – just couldn't believe it! – that at the very same moment she started to throb, there was a sharp, insistent knock at her door.

Damn damn damn! Goddamn! she thought, clasping her whole crotch in her hand and rolling across the bed in aggravation.

Who the hell could it be? David, suddenly daring? Julian? Surely not, with his glorious wife at home. The Hadeys' sex-life seemed to have extraordinarily flexible boundaries, but surely Julian didn't hop from one bed to another on his wife's first night home? As she rose shakily from the counterpane, Rosie glanced at the clock. It was still only relatively early.

When she opened the door, her visitor was the last on her secret list of three.

Smiling like a goddess, Celeste swept gracefully into the room, filling it almost immediately with her heavy, exotic scent. As the door clicked shut, she paused, almost as if posing for a camera, and Rosie felt a rush of strange awareness.

This was the most beautiful woman she'd ever seen. A woman whose attractions seemed to over-ride the strictures of gender, and make Rosie want something about which she understood very little. As little as David understood about heterosexual sex.

Celeste's nightdress made everything in Rosie's collection seem chaste. It was made of a satin so thin it looked like fluid. Peach-coloured, and suspended from the narrowest of shoulderstraps, it seemed to drip from the points of Celeste's dark nipples; it snagged on the wiry black tangle of her pubis; then trickled on down to her ankles. Rosie could see

everything through it. Breasts. Pubic curls. Navel. All
of it sexual and wantable. Her own body surged with
feeling.

'Well, did it happen?' Celeste enquired, taking
Rosie's hand and urging her to sit on the bed.

For a moment Rosie was confused. Had what
happened? Her orgasm, just now? She glanced across
quickly to the mirror and saw her own flushed face,
and beside it Celeste's inquisitive expression. Julian's
wife had removed her make-up now, but somehow
her face looked equally vivid without it. Her hair hung
down in thick glassy sheets, curving neatly around the
line of her chin in its perfect Egyptian-style pageboy.

'Did you and David make love, Rosie?' she said
softly, re-stating her enquiry.

'N . . . no,' Rosie stammered. To describe what had
actually happened might make it sound like a failure.
The success was too vague and non-definitive. To a
woman like Celeste, it would just be an embarrassing
fumble.

'I think – perhaps – you mean "yes",' said Celeste
with a warm, gentle smile. Her long, scarlet-nailed
fingers rested lightly on Rosie's blushing cheek. 'There
are lots of ways to make love, Rosie . . .' Her thumb
grazed Rosie's jawline as if framing her face for a kiss.
'And something tells me that you've made a good
start.'

'Sort of,' Rosie admitted, imagining David's tortured
groin and how it had leapt and pulsed beneath her
fingers.

'Good,' Celeste replied crisply. 'I've got faith in
you, Rosie. And now I'll show you something that'll

help you.' Celeste's eyes flashed violet with mischief. 'The best way to find out what a man likes is to watch what he does for himself.'

'What do you mean?' whispered Rosie. She had a good idea what Celeste meant, but wondered how on earth they could achieve it.

'Come with me,' Celeste purred, reaching out to grip Rosie's hand. She raised it to her soft red lips and kissed. Kissed with all the seductive power and passion that Julian might have employed. The wife was as irresistible as the husband, she realised, and she was helpless to do anything but follow Celeste wherever she led.

In a moment, they were walking along a corridor, moving between walls full of collectable paintings in a part of the house she'd not yet explored. Rosie felt intensely conscious of her body; of the luxurious carpet beneath her unshod feet, and the cool air flowing up beneath her nightshirt, playing across her thighs and vulva. Every nerve-end alive, she watched as Celeste preceded her, studying the beautiful, easy roll of the other woman's buttocks as they swayed beneath pale filmy satin. Celeste's body was fine and slender; she should have made Rosie feel fat and lumpy but she didn't. The contrast between them only served to flatter them both.

'This is David's room.' Celeste indicated an anonymous, panelled door with a toss of her glossy black hair, but to Rosie's surprise, didn't stop. Instead she continued along a little way, then paused before a more concealed entrance – one painted to blend in with the wall.

'And this is the linen cupboard.' She pointed to the featureless door, and flashed Rosie a pantomime wink. 'Amongst other things.'

The room beyond the door was dark, larger than expected, and not just a storeplace for blankets – although there was a lot of fragrant, freshly laundered bedlinen stacked neatly on slatted wooden shelves.

On the other side of the room, however, opposite the shelves, was evidence of a pastime far less mundane than laundry. A long, lowish, plushly upholstered couch was set a few feet from the wall, parallel with the heavy velvet curtain that covered most of it. Rosie suddenly had a shrewd idea what was behind the thick draping, and her heart fluttered madly as Celeste led her in, switched on a tiny nightlight, then closed the door.

'Wha–' she began automatically, as Celeste pushed her down onto the couch.

A perfumed fingertip pressed lightly against her lips, and shushed her. Celeste's pale, silk-clad body was just a drifting blur, and Rosie could hear a subdued rustling as the other woman reached around in the darkness, and found the cord that opened the curtain.

Beyond the glass was a bedroom. Just as luxuriously decorated as her own, but in a cooler, more masculine style. It was a young man's room, done up in blues and light woods, and seen through what was obviously a floor-depth two-way mirror. An angular modern-looking lamp shed a glow across the centrally-placed futon-like bed, and more light shone from what was clearly a bathroom beyond.

Rosie felt a surge of horrified excitement. They were

planning voyeurism. An invasion of privacy. They were going to slyly peep at David, and as much as the prospect appalled her, it also made her body stir with lust.

As if he'd heard her thoughts, their subject appeared in the bathroom doorway, switching off the light behind him, then walked forward into the bedroom. Rosie felt Celeste's fingers over her mouth again, stifling her cry before it started.

Wearing only a pair of pristinely white pyjama bottoms, David was even lovelier to look at than she'd imagined. His pale chest was as bare of hair as an angel's, but looked surprisingly strong and substantial, as did his shoulders and his arms. There was a faint gleam of moisture on his skin, and his hair was wet and slightly tousled as if he'd only just stepped out of the shower. His feet were neat, slender and quite bare, and Rosie had a sudden sharp longing to kiss them and suck on his toes.

David frowned as he sank down onto his bed and stretched out; and regardless of the solid glass between them, Rosie could almost taste his tension. He looked uneasy, his limbs stiff and his body uncomfortable, and even as she studied him, there was an animal-like twitch beneath the white cotton fabric of his fly. He placed his hand on his crotch and squeezed himself, then Rosie heard him moan. The clarity of the sound was incredible, and told her that an even grosser intrusion was occurring; the room beyond was wired for sound as well as being two-way mirrored.

While David rubbed at his still-hidden penis, Rosie sensed movements much closer. The fingertips that had gently stopped her mouth now began to slide across the surface of her lips, stroking and exploring. At the same time other fingers settled on her nightshirt and eased it up over her belly.

She was caught between vision and sensation. Was Celeste going to touch her? Fondle her sex? The note left in Rosie's room had indicated that Julian Hadey's wife was blatantly and joyfully bisexual, and to stroke a fellow woman's vulva would be both natural and a titillating thrill to her.

But what about me? thought Rosie frantically. Will it thrill me?

The answer seemed to be 'yes'. With barely a moment's hesitation, she eased her legs apart, then felt the velvet of the seat tickle her bottom as Celeste tugged the nightshirt from under her. For a moment her view of David was blocked, and she felt a pair of firm, commanding lips press down onto hers. Husky words whispered against her mouth.

'Touch yourself, Rosie,' Celeste urged her. 'Share his pleasure. Masturbate your beautiful pussy while David plays with his cock. Rub yourself so you can both come together. It's the next best thing to making love.'

It was one of the most extraordinary speeches Rosie had ever heard, and for a fleeting instant she remembered how Geoff had liked to talk dirty, and how it had always sounded just that: dirty. Celeste's words were equally crude, but sounded sweet and caring too. Rosie obeyed her with a harsh little sob, sliding a fingertip down her belly to her groove, and there encountering a deep well of wetness.

David was moving on too. As if too hungry for sensation to stop, he was fumbling to unfasten his flies with one hand while with the other he carried on rubbing and squeezing. His actions seemed unco-ordinated, and slightly frenzied; but after a couple of moments, his pyjamas were unfastened and he'd ceased his rough pleasuring just long enough to expose his naked penis.

Rosie whimpered and pressed her fingers in hard between her legs. Squirming furiously, she squashed her clitoris against her pubic bone and came imme-diately, her eyes filled with David as he took his reddened sex in both his hands and worked it to a full, hard erection.

She'd been right about his size. His cock was large and sturdy, rising up from his groin like a tower, and crowned with a ruby-tinted glans. The whole length of it was already gleaming with fluid, and she could see him staring intently downwards, watching the tiny love-eye wink open as his fingers slid quickly on his shaft. He was both squeezing and pumping now, drag-ging his slick, penile skin to and fro on the rigid, stiffened core that it covered. The movements were ragged and violent, and Rosie almost sensed pain within his pleasure. She watched his bottom churn crazily, rucking up the bedclothes and making his pyjama fly gape and pull apart. She could see the thick, curly mat of his pubis, which was dark and wiry, less fine than the sleek red-brown hair on his head.

She was aching herself now, her sex-lips swollen, her clitoris engorged between them. Prising herself open with her fingers, she felt the whole zone shudder, and while half her mind prayed that Celeste would help her and touch her, the other half still shrank from that final, sapphic strangeness.

When the contact didn't come, she slid two fingers of one hand inside herself, then took her tingling bud in a tight, pinching grip between the thumb and a finger of the other. She felt another hand cover her mouth, and like a baby, she nuzzled at Celeste's scented fingers, trying to focus and stay still as the pit of her belly went molten and her clitoris twittered and leapt.

David was arching himself clear of the bed now, rising on his heels and shoulders, his body a long stretched curve. His eyes were closed tight in his grimacing face, and Rosie felt splintered by the loss of them. She imagined their bright, golden beauty looking in at her, boring through the shadows, growing huge when they saw her fingers attacking her own sex.

In an instant, they were coming together; both spasming, both flowing, the liquids of their crisis rich and copious. Semen shot high in the air from the tip of David's prick, and Rosie felt her fingers, her quim and her thighs become trickly with her thick clear juices. Her belly shimmered wildly, then went taut, and when Celeste's hand pressed flat across her mouth, she was glad of it. If she'd screamed as loud as she needed to, it would certainly have been heard through the glass. As it was she let her own heart rise up with David's cry, soaring high and free on his long, orgasmic moan.

After many protractedly exquisite moments, she fell back into herself and away from their strange, sweet joining. She no longer needed to see David now. Their climax had been apart, yet mutual all the same, and though there was no way he could know she'd been with him, Rosie felt alive with his presence. What they'd shared had marked her; she could still see him coming, hear his sobs, almost smell and taste his semen. Yet as she opened her eyes in the darkness – hardly aware that she'd even closed them – she found the curtain had been drawn across the mirror and all she could see was deep, deep shadow.

'Remarkable, isn't he?' murmured Celeste from close by, her perfume assaulting Rosie's nostrils. In the darkness, she was just a silvery flicker in her pale nightdress, and yet Rosie felt a strong urge to touch her. She wanted to acknowledge Celeste and caress her, but she felt too weak and lethargic. Her limbs seemed to be weighted with sex, yet to her surprise she felt hunger stir anew between her legs. She put her hand out for Celeste, all her qualms dispelled by the cosiness and intimacy around them.

'Oh no, love. Not me,' laughed Celeste, her voice teasing. 'At least not yet.' As if in compensation, she crushed her mouth against Rosie's and kissed her, the contact as deep and lusciously punishing as genital sex itself.

Rosie felt completely at a loss. What was happening now? There had been a strange prophetic lilt in Celeste's husky tones, as if there was more yet to come. More than a strong, thrusting tongue; more than the delicacy of long, tapered fingers as they slid over Rosie's damp thighs.

'Wait here, Rosie,' said Celeste, in a voice that

brooked no resistance. And Rosie didn't move because she couldn't. Pinned by inertia, her hands and arms limp at her sides, she let Celeste push her nightshirt up over her breasts and kiss each nipple in turn. Almost floating in the dim, ghostly light, Rosie felt the other woman licking her, laving her generous curves with spittle, mouthing and nipping. The feeling was shocking and wonderful, but just as she was rising to its sweetness, it disappeared. She sensed Celeste draw away from her, and as she did, even the night-light snapped off. There was a momentary slice of brilliance, and then Celeste was gone through the door, leaving Rosie alone, waiting.

Completely black now, the room had the womb-like quality of an isolation tank. Rosie had never been in such a structure, but this was just how she imagined it would feel. The featurelessness, the dense, yet comforting darkness, the blankness that let the mind range free; especially a mind like hers with so much to range over. There was so much that was new and exotic that had happened in a few short days.

Backtracking just a little way, she considered the tableau she'd just witnessed: David in his solitary lust; his pure, private desire, untempered by company or censure. She wondered if she'd ever see it again, and then desperately wanted to. She longed to see it with his knowledge and his trust. She yearned to watch first and then, in tenderness, participate; caressing his firm young flesh just as he'd done.

Other faces swam into her mind's eye: two faces, that were disparate, yet strangely kindred; dark, exotic Julian and his beautiful wife beside him. Suddenly,

Rosie had a yearning to see them together. Really together – their naked, contrasting bodies entwined in a sweating dance of love. She wondered fleetingly if there were any other cupboards around like this one. Oh God, what if there was a cupboard next to *her* room? What if Julian had watched her stroking herself, and seen the thrilling red vibrator at work between her tensing, jerking thighs? It was possible, in fact probable in this house. And how could she even feel outraged when she herself had so blissfully watched David?

The air in the room was warm and still, yet it seemed somehow to be stroking her, pressing down in waves on the soft, bare skin of her belly. Her sex was provoked by it, and the hair of her pubis felt sticky. More than ever, she wanted to touch herself, to play with her needy clitoris while her head filled with strange new visions.

She saw herself bent backwards, stretched across the leather arm of one of the library chairs while Julian stroked her vulva with a feather. Like an image from one of Julian's rare books, she saw Celeste in a bizarre leather harness, her sleek white body possessed by two bulbous vibrators. Beyond this, she saw Julian himself, hooded and gagged and being fondled by a faceless male lover. The last 'flick' was David, astride the end of his piano stool with his flies unzipped – while she, Rosie, sucked keenly on his thick, ruddy cock.

She was wriggling now, her bottom-cheeks split against the sofa to stimulate her dark, forbidden entrance. Between her thighs, she felt puffy and irritated, voracious for more pleasure; but when she reached down into her wetness to stroke it, a small warning sound stayed her fingers. The cupboard door opened slowly, then closed again. For a few seconds she saw the image of a figure, then nothing.

Not that she needed to see. Or ask. She knew who had come in. Celeste had said 'not me', and it was hardly likely to be David. Which left just one other person. One man, come to sample her body.

The footsteps were light, almost weightless, but the approach was swift. Someone confident was here, someone purposeful and skilled. She gasped as hands settled strongly on her thighs, drew them obscenely wide, then pulled her bodily forward on the couch until her tailbone lay on the front edge. A naked body moved between her legs, and an erection brushed the soft, inner slope of her rear. She sensed that the man had sunk gracefully to his knees so their sexes were precisely aligned.

The height, the angle and the moment were perfect, and Julian – wreathed in his telltale cologne – moved smoothly into the niche he'd created. Rosie tried to reach out and touch him, but he caught hold of her wrists before she could, and placed her hands on her own waiting body. One on her breast, one on her softly-curled pubis.

'Stroke yourself,' he said, echoing his wife's sultry order. 'I want you to be ready. I want you to be ravenous when I enter you. Starving. I want to coast straight into your flesh, ride in on a hot wave of hunger.' She heard him draw breath, moan almost, as if his own words excited him powerfully. 'Oh, Rosie . . . Oh God, yes, Rosie,' he hissed, grabbing her hard by the flanks as his velvet tip pushed at her entrance.

Mad for him, she pinched her tingling nipple and drummed on the bud of her clitoris – all the time shuffling and hitching herself forward in an effort to enclose and engulf him.

'Be still!' he commanded, his fingers closing on her body.

Rosie obeyed and let her muscles relax. At the same instant, and with total assurance, Julian began pulling as he pushed; dragging her hips towards him, as his penis drove in and took her. Rosie felt her sex-flesh give way and submit, her membranes deforming to take him.

The process was slow, deliciously slow. A lesser man couldn't have managed it, and would have come – in seconds – from the extenuated caress of her tightness. For an instant Rosie thought of David, and imagined him plunging in and losing it because the pleasure was too much and too soon. He'd cry out with agonised despair, slump across her, sob as the sensations overcame him.

But Julian wasn't David. They were both entrancing men, but Julian was – she realised happily – a lover of infinite experience. His mastery of his own body was unswerving, and the entry of his sex into hers was an event both extended and delightful which brought Rosie to a sudden sweet climax.

As her vagina throbbed and fluttered, she felt, sensed, and seemed to see in her mind that Julian lifted her up from the sofa; raising her hips and thighs so he could improve both his power and his leverage. He was handling her like a doll, a toy, a pretty, malleable indulgence to satisfy his whimsical desires – something she should hate with all her heart after Geoff. She'd come to this house fed up of being used – but now, in the blackness, she adored it, rippling around her possessor's fine stiffness, and crying out as her inner self massaged him.

'Ah!' was the only sound Julian uttered, but his fingers and his cock were more eloquent. His fierce grip hurt her unintentionally, and in her channel, his penis bucked and leapt – as if emitting a sharp burst of pleasure that made his climax become one with her own.

He held her until long after they were still, his cock resting in her, their crotches joined in heat. His only physical action was to curve himself over her, kissing her upper body and nuzzling at her throat and shoulders.

Rosie felt as if she were still in that imaginary tank. Her thoughts were as loose and drifting as the water might have been; moving languidly between her recent, and most exotic memories. She made no comparisons or judgements, but just revisited the beauty and pleasure of each of them: the solemn shyness of David, and the challenge of his innocence; Celeste, and the lure of the utterly new; Julian, who was both exploitative and giving, and who used her body like an artist.

It seemed impossible to believe that only a week or so ago, she'd been barely more experienced than her 'pupil', and prone to blushing over her burgeoning libido. Sex had been private – between her and Geoff – and restricted to bedrooms at night.

Now, instead, she had erotic thoughts all over the place: any time, anywhere. And it was no longer just thoughts. She'd been made love to in the library by Julian and Celeste, and now, here in the linen cupboard, pleasured by them again.

And she had a feeling that this was just the beginning; that before long, lovemaking would be integral to *all* of her life, and as much her *raison d'être* as the study of fine literature was.

As she dreamily absorbed this fact, she felt Julian stirring. Very carefully, very considerately, he eased himself out of her and rose with noiseless grace to his feet, caressing her thighs gently as he did so. Rosie felt almost too sleepy to respond, too close to the edge of consciousness to reach out and touch him in return. She wanted to say 'thank you', to acknowledge what he'd done for her, but she was too tired to even lift up her arms. Somehow, though, she knew it didn't matter, and that Julian was aware of how she felt.

After the closeness of their joining, it was chilly to find oneself a separate body. Rosie shivered, then trembled in a different way as her legs were lifted and moved. She was being rearranged, she realised. Julian was shifting her into a new and more comfortable position, lengthways on the couch, and lying down. As she curled up foetally, smiling a smile he couldn't see, she felt her nightshirt being tugged down to keep her warm.

That was the most special thing about Julian, she thought contentedly. His most appealing quality. He was a Lothario, obviously, but he cared. He had respect for the women he slept with, and even though he made love powerfully, and drained you dry with his ravenous demands, there lay beyond an unexpected thoughtfulness. It was the very same tenderness that was making him drape fluffy blankets around her limp, drowsing form.

'Bless you, Rosie,' he murmured, easing her hair back off her face, purely by touch. 'You're a treasure.'

As his fingers slid over her cheek, she rolled and took the caress on her slightly parted lips, kissing his fingers and sighing with a voluptuous well-being. She'd have to come out of this cupboard eventually, she decided vaguely, but not just yet. She mumbled a muddled explanation, and Julian's mouth brushed her forehead, his breath like a soporific breeze.

'Go to sleep, sweetheart,' he whispered in her ear before he left her – and like a dutiful employee she obeyed him.

8

What the Little Bird Said

Oh God, I spent the night in a cupboard! thought Rosie as she showered the next morning.

Crazy as it seemed, she'd fallen deeply asleep when Julian had left her, and remained that way, perfectly dreamless, for several hours thereafter. Sometime in the early hours, she'd woken with a start, but remembered immediately where she was. The black velvet darkness hadn't frightened her.

Outside in the corridor, someone had thoughtfully left a light on, and in a couple of minutes Rosie had been safely and silently back in her room.

Now she had the same problem as yesterday – was it only yesterday? – which was how to face a lover over breakfast. There were three this time, but ironically, she felt less nervous instead of more so. She even found herself looking forward to it. She imagined herself swanning into the dining room, and meeting three sets of questioning eyes. Three intimate, remembering smiles.

This is so weird! she thought as she soaped herself.

Her skin felt smooth and glowing to her fingers, as if it thrived and bloomed on excess. She looked down at her own body and found it improved somehow. She'd eaten well in Julian's house, but she didn't seem to put on any weight. There was even a finesse about her shape this morning that she'd never noticed before; a harmony to her curves that made her feel happy to have them. People in her old life – some people – had made it clear that they found her unfashionably podgy; but now, in this new and more sensual world, her lush form was prized and admired.

Breakfast, when she went down to it, was a peculiar meal. The events of last night weren't mentioned, but their echoes were real and perceptible; as tangible as the table they ate at, or the excellent coffee and food.

Julian had a full breakfast and looked disgustingly pleased with himself. As well he might, thought Rosie, sipping at her coffee and trying to stop her body wanting his. He'd taken – and given – great pleasure in that damned linen cupboard; it was no wonder his eyes were twinkling. Celeste seemed in good spirits too, although she ate very little, and Rosie wondered if the Hadeys had made love to each other after they'd finished their games with her. It seemed highly likely. She imagined them together in their marriage bed, writhing and shouting with passion, while she, Rosie, slept the sleep of the innocent in the linen cupboard.

And what of David? she thought, nibbling at a triangle of toast, and eyeing him over it, as discreetly as she could.

The boy seemed as quietly composed as ever, although he had blushed beautifully when she'd arrived at the table. He appeared to be quite calm now, but there was suppressed excitement about him. Her own heart started pounding as she realised he was waiting for something; expecting something from her. He was probably a little embarrassed about what had happened in the library, but he didn't seem crippled or upset by it. What Rosie sensed most was only his sweet and rather titillating shyness. His natural, almost juvenile modesty was as endearing as it was a huge turn-on.

It occurred to her, as she watched his neat, elegant way of eating, that he'd subconsciously accepted her role: her secret place in his life. His intellect might reject the true facts when they were presented, but his body wouldn't. More than ever she felt she was his tutor, and she liked both the word and what it signified. She was learning herself, at an astonishing rate, and whatever she discovered, she'd pass on.

After breakfast, everyone moved with purpose.

Julian was first on his feet, preparing to leave for his domain in the City. Rosie hadn't worked out what he actually did; but whatever it was, it earned him an obscene amount of money. Everything about the Hadey establishment was rare and opulent, and this was only one of their homes. Rosie had been intimidated at first, but it was funny how easy luxury was to get used to. She stared down at her Irish linen napkin, her bone china plate and her sterling silver knife, and realised she'd taken them all for granted.

Celeste didn't work, and certainly didn't need to, but this morning she was a demon of activity. She'd be shopping, meeting friends, keeping various appointments, and she'd be out all day. And she'd be taking

David with her. He was to see his analyst, for the last time, and an educational advisor – to help him plan his future academic career. Tied to his grandparents he'd missed out on going to university, but that was now in the process of being rectified.

For a moment, as the others mapped out their days, Rosie felt slightly aggrieved, left out of things. But after thirty seconds' further consideration, she almost laughed out loud.

Good grief! What the hell was she thinking of? Totally absorbed in her bizarre sexual duties, she'd lost sight of her genuine bona-fide job! She was as much on the Hadey payroll as Mrs Russell who'd served their breakfast. Remembering her place, and feeling strangely glad of it, she smiled, stood up and excused herself.

'I'd better get along to the library,' she said brightly. 'I've got a date with some books that need cataloguing.'

'I hate to think of you slaving away in there all day,' said Celeste, making Rosie smile again, but inwardly this time. It wasn't as if she was heading for the dark, satanic mills. She loved Julian's marvellous library, and even without all the esoteric perks, working in it was a dream come true in itself.

'Perhaps you could take the afternoon off and we could meet for tea or something?' the dark-haired woman persisted. 'I'm sure David would like that.'

It was tempting, oh-so-tempting, but Rosie felt a pang of guilt. She hadn't done much here yet on *either* of her projects, except enjoy herself, and the salary she was receiving was humungous. Shouldn't she at least *try* to earn it?

'That's really kind,' she said, wondering how to refuse without seeming ungracious, 'but the library is so huge and there really is a lot to do. It seems a bit much to bunk off when I've only just started. You don't mind, do you?'

'Of course not!' replied Celeste breezily. 'We'll do it another day.' She smiled then, a narrow, creamy smile, and something in her pansy-coloured eyes harked back to last night and their intimacy. 'We'll have a big shopping binge . . . Harvey Nichols, Bond Street, the works . . . Just us girls together, eh?' She walked forward until she was just inches away, then touched Rosie's arm, her aura overpowering. Rosie thought of those glossy red lips kissing hers, those delicate, manicured fingers in her mouth. Communication moved silently between them and she suddenly felt able to smile, and to promise.

'I'd love that. I'll look forward to it,' she said, imagining what David and Julian would think if she followed her instincts right now, and bestowed the kiss that Celeste so obviously wanted.

'You're a conscientious girl, Rosie. I'm impressed,' murmured Julian, moving to stand behind his wife, his expression intent and challenging. Those dark, middle-eastern eyes had been hidden last night, but had watched her all the same, she was sure; watched her as she'd bucked and heaved with pleasure, her body impaled and in orgasm.

He was teasing her, and for a moment it was infuriating. Men, with the notable exception of David, were such chauvinists. So sexually smug. Even the better class of men like Julian, the kinder ones. They all had that same irritating quality of believing they were God's gift to women – that because a woman had a climax with them, it made them Superman.

She had an urge to make a tart remark, then for the second time in a minute, felt like laughing.

Julian's faults were a good thing! They reminded her that the world outside was real and life was sometimes a bitch. One day she'd have to go back to an existence full of Geoffs and various other bastards. Living with the Hadeys was like living in a cocoon, a space capsule; it wouldn't do to forget the hard knocks.

'Thank you. I aim to please,' she said, flirting slightly, though she knew it was extremely foolhardy. Those scrutinising eyes were upon her. Pansy-purple ones; sharp, spice-brown ones; mind-bending, amber-gold ones.

'So I've noticed,' said Julian quietly. Rosie watched his hand drop lightly onto Celeste's shapely hip, and saw the other woman respond, swaying slightly, her lovely face softening for a second as if the touch granted instant, erotic pleasure.

'Me too,' Celeste mouthed, winking as she recovered her composure, then spinning away, her black hair swirling out around her in her eagerness to get started on her schedule. 'Come on, Davy, let's go,' she said, turning away towards David, who was on his feet already and pushing his chair beneath the table.

'I'll just get my jacket,' he said quietly, then made to follow his cousin from the room.

As he passed by Rosie, he seemed to hesitate, his eyes questioning. She could see a dozen strong emotions in their depths, but her heart hammered crazily when one of them came to the surface. He hunched his shoulders in a graceful shrug, then grinned at her. A real, beautiful, boyish gem of a grin that made her knees go genuinely weak.

'I'll see you later, maybe?' he said softly, his strange eyes as bright as sovereigns.

'Er, yes. Yes, of course,' she stammered, their roles all of a sudden reversed. She felt flustered, naïve, right back to square one; her experience cancelled and nullified by the beauty of the young man before her. 'I'll be in the library if you need me,' she finished lamely, watching the flip of his long pianist's fingers as he cheerfully bade her '*au revoir*'.

If you need me for *anything*, she added with silent emphasis, watching his precise, long-limbed walk as he followed his cousin from the room.

'Not long now,' murmured Julian, as he passed close by her, and Rosie trembled because she knew he was right.

In spite of her desire to work, Rosie found the library difficult that morning. The tasks there weren't beyond her, in fact under normal circumstances she would have relished them. It was just that she simply couldn't concentrate, couldn't focus her attention. A fact that didn't surprise her at all.

The books themselves didn't help her. The beautiful leatherbound volumes around her were as much works of art as the pictures on the walls, and the antique rugs beneath her feet. She couldn't just stick them in an arbitrary order, because most of them were bound as sets – even though their contents had little in common. She was going to have to create some sort of locational index as well as a classification sequence. The shelves themselves would have to be marked somehow, and in a way that didn't mar the elegance of the woodwork.

It was all a headache at the moment, no matter how good the computer, and how marvellous the books were to handle. And matters weren't helped by her inclination to open the private cases. She almost felt the books were calling her. She kept finding herself with one in her hands, scanning through it for particular words and images, for things she could teach David; things she could ask Celeste or Julian about.

At ten thirty, she gave up the ghost, knowing she could no longer function with a mind full of received eroticism, and a body that was yearning for release.

She decided to follow a suggestion of Celeste's, and take some physical exercise. One of the last things Julian's wife had said, before she'd left, was that Rosie should take a look downstairs if she wanted a change, and check out the gymnasium and the pool.

The more Rosie thought about this idea the more she liked it. In the shower, she'd been quite entranced by her positive new self-image, and exercise would only reinforce that. She'd always gone to Step classes when she'd lived at her flat, and she'd been wondering what to do instead. A gym on the premises was the perfect answer, and no doubt as de luxe as everything else in the house.

It was a simple matter to slip up to her room and change into a tee-shirt, some leggings and her Reeboks, then tie back her hair in a bunch. Grabbing a swimsuit and towel, and clean undies, she made her way down to the bowels of the house, in search of a hard, energetic, and hopefully distracting workout.

The gym wasn't as small as Celeste had led her to believe, and Rosie was impressed by the excellent array of equipment. There were benches, static weight machines, a couple of exercise cycles, and even the ubiquitous Step if she wanted it. There was also a mini-trampoline, and an elaborate looking rowing machine. The swimming pool wasn't huge, but it looked good for a decent length's lap. The whole complex was as beautifully appointed as the rest of the house, all done out in clean, aquatic blues, and complete with a spacious, towel-filled shower and changing area.

Static-cycling was the logical warm-up, and Rosie was pleased that there was a music centre in the room to offset the boredom. There were plenty of tapes and CDs to choose from, but it was a selection of what looked like home-recorded tapes that took her fancy. She smiled as she saw they were all clearly labelled, something she – a librarian – never did. She dithered over a collection of piano classics, presumably David's, then rejected them. A mental picture of *him* working out would defeat the whole object of her being here, so she picked out a rather cool-sounding dance tape instead. As the pounding beat filled the room, she climbed astride the nearest bike, set the resistance to moderate, and began to pedal at a fast but steady rate.

The rhythm of her cycling legs was hypnotic. Rosie felt her mind empty of all ethical debate about being a conventional woman in an unconventional situation, and her body found a deep relaxation.

Endorphins rushed strongly through her bloodstream and she thought only of her rising metabolic rate and the burning off of excess calories. She'd never be a sylph, and it didn't seem to matter, but there was no harm in helping things along.

Grooving along smoothly with her eyes closed, it was a while before she realised she had company. There was a muted footstep on the rubberised floor, and in the split-second before her eyes flew open, Rosie imagined either Celeste, or Julian, or David standing there. Any one of them was likely to be grinning.

But the newcomer was a stranger, a young woman Rosie had never set eyes on before. She was tall, with thick, softly-curled titian hair and she wore a track suit. Her figure was one of the best Rosie had ever seen.

There was an awkward, music-filled moment, and Rosie stopped pedalling. The young woman walked over to the stereo and turned it down to a muted background pulse. 'Hello, you must be Rosie,' she said pleasantly as she moved towards the bikes, her tread very light and athletic. 'I'm Angela Byrd, Celeste and Julian's fitness trainer, but you can call me "Ladybird" if you like. Everyone else does.'

Rosie's 'how do you do' sounded stilted even to her ears, but 'Ladybird' smiled sunnily and began stripping off her tracksuit – a process that probably made everyone feel fat, not just chubby librarians.

'I expect you're wondering what I'm doing here,' she said, kicking aside her tracksuit bottoms and revealing the longest and sleekest pair of legs: perfect pins in vivid pink lycra. 'Celeste offered me free run of the place when my usual gym's too crowded. You don't mind, do you?'

There was genuine concern in her eyes – eyes that were large and green with darkly mascara-ed lashes.

'No, it's fine. I'm glad of the company.'

It was hard to imagine anybody not wanting Ladybird around them. She seemed to radiate a natural good humour that was instantly attractive. To women as well as men, Rosie thought with a pang. The other woman's movements were neat and economical, and in seconds, she'd caught her pretty red hair into a ponytail and was slewing her lithe, shapely body across the bicycle next to Rosie's.

They pedalled without speaking for a while, although from time to time, Rosie found it hard not to turn and glance at her companion.

Ladybird was extraordinarily beautiful, though not in the classic sense, like Celeste. It sounded judgemental somehow, but the trainer's beauty had a commoner touch. Celeste had the look of a goddess descended to Earth, but Ladybird seemed more like someone who'd started with the same raw material as any woman, but just worked harder. To achieve a body like hers wasn't easy, and the grooming, the artful hair colour, and the carefully co-ordinated work-out gear that went with it, all spoke volumes about a determined desire to look wonderful.

And Rosie couldn't resent her. Especially when Ladybird breached the unrelenting whir of their cycling and began chatting, with a wry, pungent wit, about the Hadeys, their houses and their opulent, freewheeling lifestyle.

'So what do you think of Julian?' she enquired after a while, her voice warm and mischievous.

Rosie felt her emotional antennae start to quiver, and sneaked another sly look at the redhead.

Good God! Of course! The trainer and her boss had slept together! As the idea formed, she realised she should have known. Julian was a connoisseur of fine women and an unbridled sensualist. Ladybird was just the sort of choice female morsel he'd consume with the greatest of pleasure.

'I like him very much,' she answered cautiously. 'He's intelligent, kind, easy-going . . . The perfect boss really. I couldn't ask for better.'

'But don't you think he's sexy?' Ladybird's voice was intent and charged now, and even though so far the relentless pace of their cycling had had no visible effect on her, she suddenly started to blush.

'Yes, very much so,' said Rosie, deciding that here, perhaps, was a feminine friend she could truly confide in. 'Too much in fact . . .'

'Far too much,' echoed Ladybird, with feeling.

Their glances locked, and they both stopped pedalling. Rosie felt her instincts suddenly validated as a silent agreement flashed between them. A pact to be frank.

'I can't get into this today,' said the fitness trainer, leaping lightly from her saddle. 'Why don't we take a shower, then have a cuppa or something. Then we can really dish the dirt!'

Yes, the dirt, thought Rosie as she followed Ladybird's sleek shape into the showers. But whose dirt would be the dirtiest?

*

I like her. I really do like her, thought Ladybird as she emerged from the shower, and found a nervous looking Rosie trying to dry herself without dropping her towel or exposing her lush, exquisite curves.

Although it was partially her own doing that the librarian was here in the first place, Ladybird had – against her will – felt an initial inclination to resent her. This was irrational because she herself had declined the job anyway – the strange, sensual job that Rosie had so obviously accepted.

'So then, let's compare notes,' she said, dropping her towel and hoping Rosie would do the same. Ladybird worked killingly hard to keep herself slender, but for some strange reason she didn't understand, she liked the sight of flesh on others. Especially on women she fancied.

'Come on, what do you think of Julian?'

In essence, it was the question she'd asked in the gym, but she sensed that Rosie understood its true meaning now.

'He's gorgeous,' replied Rosie softly, her eyes dreamy and her grip on the towel less vehement. 'One of the most handsome men I've ever met. And he's . . . he's . . . Well, he's what I'd call overpowering.' She paused, as if trying to say delicately what Ladybird confidently expected. 'I suppose it's a cliché to call a man irresistible, but . . . well . . . I didn't. I didn't resist him.'

'Me neither,' answered Ladybird, moving across to sit on the slatted wooden bench beside her new found friend. 'I had sex with him the very first time I met him. In the middle of a training session, would you believe?'

'I can believe it,' Rosie answered, grinning. With a curiously fatalistic shrug, she let her towel fall away from her bosom and started rubbing at her still-damp legs.

Ladybird tried to stay cool. 'Ah, but would you believe that after he'd had me, he went on and did the second half of his exercise programme?' she continued, trying not to ogle the glorious body beside her. Rosie was clearly fighting the giggles, which made her breasts shake softly and delightfully. 'And he'd hardly even broken sweat, the swine!'

'God, he is one, isn't he?' Rosie was laughing properly now, a sight that Ladybird found dangerously stirring. Her new friend was extraordinarily beautiful, and seemed prepared to confide, but that didn't mean she liked women in the way that Ladybird herself did.

'And how!' she answered, fighting her urge to touch Rosie's dark nipples. 'But he's nice with it, isn't he? You don't mind if he takes advantage, because basically, he makes you feel safe too.'

'That's exactly how I feel.' Rosie's voice was soft with wonder. Ladybird watched her closely, as ideas turned over in the other woman's mind. She found herself holding her breath, and hoping hard as Rosie spoke again. 'And I . . . I feel more or less the same way about Celeste too.' It came out in a rush, as if it had been an effort, and Ladybird felt her own body tingle as she sensed her hopes being answered.

'Yeah, she's quite something, isn't she?' she offered, trying to be non-committal. 'They're a very well-matched couple.'

It was an unbearably fragile moment. There were many possible futures in the balance, and Ladybird knew from bitter experience that to push now was foolish. What would happen would happen, and in the meantime, it was easier to concentrate on their mutual interest in men. And in Julian in particular.

'Shall I tell you about that first time with Julian?' she asked coaxingly, hoping that such a blatant offer would disguise her subtle change of subject. It seemed to work because Rosie's face became a picture of almost school-girl curiosity. She nodded, her blue eyes glinting as if she relished the thought of juicy revelations.

'Well, I'd spoken to him on the phone beforehand to make the arrangements, and believe me, that yummy voice had me creaming my knickers before I'd even seen him!' As she launched into her account, Ladybird felt surprised at how the memories affected her. The tips of her breasts were throbbing already, and between her legs was a hot well of stickiness.

'It was a job I was really looking forward to, I can tell you, and when I saw him I wasn't disappointed.' She cast Rosie a conspiratorial look. 'Well, you've seen his body, haven't you? And a pair of satin shorts don't hide anything! To be honest, he hasn't the slightest need for a personal trainer, but who am I to argue? The salary is unbelievable, this place is a dream . . . I'd have to have been mad to refuse.'

Rosie's eyes were wide, and Ladybird wondered first whether to edit her account or embellish it, then decided on the simple, delectable truth.

'He was in the gym early – on purpose, I presume

– and just lying there on the pressing bench with his eyes closed. Rubbing his crotch!'

'You mean he was masturbating?' Her companion's voice was soft, but not shocked somehow, and Ladybird wondered if Rosie had seen something similar.

'You named that tune,' Ladybird replied. 'I often see men fiddling with themselves in my work, but it's not usually so deliberate. He wasn't just doing it without thinking. He was doing it on purpose. Putting on a show. For *me*.'

'And what did you do?' Rosie's voice was a breathy whisper.

'Well, I introduced myself and got on with the session . . . In the meantime trying to ignore the fact that he had a hard-on the size of a house!'

She could see the image now. Luscious, swarthy Julian in king-fisher blue shorts, his penis pushing like a ramrod against the satin that covered his groin. She could see his eyes too: dark and challenging; cheeky, if you could use such a word about a man in his forties.

It had been difficult for her to concentrate, although Julian had been totally unflustered. He'd listened intently to her instructions, and performed her carefully planned warm-up routine with just the right degree of concentration.

By the time both he and she were thoroughly loose and ready, his face and arms and legs were gleaming with the lightest of sweats – and his erection had barely diminished. It even looked as if it had stiffened slightly: aroused by the sensuality of the exercise, and by the sight of her lycra-clad body.

Ladybird knew she looked good in her workout gear, and Julian wasn't the first man who'd got hard for her in the gym.

Then they began the weight training. Already armed with his health profile, Ladybird had a good idea of her client's capabilities, and had drawn up a general toning and hardening programme rather than intensive muscle-building for particular areas. For today, she'd set a target of two full circuits of the entire apparatus, but with only a few kilos on each.

At every station, she demonstrated the form she required for the exercise. It should have been child's play for her, doing routines she'd done hundreds of times, but instead it was extraordinarily gruelling. She could feel Julian's eyes following her every minute move, and even though that was what she *wanted*, professionally, she sensed that his scrutiny was twofold. He was studying the exercises, but he was also examining her body as he did so: staring at her breasts, her bottom, and the divided groove of her sex where it was visible through thin layers of nylon and cotton. As they approached the end of the first circuit, she could feel she was moist at her centre and suspected that it showed. She was certainly sweating far more than usual.

After a set of free weights, Julian suddenly placed the dumbbells on the floor and rolled them away. Sitting up, he looked her squarely in the eye, but made no attempt to begin the next exercise.

A hot, familiar terror flared in Ladybird's belly. This was it. The way he'd been exhibiting himself when she'd arrived should've warned her he wanted more than a work-out, but somehow she'd expected a far

subtler approach. His dark eyes were inviting her to
enjoy him – luring her sweating body to his, and her
musky crotch to his penis. Like a mesmerised doll she
moved towards him, and gasped when he took hold
of her wrist and pulled her down roughly onto his
lap.

No words were spoken, but none were needed. His
fingers slid knowledgeably over her nylon-encased
breasts, flicking at the already peaked nipples. She
groaned when the hand moved on with purpose, and
pushed rudely at the vee between her legs.

He cupped her, thumb pointing to her navel as his
palm circled slowly on her mound, rubbing both the
cotton of her panties and the lycra of her leotard deep
into the channel of her sex. Without conscious thought
she wriggled, squirming her tautly honed bottom
against his muscular, lightly haired thighs. She felt
his lips settle on her neck, making the skin there quiver
as he nibbled and sucked it. He was licking at her
sweat in neat, delicate strokes, entirely unfazed by
the sticky tangled strands of her hair, where it had
come unbound from her ponytail. As his pressing
hand dove further, and her clitoris leapt, she felt his
white teeth close lightly on her throat.

The way he worked her was remorseless. His
fingers pushed the layers of cloth right into her vulva,
soaking them through and forming them moistly to
her shape. She felt him rubbing at her clitoris, her
labia, the fluttering mouth of her vagina, then pushing
the juice-soaked fabric inside her, as another finger
stabbed at her anus.

Ladybird screamed, her climax immense as her

arms tightened around Julian in a death-grip. She felt herself almost falling, almost flying, her flailing body sliding on his knee. He was using his fingers on her bottom and sex like an infernal, prodding fork, while at the same time biting her neck – and it was the most erotic experience of her life. She screamed again, half choking as his supple wrist twisted and he thumbed her throbbing, pulsing clitoris and pressed it against her hard pubic bone.

But as she gasped and gobbled uncouthly, she felt his ruthless hands withdraw. Nearly tipping her off him, he made her stand for a moment, swaying on wobbly legs as he peeled away her sweaty sports clothes. First leotard, then leggings and pants, all in one bunch, although he ignored the snug white band of her bra. When he had everything as far as her knees, he took her and turned her; then laid her face down across the bench, her bare bottom high, and her upper body dangling down over the shiny black leather of the seat. She felt fingers prising at her thighs, opening her as far as the restriction around her legs would allow.

The same fingers tested her wetness, then teased her tiny pink bottom hole, making her eyes bulge with fear.

'And did he?'

Rosie's voice made Ladybird jump and her unfocused eyes see the real world. She'd been so entranced, so hypnotised by her own dream-filled voice, that she'd almost forgotten the woman beside her.

Almost forgotten? Completely forgotten, thought Ladybird, looking down. Her hand was wedged between her legs, pressing nearly as hard as Julian's had all those months ago, in the gym next door. She'd been masturbating, she realised, and for quite some time. She must have begun almost at once, unaware of her actions, although she was now keenly aware of their consequences.

Her flesh was heavy and aroused, and she could smell her own scent – fresh and thick and gamey in spite of her recent shower. She saw that Rosie's face was flushed, and that she'd been watching as well as listening; and yet she, Ladybird, didn't feel embarrassed. She'd often caressed herself to climax for a girlfriend; and often, in this house, for Celeste. She could even recall times when she'd done it for Celeste and Julian together.

But that was another matter. The Hadeys were freethinking libertines who had an open marriage. Rosie, she sensed, had only just begun to shed her inhibitions, and take the first, tentative steps.

And it was necessary to ask her permission, Ladybird decided. 'I need to come,' she said softly. 'Would it bother you?'

'No . . . Please . . . I . . .' Rosie's face was almost puce, but her eyes were twice as hot. 'Please, go ahead . . .'

'Thanks,' whispered Ladybird, her blood pounding, her heart elated. The woman at her side was cautious and still scared, but the sensual promise was there. And as Ladybird closed her eyes and leant back against the cool, tiled wall, it was Rosie who triggered her pleasure.

*

Last night David, and now Ladybird. Why oh why, pondered Rosie, do I keep on seeing people's closest secrets?

Nevertheless, she watched, enchanted.

Ladybird's body was as beautiful nude as it was clothed, and she seemed entirely without inhibition. Her long, sleekly-tanned legs were stretched out in front of her, and parted to display her precision-trimmed russet-brown pubis and the orchid pink lips it protected. A finger flickered in that pinkness, and as she rubbed furiously, her bottom wove and worked on the seat beneath her, and her small round breasts bounced and shook. Jerking towards a climax, she caressed one nipple too, pulling at the thick, roseate peak in time to her strokes down below.

Suddenly, the squirming girl stiffened, pointed her toes and whimpered very quietly. 'Oh! Oh! Oh!' she moaned, her fingers stilling and her knuckles turning white with pressure. For a moment, Rosie longed to do the same – to make herself climax. The urge was potent and compelling, but she couldn't quite obey it. The feelings were too sudden and too strange. She'd do it one day, but she couldn't now. Her body was left with frustration.

'Wow! That's better,' said Ladybird presently, her green gaze bright, yet still hazy. As she seemed to focus again, on Rosie, she frowned, her smooth brow crumpling with concern. 'I didn't embarrass you, did I?'

'No, it's alright . . . It's just the first time . . . with a woman,' she admitted, then smiled, thinking of David.

Ladybird's eyes narrowed. 'But not with a man?'

Rosie felt blood rush into her face and throat; she *was* embarrassed.

'It's okay. You don't have to tell everything,' the other woman said amiably, rising to her feet, all nimble, athletic grace. 'I'm going to take another shower. For some reason I'm all hot and sweaty again. See you in a bit.' With a grin and a flip of her fingers she walked through into the shower area – closing the connecting door firmly behind her.

Rosie blessed Ladybird's tact. She needed solitude now, and her new friend the trainer understood that. Without wasting a second she slid a hand between her thighs, and sighed with relief at her own hungry touch. Just a few long, slicking strokes and she burst through the barrier, biting her lips as her quim throbbed deeply and gratefully. Sighing with relief, she slumped back against the wall, turning her head first to one side then the other to cool her glowing cheeks against the tiles.

By the time Ladybird returned, Rosie was composed again, and pristinely clad in her clean bra and panties as she combed her hair at the mirror.

'So, who's this man you've seen tossing off?' Ladybird enquired salaciously as she slid into her own undies – a pretty lace-trimmed bodysuit, Rosie noticed, that made a perfect shape look even better. 'Is it the sumptuous Julian?'

Rosie could quite imagine that, and thought Ladybird's adjective well chosen. The vision of Julian touching himself was intoxicating; but somehow it couldn't match what she'd seen from the linen cupboard. Julian's self-pleasure lacked the perfect jewel-like innocence of David's. With him there was no delicious aura of guilt, no atavistic, juvenile dread of indulging in a vice. Masturbation would be an everyday experience for Julian, with no sinful overtones. A de luxe way of scratching an itch.

'Well, is it?' persisted Ladybird, grinning.

Rosie shook her head.

'Stephen?'

'Stephen?' Rosie couldn't say she hadn't noticed the handsome chauffeur, but she hadn't really considered him sexually.

There was no denying that Stephen was a gorgeous piece of work. He had a strong, muscular body beneath his uniform, and an exceptional smile: strong and white in his smooth-skinned, oak-brown face. There was something in Ladybird's glittering eyes, Rosie observed, that said she'd noticed these assets too. More than noticed them.

'Yes, why not?' the trainer said questioningly.

'I've never been near enough,' replied Rosie, 'except in the car.'

'I have,' Ladybird said, quirking her pretty pink mouth, 'and much good it did me!' She adjusted the fit of her bodysuit as if it were suddenly too tight. 'I know he fancies me, because he's started coming to my gym occasionally instead of working out here . . . But can I get him to fuck me? No! He's playing hard to get, the bastard! Either that or he's completely gay and he's getting what he needs elsewhere and only teasing me out of spite.'

Rosie analysed this astonishing statement carefully, and realised how tame her life had been until these last few hectically erotic days. She'd thought herself quite daring trying new things with Geoff, but now lesbianism, bisexuality, voyeurism, and Lord alone knew what else, all seemed to be almost common practice!

'He looks so macho,' she said in a small voice.

'Oh, I'm sure he is,' replied Ladybird evenly. 'But he's certainly into men some of the time, because . . . Well . . . I've seen him with one!'

The beautiful redhead hesitated, her inner debate obvious. There was another revelation imminent, and with her appetite now thoroughly whetted, Rosie couldn't resist the question.

'Who?'

Ladybird still dithered. She bit her lip, looked troubled, then made a small gruff sound of resignation. 'Well, considering why you're here, I suppose I'd better tell you everything. I once came in here quite early one morning and found Stephen making love to Julian. Right there on that bench . . . He had him doubled up, nearly folded in two. Neither of them noticed me. Julian was sobbing and moaning, in seventh heaven, and Stephen was pounding away like a steamhammer.'

It was an appalling picture, yet unthinkably arousing. Rosie tried to imagine her all male Lothario boss being taken and used like a woman, and the thought made her ache with desire. She wanted to see it for herself; see the strong, assertive Julian made weak by the act of sodomy.

'It seems unbelievable,' she breathed, wishing she had the courage to touch herself again.

'Believe it,' said Ladybird firmly, reaching for her tracksuit.

The two of them stayed silent for a while, and continued getting dressed. Ladybird put on her tracksuit and began to pack her various belongings, but Rosie just pulled on her white tee-shirt. It was voluminous, and covered half her thighs, so she didn't need her tight sweaty leggings.

'What did you mean by "considering why I'm here"?' she asked, as the significance of the phrase suddenly dawned.

'Uh huh . . .' Ladybird looked evasive.

'Just how much do you know about me, Ladybird? About my job, I mean?'

'Well, I know there's some pretty strange things in your job description . . .'

Rosie felt confused and angry. It seemed that all and sundry knew about the tutoring. She wondered how many more members of the staff were in on it. Stephen? Mrs Russell?

Sounding worried, Ladybird rushed on: 'Don't take this the wrong way, but they asked me first. They asked me if I'd take David under my wing –' She grinned nervously. 'Joke! Ladybird? Wing? Get it? No? Oh well . . . They asked if I'd teach him about sex, and help him get rid of his virginity.'

'So I'm just the second choice?' Rosie said tightly. 'The substitute.'

'No, it's not like that at all!' Ladybird seemed cross with herself now, her ruddy hair tossing and her eyes as sharp as green glass. 'I fancy the lad . . . He's beautiful. But I couldn't take the job 'cos I'm too thick!'

She thinned her mouth, as if admitting to shortcomings wasn't pleasant. 'He's too clever for me. Too intellectual. Always reading and playing the piano and stuff. I'm a body person, not a mind person.' She touched her breast lightly to illustrate the obvious. 'He needs someone a bit brighter to relate to . . . Someone to talk about sex with, not just screw. And someone who isn't *too* experienced, so he won't feel put off and fail . . .'

'Enter the naïve librarian,' commented Rosie dryly, although her initial irritation was fading.

'No. Honestly. You were the first *real* choice. They only asked me because I was handy. I don't think either Julian or Celeste really thought I was suitable.'

The irritation was gone now. Ladybird was too open, too honest – and far too attractive! – to resent. She was also doing herself down, Rosie decided. The other girl was perceptive, considerate, and physically beautiful; David couldn't have been put in better or more tender care.

'Will you help me?' Rosie asked on the spur of the moment, reaching for Ladybird's hand in a purely instinctive gesture. When she squeezed it, she felt her shaking. 'I'm not as green as David, but there's a lot I don't know either. I could use some guidance. A list or something. An A–Z guide to sex!'

Ladybird laughed full-bloodedly. 'On index cards, maybe?'

'I don't think so,' replied Rosie, grinning. 'Although when I want to find out how to do a thing, I do usually try and find a book on it.'

'What a logical girl.' Ladybird reached into her sports bag and took out a shorthand notebook and a pencil. Rosie could see what looked like lists of exercises on the top sheet, but Ladybird flipped this over, and wrote the figure 'one' at the top of the next sheet. 'Okay then, here we go.' She chewed the pencil, then her lip, then made a quick note.

'Well first you've got to teach him anatomy. Sexual anatomy, that is. What makes *his* body feel good and what makes *your* body feel good.'

'He knows what makes *his* body feel good. He's the one I saw masturbating.'

'I might've known in this bloody house! Was it one of Julian's trick mirrors?'

'Yes, it was,' Rosie admitted. 'Celeste thought it would be helpful.'

'And was it?'

'Oh yes . . .' The memory was dreamlike, almost unworldly. The sight of a beautiful innocent exploring his pale, almost saint-like body.

'Ooh, I bet he's lovely,' purred Ladybird, licking her lips. 'I've seen him in his swimming trunks . . . and I was impressed! He isn't a little boy, is he?'

'No, he isn't,' whispered Rosie, seeing nothing at that moment but David. David with his hands on his sex, and his eyes tightly closed in ecstasy.

'Does Julian have many little hidey-holes?' she asked, after a pause – still wondering if she'd been watched too.

'Oh yes. Lots,' replied Ladybird. 'Both here and at Stonehaven . . . They're behaving themselves at the moment, I think. Because of David . . . But some very strange things go on at Chez Hadey, I can tell you. I've seen things you could hardly credit. Honestly.'

Rosie could imagine the concept if not the acts, and felt intensely curious. Would she get her chance? she wondered. Would she be allowed to sample these barely credible pleasures? It all still felt vaguely sinful, but she couldn't help hoping just the same.

The two women got on with their list; stopping from time to time for wild fits of giggles and heavy, arousal-charged silences. The compilation was a work of erotica in itself, given all the extravagant acts they'd itemised.

'Now most men turn to putty in your hand for oral . . . Or maybe not putty.' Ladybird chuckled knowledgeably. 'So I think you'd better do lots of sucking and licking and nibbling. He'll love it, and then, when you've made him your absolute slave, you can get him to go down on you!'

Rosie mentioned some of the books she'd perused. 'There's just about everything in Julian's collection. If I can't find a way to talk about something, I can always give David a book!'

'I should read more,' Ladybird said pensively. 'I bet there's still plenty I could learn.'

'You want to experiment with a few simple positions, Rosie,' she said later, scribbling more notes. 'Nothing too fancy. No performance tricks. And then you could try a little gentle kinkiness. Show him how to use a vibrator on you, perhaps? Or tie him up with silk scarves. Keep it light though. Just fun.'

'You should be a sex therapist,' said Rosie, feeling a great rush of fondness for this raunchy but sensitive woman. 'You'd be wonderful at it!'

'I'm wonderful at screwing!' replied Ladybird

smugly. 'But I'm a doer not a talker . . . I can teach people how to make themselves fit, but when it comes to sex, I'd rather just get on with it!'

'Maybe so,' said Rosie cautiously, 'but I'm still grateful for your help . . . Are you here often?'

'Two or three times a week,' replied Ladybird, suddenly frowning. 'God, what a dummy I am! I should've given you a massage . . . Shown you how to do one . . . It's a perfect way of getting into sex!' Her frown changed to a deep, glowing blush. 'For David, I mean . . .'

Rosie knew what she meant, and either way, she liked the idea. She liked it very much. To either give or receive a massage was a delectable prospect. 'I'd love that. Maybe we could do that next time you're here? They don't seem to be too bothered about me doing much in the library.'

'Well, it's only one of your jobs, isn't it?' Ladybird winked, then got back to her point. 'Yes, I'll give you an aromatherapy massage.' Her lively voice became softer, deeper, and more intimate. 'And then you can practice giving me one.' She moistened her petal-pink lips. 'You'll enjoy it both ways, I promise you . . .'

'I'm sure I will,' answered Rosie, part certain, part fearful, and wholly excited. 'Believe me, I'm sure I will.'

9

On and Off the Road

'Change of plan indeed!' muttered Rosie as she threw clothing willy nilly into a holdall. 'It's alright for her. She's used to all this! I'm not. I haven't even settled in here yet, never mind slogging all the way out to the wilds of Norfolk!'

Rosie knew she wasn't really all that cross, but letting off steam reassured her. It was normal and manageable and ordinary, while almost everything else around was extraordinary.

The 'she' and 'her' in question was Celeste. She'd come home unexpectedly – with David – just as Rosie and Ladybird were coming upstairs from the gym.

'Change of plan, Rosie,' she'd said with a smile as winning as it was imperious. 'We're all going to Stonehaven for a few days. Ju and I can't drive down until tonight, but you and David can go this afternoon. David knows the way, and he's good with maps. Can you drive?'

'Yes, I can,' Rosie had replied, then added with some smugness, 'And I'm pretty good with maps too!'

It was true, she did have a knack for routes, but she wished now that she hadn't been so pert with her employer.

Fortunately, Celeste had seemed oblivious.

'Marvellous! That's wonderful!' she'd continued cheerfully. 'I'll run you off some directions on Julian's routeplanner, just in case, but in the meantime pack a few holiday type clothes, and I'll have Stephen bring the small car round.' She'd paused for breath then, as if sensing Rosie's irritation. 'I'm sorry, I didn't think . . . Have you had lunch? Perhaps Mrs Russell can whip up a picnic for you? Would you like that?'

'I've not much option,' observed Rosie wryly as she stuffed the last item in her bag and zipped it up. Picking up a fresh white tee-shirt from the small pile of clothing on the bed, she began to dress – all over again – for the journey.

Twenty minutes later, after a detour to the library, she stood on the pavement outside the house juggling with her bag, her holdall, and a dozen or so carefully chosen books – feeling nonplussed by what Celeste had considered a small car.

Although no expert on the matter, Rosie could still recognise a Mercedes when she saw one. And this one was a sleek, black two door number that crouched by the kerb like a panther. It would be by far the most luxurious vehicle she'd ever ridden in – apart from the Hadey limousine – and the first, and probably only supercar she'd ever actually drive.

'Beautiful, isn't it?' said a soft voice behind her, and when Rosie turned around, David was with her, changed into a black cotton tee-shirt and jeans, and carrying a soft, squashy holdall of his own. In his other hand were the keys to their technological chariot, and he was holding them out towards her.

'Can you take these?' she asked, gesturing with the books she was precariously balancing. Exchanging their various belongings, and getting organised in the car was quite a performance; something Rosie suspected had been contrived on purpose. The two of them were being thrown together as innocent travellers on a voyage into the great unknown. This was a perfect parallel with their bigger adventure, and she tipped a silent salute to the clever, but absent Celeste for her highly effective strategy.

'Where's everyone else?' she asked, surveying the dashboard layout while David fastened his seatbelt, the routeplan dutifully on his lap.

'Celeste's gone to lunch with someone. Stephen's driving her. And Ladybird's gone back to the gym she works at . . .' He paused, faintly frowning, 'Celeste's invited *her* down for the weekend too. She's coming tomorrow.'

Good, thought Rosie. Ladybird was beautiful and kind, and to have her on hand would be invaluable.

'Let me have a look at that,' she said, nodding towards the sheet of directions.

David passed it to her and she perused it quickly, recognising place names and road numbers, and seeing the way quite easily in her head. The distance was 136 miles and the programme said it would take them three and a half hours. She checked the dashboard clock, and it read just before one. They could get there for teatime, no problem. If there were no interruptions.

'Here, thanks. I shan't need this.' She passed the sheet back to David. 'Are you hungry? Celeste said something about a picnic . . .'

'Yes, there's a basket in the boot,' answered David. His voice was soft, slightly husky, and she wondered how nervous he was, and whether he was still thinking of last night, and what had happened in the library. He was all hers now, with no outside influences; and the idea of having him cocooned inside this close, luxurious space with her, strapped in and with nowhere to go, was sharply and viscerally thrilling. She only hoped it wouldn't affect her driving.

'Shall we get a few miles under our belt first, and then eat?' she suggested. 'I'm not really hungry myself.' For food, that is, she amended silently.

'I'm not either,' he replied, his voice still muted. 'Do you want me to shout out when we're getting towards junctions and things?'

'No thanks . . . It's alright. Trust me,' she said, hiding a grin. 'Why don't you put some music on, then take a look through those books.' She'd slid a few of the choicest volumes into the well beside his seat; ones she'd selected after her talk with Ladybird.

While David sorted through the CDs in the glovebox, Rosie snapped her seatbelt in place, flipped the ignition and set the car in gear. There was no traffic in the quietly exclusive Gardens, and as she pulled away from the kerb on the very first stage of their journey, she revelled in the effortless response of the Mercedes. By the time they got to Norfolk, she decided, she'd be too spoiled for anything less.

It took them forty minutes to clear the northern

periphery of London, and while Rosie's attention was mainly on the roads they were travelling, she was still intensely aware of David. She sensed he was uncomfortable, but trying not to show it. There was a Mozart sonata playing, but even so she could hear every nuance of his breathing, and the delicate rustle of paper as he turned the pages of his book. He'd chosen Anaïs Nin's *Delta of Venus*, and that pleased her. Her hopes soared as she realised he was becoming absorbed in it. Would its gallic eroticism arouse him? And what about the fact that it was written by a woman?

'Good book?' she enquired, as the car slid out onto the M11 and she could relax on a long straight road.

She felt him look at her sharply, and sensed him wondering whether *she'd* read the book too. And if so, could she still remember it.

'Yes, it's very good.'

His voice was contained but slightly unsteady, and his attempt to seem unconcerned made her smile. She decided to let him stew for a few minutes, and just listened to more pages being turned. When finally she did steal a glance at him, she felt a powerful surge of excitement. He was blushing.

'Do you find it arousing?' she asked, and though she couldn't look at him just then because she was overtaking, she could almost feel the intensity of his colour. She heard the rustle of cloth as he moved again, adjusting his body in his seat. Was he hard? she mused. Was he trying to ease the pressure on his penis?

The answer to her question was a long time coming.

'Yes,' he whispered, the word barely audible, but

heavy with embarrassment. The effort it took him to speak told her that he *was* erect. That he was aching and swollen in his jeans, and plagued by a sensation not dissimilar to the sensations she was feeling herself: heat, fullness, engorgement; the delicious hunger for sex.

Her own jeans were uncomfortable too. The seam between her legs had ridden up into the cleft of her sex and was caressing her clitoris like a lover. She longed to be able to close her eyes and surrender, but she was trapped by the road and the car. The motorway ahead seemed to mock her; all she wanted to do was screech the car to a halt, embrace the boy beside her, and bring relief to their mutual torment.

Across the screen of the dull grey road, she saw the sight she'd seen last night – a penis that quivered and was beautiful – and she wanted it so desperately it stunned her. If she could stop the car now, there would be no doubt, no hesitation. She'd engulf him. Possess him. Feel his nervous majesty within her, filling her warm female body with reality instead of just fantasy yearnings.

'Read to me,' she said suddenly, wanting his voice if she couldn't have his flesh. 'Please. Read me a story from your book.'

She felt him glance at her like a startled fawn, his golden eyes wide with astonishment.

'I . . . I'm not sure if I can,' he stammered, but even so, she felt his psyche rising to the challenge, and trying to shake off fear and inhibition.

'You can,' she said, making her voice confident, so

his would be too. 'You've got a nice voice, David. You'll be a wonderful reader.'

As she overtook another car, she heard pages flicking quickly, as if he were looking back, searching for something he'd already read.

'It's called "The Veiled Woman",' he began without preamble, then launched straight into a story that Rosie knew quite well. It had recently been reprinted in a magazine.

In spite of everything, David's voice was strong, and his familiar accent evenly modulated. He spoke every word with a strange, telling clarity, and caught the natural rhythm of the sentences with an aptness that was almost uncanny.

Rosie found herself entranced, and aroused all over again by the story of a mysterious woman who'd enslaved a complete stranger in a bar – purely because he *was* a stranger. She drove the car as if on auto-pilot, listening to the erotic tale of 'George', and his dealings with a nymphomaniac temptress who seduced him in a bedroom of baroque and mirror-filled splendour.

The mention of mirrors made Rosie quiver and grip the wheel tightly. David had made love before a mirror last night, and his natural, solitary pleasure had been as sensual as anything by Nin. For a second Rosie wondered if David had been aware of his watchers, then commonsense told her he hadn't. He was too honest and guileless to dissemble.

Should she ever tell him what she'd seen? At the end of the story George had felt betrayed because the veiled woman had only really wanted him as a performer. For a paying audience.

What would such a situation feel like? she wondered. Could she 'perform', sexually? Staring at the road ahead she saw a different vista – herself on a bed, entwined with David, while Celeste, Julian and even Ladybird looked on. The shock of the thought was so immense that she had to concentrate hard on holding the wheel while her centre throbbed and vibrated. She was having a secret, hidden orgasm and it was a battle to keep the car steady.

As David finished the story, it was Rosie who had to lick dry lips. She heard the book slide away onto the floor of the car, and when she dared look quickly across, she saw that David was slumped in his seat with his eyes closed. His face was tense, he was biting his lip, and his hand was resting squarely on his crotch.

'I'm sorry,' he muttered, his fingers squeezing involuntarily.

'What for?' she enquired, keeping her voice light. She had the sensation again that she was dealing with a wild, young animal – a creature whose nascent trust would be shattered by the slightest false move.

'For this,' he gasped, his fingers tightening. 'For last night . . . For getting all worked up and being too young and too stupid to control myself!' Rosie didn't even have to look to know that his face was agonised.

'But you'll learn . . . It'll happen naturally when you get used to sex,' she said reasonably, even though her heart was pounding fit to burst. She sensed the approach of some indefinable, irrevocable watershed and she wanted to reach out and touch him, to help him cross it. Words teemed in her mind, but she realised – in a moment of astonishingly cool rationality – that they were almost at their motorway exit. Praying that a great chance hadn't just been lost, she negotiated the traffic stream, slid neatly into her lane and indicated.

'But how can I get used to it if I don't do it!' he almost sobbed as they cruised along the slipway.

Braking at the junction, Rosie had to concentrate for a few more eternal-seeming seconds, but mercifully they were soon moving smoothly forwards, along the road that would take them to Newmarket.

'That can be changed,' she said quietly.

'Wha . . . What do you mean?' He knew, she could tell, but she could also tell he was having a hard time making himself believe it.

'You can "do it". You can have sex. Make love. Whatever you like to call it.'

'When?'

'Whenever you're ready.' He hadn't asked 'who with', she realised, as if he knew he didn't need to. An idea formed in her mind, and she glanced at the passing scenery.

Soon, she told herself. There was a magic place somewhere, but she knew they hadn't yet reached it. She pressed her foot to the accelerator as her wild idea became a plan.

'Read some more,' she commanded quietly, feeling her loins thrill at the sound of her own controlled voice. Did she really know what she was doing?

David started reading again, this time a longer story, about a woman called Elena who discovered certain inner hungers whilst reading D. H. Lawrence on a train. It seemed an ironical choice, and prophetic; it was the written word that had brought David to the brink too.

They drove for nearly an hour before Rosie saw what she needed. David had already finished the story by then. He seemed distracted, lost in a deep sexual fugue, and she wondered what on earth he was thinking. He wasn't touching himself any more, but his erection was still clearly visible, pushing against the fabric of his jeans.

Turning from their route, Rosie followed signs for a forested picnic area, and when she found it, she parked the car. The place was beautiful, but deserted, and she thanked whatever kind spirit was protecting them for making conditions so ideal for her scheme.

You're crazy, Howard, she told herself as she swung her legs out of the car. This is all mad, self indulgent and ill thought out – and if it goes wrong it'll be David that suffers.

Even so, she felt confident. It was the most foolhardy decision she'd ever made in her life, but the simple act of making it was exciting. As was the sensation of being in control, instead of controlled.

'Let's see what's in this boot,' she said crisply to David who'd followed her example, and got out of the car. She could see his nervousness in every gesture, in every facet of his expression, but in a strange way that made her admire him more. He was scared to death, yet he still stood tall and straight, and made no effort to hide his tumescence.

Rosie decided not to insult him with euphemistic talk about picnics. Instead she just pulled out a thick, luxurious car rug and passed it to David; and then took out a half bottle of wine and two glasses from the picnic hamper. It came as a surprise that it was actually champagne this time, not her usually 'sweet and fruity', but somehow the fine vintage wine seemed totally appropriate. Hopefully, they'd soon be celebrating.

'Come on,' she said, nodding to a path that led further into the woods. 'Let's find somewhere a little more secluded.'

After a few minutes of silent walking, they broke away from the established trail, and passed through a thick shady copse. Further on, they found themselves in a sort of half clearing where the sunlight was broken and dappled. To one side was a softly mossed hollow which could almost have been designed for their purpose.

Thanks again, whoever you are, thought Rosie, feeling amazed and grateful that sometimes in life, things just went right without you even trying. Almost as if he'd read her mind, David flicked open the rug and spread it out across the moss.

As he stared intently at the soft, tartan fabric, Rosie wondered if he was having second thoughts. Sitting down as elegantly as she could in her tight jeans, she patted a space on the rug beside her.

'It's time, David.'

The serenity of her own voice amazed her. Now the moment had come, she felt calm and assured. Somewhere along the road from London, she'd left behind the last remnants of her girlish gaucherie, and become completely and powerfully a woman; and everything that David needed.

As if protected by the same magic spell, even the champagne opened perfectly, and Rosie poured them both a brimming fluteful.

'Here's to knowledge,' she toasted, clinking their glasses together. David said nothing, but just looked back at her, solemn and unblinking. When he finally put his wine to his lips, he drank it all down in one swallow.

Rosie watched his pale throat undulate, then followed suit, swallowing the crisp golden wine, and for the first time in her life, truly enjoying it. The dry, mellow taste had an effervescent radiance that warmed and enlivened her, titillating not only her mouth and palate, but the whole of the rest of her too. Her limbs, her belly, her sex.

Together they put their glasses aside, and then Rosie reached out, slid a hand behind David's head, and pulled his mouth on to hers for a kiss. She felt him shake as she touched him, but his lips opened eagerly and his champagne-drenched tongue found hers, stabbing forward with an unexpected boldness. His arms came around her too, holding her in close to his body, his fingers massaging her back as her breasts met the heat of his chest. He made a low, anguished sound as she shimmied against him, caressing his body with her own and revelling in his muscular, young torso as it pressed against her aching nipples.

Every part of her felt sensitised, every nerve end sang with rich feelings. She cooed with approval as she felt him tugging at the edge of her tee-shirt, then smiled into his kiss as his warm hand touched her bare back. Her shy-boy had taken the initiative.

She didn't want to rush him, or damage his fragile confidence, but her breasts felt so tender and needful she could almost have described it as pain. Crushed against him, they were tense and swollen. She wanted him to squeeze her, explore her, be a little rough, perhaps – anything to distract her from the greater ache lower down; the wet, burning need to be filled by him, and to possess his rampant young beauty in the very act of him possessing her.

Novice or no novice, David seemed to read her effortlessly. He fumbled, but within moments he had her tee-shirt pushed up to her armpits and was working on the single front catch of her bra. The small hook yielded easily, and as the pretty silk cups slid away, her full breasts swung free towards his hands.

'Oh God,' he groaned, sitting back a little so he could study what he'd revealed. Rosie guessed it was the first time he'd ever seen such a sight in the flesh, and she cupped her own lush shape in her hands and held her breasts up towards him like an offering.

David's great golden eyes were enormous now, with discs of pure black at their centres, his pupils dilated with arousal. He reached forward with a trembling hand, and brushed his fingers to first one nipple then the other, exploring their absolute hardness. Rosie gasped, shocked by the delicate, ghostlike contact that shot directly to her quim and her clitoris. She hadn't expected an orgasm from this encounter – it was David's time, not hers – but suddenly she was balanced on the edge of one. As his fingertips flexed, then squeezed her, she started rocking convulsively on the blanket, working her furrow against the seam of her jeans until a great wave of pleasure engulfed her.

As she throbbed and swayed, David let go of her, an alarmed expression on his face. Through her haze, she realised he was frightened he'd hurt her, and quickly, she took his hand, pressed it to her breast, and curled it round the firm white flesh.

'Squeeze hard! I like it!' she hissed, one hand still folded around his, the other rubbing furiously at her crotch.

David frowned for a moment, then smiled and obeyed. Rosie couldn't help herself now, she was writhing and panting, and it was obvious what was happening to her. With the hand he had free he reached for her, pulled their faces together, and in a move that was exactly what she wanted, needed and craved, he kissed her through the tumult of her climax.

When she was finally calm again, or as calm as was possible, Rosie reclaimed the kiss. Abandoning her own needs, she let her hands run freely over David, examining his body through his clothes.

The process made him gasp, his breathing coming hoarse and heavy as her fingers flowed indulgently over him. And just like her, he seemed to be unable to keep still, shifting this way and that on the rug, and shivering as she discovered first his nipples, then the bulge at his groin.

'Let's get these clothes out of the way, shall we?' she murmured, pushing him gently backwards until he was lying before her on the blanket. Working quickly and deftly, she eased his tee-shirt out of his waistband and pushed it upwards. His chest was white as milk against the dense black cotton, and his nipples were as sweet and dark as berries. Running her tongue across her lips, she leaned forward and nibbled him, mouthing at his tiny male teats. As she sucked one, then licked it, she pinched its twin with her fingers and made David groan softly in response. Surrendered beneath her, he rolled his slim body on the rug, his hips weaving this way and that. Out of the corner of her eye Rosie saw him reaching downwards, rubbing at his groin in desperation.

'Oh, please,' he gasped, his voice so sharp and clear and young that she could deny him no longer. Now it really was time, and with a last swirling lick at his nipple, she straightened up, then started unfastening his jeans.

Underneath his black denims, he wore plain white jockey shorts, and as his fly slid open, his erection forced them out through the gap. She could see the shape of his cock quite clearly, pressing up against the thin white fabric and deforming it with the power of his lust.

Rosie considered simply easing him out, letting his flesh spring up, then sliding down on it straight away. It would be a perfect poem of rudeness. Instant gratification. A gallop in jet black, silky russet, and vital quivering red. She imagined his penis rising up like a tower, questing towards her, reaching out for a new world of sex.

Sunlight glinted on the teeth of his zipper, and those sharp little points changed her mind. 'Hup,' she said softly. 'Lift your bottom.' When he obeyed, she pulled his jeans and underpants down to his knees, and made him bare from armpit to thigh. His chest and belly were a pale, naked band with his burgeoning cock at its focus.

She watched his flesh sway, as if played on by a breeze, and felt her own sex ripple in answer. She wanted him, she desired him, she needed him and hungered for him as much, if not more than he was hungering for her. It would be cruel now, to wait or delay, and in a flurry, she pulled off her trainers, then her jeans and panties. Moving as gracefully as she could, she stood astride his body, nude below her tee-shirt, and showed him the treasure he longed for.

The sensation of displaying herself was intoxicating. She saw David swallow, take huge breaths, then try to struggle upwards, reaching for her. But with a slow smile, she brushed aside his hands, then steadied herself, placing her feet squarely and strongly. Very very gradually she began to sink down towards him, revelling in the way her thighs opened and stretched. Reaching down, she parted her labia, showing him her bright, swollen pinkness as she descended. His golden eyes grew wider than ever at the beauty of her folds and her clitoris.

Her thighs were taut and aching, yet the discomfort barely touched her. She held herself, hovering, her jewel just an inch from his glans. She could almost feel the heat of him, the tip of his burning hot penis, and as her muscles screamed in protest, she sank down a minute degree further. Her body tried to waver and unbalance, but she fought it, stabilising her pose with her weight and the elegant outstretching of her arms.

Seconds ticked, and somewhere a bird sang, then

Rosie forgot the awkwardness, forgot the tension, forgot everything but the thick, hard pressure of David as his stiff flesh made contact with her entrance. It was suddenly the easiest thing she'd ever done – the easiest thing in the world – just to let gravity carry her downwards and onto him.

It's the easiest thing in the world! shouted David in the silence of his mind.

He felt relieved. Triumphant. He hadn't had to struggle. He hadn't had to fumble. He'd just lain there almost serenely and let her beautiful body slide over him, then watched in gratitude and wonder as she'd neatly rearranged herself into a kneeling pose, tucking in her sleek legs beside his hips. The only thing David found difficult was stopping himself thinking he was dreaming!

A strange laden stillness seemed to engulf both the glade and their bodies, a crystalline quiet that astonished him. In every sex-dream he'd ever had, in every masturbation fantasy, he'd always pictured thrusting and wild, violent action. A headlong dash towards the peak. But in reality, everything was calm. He felt steady. Almost composed. He didn't have to rush or thrash, just lying still brought the sweetest sensations. Even his eyelids – closed now – were motionless, and perhaps in a way that was best. If he opened his eyes, he might discover he was imagining things. Rosie might be just a warm, perfumed illusion; and the delicious containment of his penis might only be his own gripping hand.

But his hand had never been like this; never felt

like both satin and velvet at once; never been so exquisitely warm and snug; never pulsated; never fondled
every inch of him so lingeringly.

Was this marvellous phenomenon natural? he
wondered – aware that he was grinning like an idiot,
but unable to prevent it or worry. Did all women
ripple like this, or was it something special and skilled
she was doing? His captured body didn't care which,
but there was a part of his brain still thinking. Thinking
– and hoping – that this particular and magical effort
was contrived to increase *his* pleasure.

As she began, very slowly, to move up and down,
he took the huge risk of opening his eyes.

He needn't have worried. Rosie was real. And her
own eyes were closed in an expression of rapt, almost
trancelike intent. She was concentrating utterly on
the even rise and fall of her body. Her face was a
flushed pink mask, finely shining with a light trace of
sweat, and David had never seen anything so lovely.
She exceeded every fantasy, every fevered, passionate
dream, and he was too excited and enraptured to
breathe. When he did remember to do so, he gasped
in air like a bellows, his head as light with happiness
as his loins were heavy with desire.

Not knowing what to do with his hands, he started
stroking the slopes of her thighs. Running his fingertips up and down them, he travelled closer to their
apex with each pass, yet felt afraid to take the last step.
He wanted to reach up and hold her breasts too, but
he held back, not wanting to still their delicate, syncopated jiggling.

Framed by her pushed-up clothing, Rosie's bosom

was a glory to his eyes, each individual breast a harmonious, delicately pointed round that was capped by a dark, puckered nipple. As he watched, she lifted her hands and cupped herself again, her delight in her own beautiful body just as obvious as his would have been. He longed to copy her action, and hold the full, veined weight of her – a breast in each hand – but awe kept his fingers on her thighs.

'Touch me, David,' she said suddenly, her voice an urgent purr, like a cat requesting attention. For a moment he was puzzled. She was gripping her own breasts tightly now, squeezing in an arcane, complex pattern that forbade interruption. She didn't seem to need *his* hands.

After a couple of seconds, though, he understood the significance of her words. She didn't want him to touch her breasts. She wanted his fingers between her legs, touching the place, almost, where he was inside her. The tiny, tender spot that even he knew was a woman's greatest pleasure. Her bud. Her berry. Her clitoris.

Tentatively he reached forward, letting his fingertips comb her silky hair and travel in search of her centre. The lips of her quim were slick and puffy, and seemed to stand away from her body, stretched, engorged and pouting. Using both hands, he parted the tangling curls so he could see what he was doing, see the gem he sought to plunder, the tiny pink droplet he could almost hear begging to be rubbed. He could actually see it moving, twitching in its niche like the beat of a miniaturised heart.

'David! Please!' she groaned, rocking on his body

to push her clitoris towards him. 'Rub me . . . Please! Just do it! It doesn't matter how!'

Her tone was both urgent and commanding. She'd said – gasped, groaned – 'please', but she wasn't pleading at all. She was telling him, ordering him to pleasure her with his fingers while his cock remained lodged in her body.

Remembering books and pictures, and drawing on his deepest internal instincts, David let his fingertip settle on its target, then pressed, lightly. Rosie cried out, her voice incensed, her head tossing, and her long hair swirling around her like a cape. Her body was in heaving, thumping motion, riding him; yet he knew that the contact between them must stay constant. Concentrating when it should have been impossible, he swirled her clitoris with his finger, delighting in its subtle mobility and the way it leapt and throbbed beneath his touch.

Rosie howled, and suddenly her whole body went rigid. Her neck, back, and thighs all tensed before David's astonished eyes – while her inner muscles spasmed around him.

She was coming, he realised, but even as the knowledge hit his brain, his own senses blanked out the thought. Long, gut-wrenching waves of feeling slammed up through his belly and loins, eclipsing everything he'd ever felt before. It was like being hit by a cattle prod or a massive electric shock, yet it filled his whole world with raw bliss.

There had never been sensations like these, not even in his most successful dreams. His penis felt indescribably wonderful, pulsing and jumping in her silkiness, his ecstasy blending with hers as he too shouted and groaned.

At the very pinnacle of his pleasure, David suddenly had to be closer. Closer than having her. Closer than in her. Curving himself up from the ground and the rug, he slung his free arm around Rosie's body, caressing her back, her spine and her rib-cage while his fingers still moved at her core.

'Oh David,' she whispered, bending down to hug him to her in return, then pressing her lips to his mouth.

'Oh David,' she seemed to say right inside him – lighting up his yearning soul with her spirit as their joined flesh danced in the sun.

10

Stonehaven

So this is the famous Stonehaven, thought Rosie, lying in – or more properly on – her very first four poster bed.

The canopy above her head was made of elaborately tented canary yellow silk, and if the librarian's bedroom was as beautiful as this, she decided, then the master bedroom must be beyond all imagining. The whole place was like a film set, and twice as opulent as the London house – and that was certainly no hovel.

She supposed she was musing about interior design to distract herself. The 'event' that had occurred on the road was so special, so marvellous that it was difficult to believe it had even happened. It was as if one of Anaïs Nin's stories had come to life; the little-known one about the boy virgin and the woman who looked after books. Even the setting had been too perfect to be real.

David, she reflected, was a revelation. As simple as that. He'd been shy, understandably, but he'd taken to sex like a natural. An adept. She'd sensed him wanting to please her, felt him trying to please her, and then instinctively getting things right. She was physically tired now, from the drive, and from their time in the glade, but at her innermost core she was awestruck.

And David felt the same, she could tell. It was obvious he'd surprised himself. She thought of his face, and how it had looked as he'd lain beneath her after his orgasm. His expression had been a blend of pure shock, and grinning, almost imbecilic happiness – the classic ear-to-ear grin of contentment. She'd been on the point of kissing her way from one end of that grin to the other, when a faint sound from the direction of the picnic ground had set both of them struggling with their clothes, each helping the other with garments that were tangled or bunched.

By the time they were decent, and free of bits of stray grass, a family of four and their dog had been visible, approaching through the trees. Rosie had been most impressed by the cool way David had gathered up the blanket and their other belongings, then nodded politely to the newcomers as they'd passed.

'So?' she'd said when they were in the car, noticing that David's dazed smile had returned.

'I never realised,' he whispered. 'I thought it'd be like . . .' He paused, and Rosie saw a blush flow up his pale throat. 'I thought it'd feel how it does when I do it myself. But it doesn't. It's not a bit like . . . like that.'

'Is it better or worse?' she asked, teasing.

'Better! Different . . . Oh God, I don't know!' He

was really quite pink-faced now, but curiously, he looked all the more handsome for it.

They both fell silent then, and the car seemed to hum with deep thoughts. A little while later, as Rosie saw a rather pretty looking roadside pub ahead, she glanced at the dashboard and realised it was just about opening time. There were rustic tables and chairs in an adjacent beer garden, and without hesitating, she pulled the Mercedes into the car park just beyond.

'Let's stop here, shall we?' she said, not giving David a chance to object. 'I need the ladies, and I could do with . . . with a breather or something.'

Within ten minutes, they were sitting one on each side of a roughly-planed wooden table top. Rosie, mindful of the champagne she'd drunk, had a tall glass of Perrier before her, but David had a pint of best bitter.

Another rite of passage, thought Rosie, smiling inside as he eyed the drink suspiciously. Real men drank pints, so people said, but although David was now most certainly a real man, he didn't seem too sure about the beer.

'Cheers!' she said, then took a sip of her icy cool water.

'Cheers,' answered David, drinking cautiously from his pint. Rosie felt a fresh spasm of lust when he licked his lips slowly, as if deciding whether he liked the taste or not. His tongue was very red and looked uncannily long and flexible; just right for exploring her body.

'So?' she enquired, nodding at his beer, unable to resist the parallel.

David laughed out loud, his golden eyes sparkling with merriment. 'It's good actually. Great.' His face coloured even more, but he was already instinctively flirtatious. 'But I think I like what I had earlier better.'

'I'm pleased to hear it,' she said softly, reaching out to touch his hand, her flesh thrilling at the thought of him: his delicious young body, his innocent *savant* lovemaking; the gentle playful wit that was emerging now the first shock was over.

It was an erotic moment, though only their hands were in contact. Messages passed between their eyes, feelings were compared and marvelled at. Rosie felt her sex rouse and her pulse race madly, then had her attention suddenly distracted by something black and shiny flashing by in the corner of her vision.

She turned quickly and saw a familiar shape speeding away along the road. 'That's the limousine!' she cried, turning back towards David. 'Julian's limousine. They're going to get to Stonehaven before us!'

David made a panicked face. 'What shall we do? Try and go another way and get past them?'

'No. I don't think so . . .' It seemed pointless. Celeste had engineered the situation anyway, and there were bound to be questions. It seemed logical to just face the inevitable.

They sat and finished their drinks, the atmosphere between them a strange mix of ease and slight nervousness. Several times, she caught David taking sneaky looks at her breasts over the rim of his glass; but they didn't discuss sex, and they didn't compare notes. It didn't seem necessary. They'd been perfectly attuned when it mattered, and Rosie had a bone-deep feeling that the same thing would happen next time. Whether in an hour or two, or several days hence.

When their drinks were done, they moved on, motoring steadily but not slowly and arriving at their august destination just as the first shades of evening were falling.

Stonehaven was a huge, gothic looking house, made of beigey-grey softly-weathered stone, just as its name suggested. As Rosie had suspected, the Hadey limousine had been sitting accusingly in the carriage yard, but when she and David had entered the lofty, pillar-lined hall there had been no sign of either Celeste or Julian. Instead, a tall, very thin woman with grey streaked black hair had greeted them.

Rosie's immediate thoughts had been of Daphne Du Maurier's 'Rebecca' and the fiendish housekeeper Mrs Danvers, but when the lean one had smiled and introduced herself as Mrs Bright, her manner had been as sunny as her name, and her welcome as warm and friendly as that of her London counterpart, Mrs Russell.

Rosie had felt a glow of old-fashioned femininity when David had insisted on carrying her bag upstairs, and an entirely different kind of jolt when his hand had touched hers as they'd paused outside her room.

'See you later,' he'd said, his voice husky, his eyes intent. And as she lay now, in this elegant room, with its gilt, its space, and its smell of spiced pot-pourri, Rosie wondered how *much* he expected to see.

She was surprised that Celeste hadn't allotted her and David a shared room. But then again that was perhaps a bit too blatant. Even for Celeste.

It was disappointing though.

Rosie had never actually slept with a man. Not even with Geoff, who'd always made a point of either going home afterwards, or chivvying her to do the same. She'd tried to tell herself this was okay, and that she preferred her space; but now she wasn't so sure. What would it be like to wake up in a man's arms? To shake out the kinks of sleep with each other? To smell another person's sweat on her body?

She imagined waking up with her lover's cock already inside her, and him moving gently and smoothly to rouse her in the nicest of ways. If all went well in her endeavour, she'd try it, she vowed. She'd spend the whole night with David, and feel his warm young body against her as she slipped into the sweetest of dreams.

This room she was occupying was more of a suite than a simple room, and when she got up to look around, she discovered that not only did she have a private bathroom, but there was also a dressing area too.

It was very pretty and very feminine-looking, and full of mirrors. Thinking of London, she wondered if anyone was watching her. Waiting behind her own reflection for the moment when she peeled off her clothes. She was tempted to strip immediately, and make a proper show of it, but her attention was distracted before she'd even begun; by a stack of boxes and parcels piled one on top of another on one of the brocade covered dressing chairs.

Rosie's stomach fluttered when she saw a note lying on the top of the topmost box. That reminded her of London too.

Dear Rosie, it said, *I just couldn't resist getting you a few things to wear for David! Just a few naughties to tickle a young man's fancy. I took the liberty of checking your sizes yesterday, while you were sleeping. I hope you don't mind. Love Celeste.*

Do I mind? pondered Rosie. Gifts of clothing were fine for an intimate friend of the family, but she still wasn't quite sure she was one. Her position was delicate, nebulous, but even so, she prised open the first box, feeling full of both guilt and greed as she plunged in, then shredded away the soft pink tissue that was printed with a world famous logo.

'Good grief!' she whispered, lifting out what seemed to be a collection of black silk cobwebs elaborately trimmed with lace. It was the product of an elitist lingerie house, an abbreviated camiknicker and suspender belt set, as insubstantial as it was exquisite. Its beautiful satin-bound edges seemed to invite the hand – the male hand – to slide beneath them and explore. Rosie could well imagine what such a whimsy would do to an excitable boy like David! Instant orgasm, just from looking. For her part, it made her think of something more lingering. Long, sumptuous bouts of tender, yet decadent pleasure.

She held the camiknicker against her, and imagined what she'd look like inside it. She'd be clothed, yet more than naked; her pale, lush breasts barely masked by the smoky black fabric. She put David's hands into the image then too, holding her through the sheerest of barriers, pressing the texture of the lace into her skin.

The rest of the clothes were just as erotic. Some more so. From a set of boxes marked 'Circe', she took a basque made of plum-coloured satin; a white voile g-string; a black net bra with holes cut in it for her nipples, and panties that were similarly punctured. Rosie's fingers shook as she pushed them through the lace-edged gap.

Some of the smaller boxes had other things in them. A slim, chartreuse-coloured vibrator to replace her red friend from London. One or two small contraptions of narrow leather straps, whose purpose she had only the vaguest idea of. A velvet *commedia dell'arte* mask. And even a fully functional pair of stainless steel handcuffs!

'Good grief,' she said again, surveying her esoteric cache. Ladybird had suggested a few mild 'kinks', but straps and buckles and handcuffs? That all seemed a little advanced just yet.

The camiknickers were okay though, and she put them aside to wear straight away.

Remembering how much David had seemed to admire last night's outfit, she picked out another 'something floaty' for the evening ahead. This time it was a long, black muslin, handkerchief-pointed skirt, with a matching tee-shaped top; and when she slipped the ensemble on over her expensive new lingerie, she smiled a slow, catlike smile. The clothes she'd chosen last night had made David want to masturbate – would this lot have the same effect?

After brushing her hair to glossy smoothness, she let it hang dead straight down her back, then made-up carefully but vividly. She added some big silvery costume jewellery to create a chic, slightly off beat effect, then finished with a rich, flowery perfume.

'How beautiful you look tonight, Rosie,' murmured Julian, ever the flatterer, as she walked into the large salon that joined onto the entrance hall at the foot of the main staircase. It was an airy, spacious sort of room, crammed with superb antiques, but because of its sheer size, not cluttered. Julian welcomed her into it as if she were a visiting monarch, not his own employee.

When he took her hand and kissed it, Rosie trembled, thinking first – and rather strangely – of David. After a second though, her thoughts went winging back to the linen cupboard, and the man who'd enjoyed her in the darkness.

'Thanks. One tries,' she murmured, wishing she could accept compliments without feeling embarrassed. She felt a brief pang of fury at Geoff. Because he'd put her down so much, she now found it difficult to believe that sophisticated men like Julian could find her extremely seductive.

Covering her nervousness, she accepted a drink. It was the same sweet sherry she'd had in London, and its delicious warmth made her innards feel delightfully peculiar: sort of warm and sparkly and randy. She realised she'd had virtually nothing to eat since breakfast, and resolved not to drink anything else before dinner.

Under the guise of letting Julian show her some of his artistic treasures, she admired him too, thinking how handsome he looked in a simple white silk shirt, and loosely tailored trousers. It seemed outrageous that after having one man this afternoon, she could now be desiring another – but either the sherry, or the situation, was making it happen. She felt her body responding to Julian's, her sex reacting to his wine-dark voice and his aura of unfiltered maleness.

'Good evening, Rosie,' said another velvety voice from the direction of the open double doors.

Celeste looked stunning too; her long, draped, off-white gown a perfect foil for her shiny black hair.

'So you got here eventually,' she continued, walking slinkily across to the drinks table and mixing a large gin and tonic. 'When I discovered we'd beaten you here I couldn't help but speculate.' She took a sip of her drink as she walked towards Rosie, then bestowed the same greeting that her husband had. A kiss on the hand, but on Rosie's palm this time, with lips cooled by the well-iced gin.

'We . . . We stopped to stretch our legs,' stammered Rosie, knowing that Celeste certainly didn't believe her. The other woman did a thing with her perfectly plucked eyebrows that said 'who are you kidding?', and Rosie felt her face start to redden.

'So you stretched your legs, did you?' Celeste's grin was perfect, beautiful wickedness. 'And what did David stretch?'

At this, Rosie went pinker than ever. She'd tried to prepare a nonchalant explanation whilst in the shower, but now the crunch was here, she'd been rendered quite speechless.

'I see,' said Celeste triumphantly. 'Well done, my dear . . . I'm tempted to say "I knew you had it in you", but that's probably just a little too crude.'

Rosie took another long sip at her sherry, then allowed an amused, but solicitous Julian to refill her glass. His brown eyes were as bright as his wife's amazing lavender ones, but they also held a spark of respect. Rosie suddenly realised that in spite of her obvious embarrassment, the Hadeys were genuinely impressed by her.

Then, as if she'd unconsciously summoned him to support her, David appeared in the doorway. He looked shy, eager, nervous, happy – a whole array of emotions seemed to shine out of his huge golden eyes. He looked as if he'd had a hundred thousand volts put through him, but in the most joyous and enriching of ways. Rosie felt herself melting all over again.

She sensed, too, the almost hawk-like scrutiny of Celeste and Julian. It was as if the couple were im- agining her and David making love, picturing them entwined together on the richly patterned carpet, their sexes meshed, their sweating limbs tangled in passion.

Their stares didn't surprise her really. If she could see such a difference in David, the Hadeys must surely be able to. There was an indefinable lustre to him now, a brilliance. His pale skin seemed to glow, highlighted by a shirt of sombre midnight blue, and trousers in the same dark shade. His sleek, nut-brown hair was as neatly combed as ever, straight back from his face, but something about its very tidiness seemed to suggest a previous dishevellment.

Expecting either Celeste or Julian to make some kind of fuss over David, Rosie was relieved when they behaved quite normally. There was a very slight atmos- phere while they all sipped their aperatifs, but as the evening wore on, and dinner was served and eaten in the elegant oak-panelled dining room, even this disappeared. It seemed as if nothing unusual had happened at all.

Perhaps nothing unusual *had* happened? thought Rosie, as she set off with Julian and David for a tour of the house, and Celeste settled down to watch a play on TV.

Two people who were strongly attracted to each other had made love. What could be more natural and normal than that? Or more beautiful? It had been straight sex in a sunny, woodland hollow. Orgasms for two. An open air idyll.

Stonehaven was as astounding inside as it was out – a moody, magnificent mansion house, straight out of a Victorian pulp novel. To Rosie it seemed more like 'Manderley' with every room they passed through. The furniture and pictures were perfectly chosen, the carpets rare, and the whole ambience a curious amalgam of the intimidating and the homely. Modernisations – to pander to conventional standards of comfort – had been made throughout, but so subtly done that the eye did not immediately perceive them. Even the heated indoor swimming pool looked 'right'.

The rooms that appealed to Rosie most were the library, of course – which was in far more of a jumble than the London one, but which mercifully contained a computer and a modem – and the conservatory, a lovely glassed-in area full of fragrant plants and shrubs. Its intense green eroticism reminded her strongly of being with David in the woods, and the whole place seemed to ring with echoes of pleasure. It was easy to imagine people making love amongst the ferns, to see Celeste riding Julian on the long, buttoned chaise, and hear their combined climactic cries bouncing back off the bright panes of glass.

From time to time, as they walked, she'd catch David watching her closely – and if their eyes met, he'd smile shyly. He was staking no claims on her, she sensed, as if he was still very wary of his own sexuality, but curiously she liked that. A cocky, boastful David would not be 'her' David and she enjoyed having a kind of control over him. The power of 'yeah or nay'. When he was an experienced lover, she knew he'd be amazing in a different kind of way, but for now his demi-innocence bewitched her. And she didn't want to rush him into changing.

When she saw him yawning, she suspected he'd had enough for one day. Probably of everything.

'I think I'll turn in now,' he said as Julian turned back towards the drawing room, where Celeste was still viewing. 'I'm really tired . . .' He turned towards Rosie, his golden eyes questioning. Was he letting her down? they seemed to say. 'You don't mind, do you?' The question was asked of both herself and Julian, but she sensed it was really aimed solely at her.

Julian nodded amiably, said 'goodnight', and strolled away; and Rosie felt a warm rush of gratitude. He was such a chauvinist in a lot of ways, but in others, his discretion and sensitivity were quite faultless.

'I feel a bit weary too,' she told David quietly. 'It must be all that fresh air.'

A complicit smile passed between them, the carrier wave for a dozen silent messages. It was okay *not* to have sex too. There was no hurry. There would be more soon, and better. No pressure.

Without thinking, Rosie leaned over and touched her lips to David's, stroking his pale face as she did so. His skin was very soft, and she wondered how often he had to shave. He was nineteen, but seemed so much, much younger. His mouth moved a little under hers, sighing slightly, and she felt a sharp, sweet stirring that ran counter to their wordless pledge. As she savoured the warm, luring velvet of his lips, she reprimanded her greedy inner self.

'Goodnight, David. Sleep well.' Drawing away, she let her fingers trail across his jaw, then turned and walked briskly down the hall.

'Goodnight,' she heard, spoken softly in reply, but didn't dare turn or halt in her stride, for fear that temptation would sway her.

When she entered the drawing room, two pairs of eyes seemed to pin her like a moth to a board.

'Have you put him to bed?' enquired Celeste, rising from the sofa like Aphrodite from the waves.

'With a goodnight kiss, perhaps?' suggested her husband, his tone light and inquisitive.

Perplexed, Rosie thought of London and the library. Separately, each of these people could easily seduce her; but together they were omnipotent. She felt boneless, without will, completely at their mercy.

'Well, did you kiss him?' Celeste was in front of her now, and deep in her personal space. Rosie quivered as the other woman's fingers curved lightly around her neck and drew their faces together.

'Did you?' Celeste persisted, her wine-scented breath fanning Rosie's face.

'Yes.'

'Like this?' Her mouth plunged down onto Rosie's, quick and hard, her tongue demanding instant entrance, then retreating to leave need in its wake.

'No, not quite,' Rosie whispered, so stunned that she let Celeste guide her helplessly to the sofa, with just the lightest of pressures on the curve between her neck and her shoulder. As she sat down, the Hadeys did too, one on either side of her, like brackets.

'But you kissed him like that earlier, didn't you?' said Julian, picking up the thread. Caught between the two of them, Rosie wondered if they were telepathic. For all their mutual, sexual freedom, she sensed that Celeste and Julian were intensely in love with each other, on a level she could barely understand. They were like two aspects of the same person, and she was trapped at the focus of their power.

She tried to remember, but her mind was numb. Yes, she and David had kissed, hadn't they? She'd kissed him, but he'd kissed her back. And with far more skill than she'd expected.

'Yes,' she said quietly, 'We kissed. It was nice. David seemed to know what to do . . .'

'Did he kiss you anywhere else? Other than the mouth?' asked Celeste, her thumb stroking Rosie's lip, then sliding down her face, her jaw and her throat. At the edge of her tee-shirt, it dipped inside, hooking in under her camisole top and resting on the curve of her breast. Acutely aware of its movements, Rosie also felt another hand at work. Julian's hand. Sliding between her lower back and the seat, flattening and going lower, cupping and squeezing her buttock through the cotton and silk of her clothing.

'Did he kiss your breasts, Rosie?' he whispered, kneading her. 'Did he put his face between your legs and kiss your wet little pussy?'

'No!' she squeaked as his finger probed her crease, and at the same moment, Celeste pushed aside the loose neck of her top and held her breast through her flimsy camisole. 'No, just my lips,' she groaned, then felt the pressure of Celeste's supple lips against hers, tasting her and making her yield.

And then there were two tongues working: Julian licking her neck as his wife probed the cavern of her mouth. Fingers also palpated her wickedly: Celeste's moulding her breast, Julian's teasing her bottom and prodding at her anus through her clothes. She was their victim, and she despised herself for her weakness, but at the same time she acknowledged their artistry. Her head, her heart and her loins all told her that they'd done this before; taken a willing, defenceless lover and quartered his or her body between them.

'Did he touch you?' The words were moist against Rosie's lips, and the fingers were cruel on her nipple. 'Did you let him fondle your breasts?' Celeste asked, pinching. 'And squeeze your nipples? Like this?'

Rosie struggled, her body alive in every pore. Celeste had asked questions, but given her no chance to answer. She was being kissed again, aggressively, the tongue in her mouth stabbing deep as the fingers tweaked rudely at her breast.

'And did he touch you here?' asked Julian slyly, letting his free hand settle on her belly. He had her loins in a sandwich now, his hands warm and intimate behind and before, but not quite doing what she craved. She felt his fingers in the channel between her buttocks and playing at the edge of her pubis. They seemed to dance there – hovering tantalisingly, but not pressing down to bring ease to her sex.

'Yes!' Her answer was garbled by Celeste's thrusting tongue, and her hips jerked crudely in Julian's unwavering hold. To her horror, Rosie realised she was unconsciously trying to entice him. She could feel herself soiling her lingerie, her juices running out like a stream across the fragile silk strip between her legs.

'And did you let him touch your quim?' asked Celeste, switching her attack from Rosie's mouth to her ear, nibbling at the lobe beside her ear-ring and sucking it like a fold of her sex.

Had he or hadn't he? She could barely remember. 'I don't know,' she whimpered, feeling Celeste on the move again. She felt her breast freed for a moment, her tee-shirt adjusted, then Celeste's hands were beneath the garment, tugging down the lace beneath and wedging it under her breasts. The thin straps slid down off her shoulders, trapping her arms and seeming to pin them at her sides. Her hands lay useless by her thighs, and her breasts were loose and free with only a thin layer of cotton to cover them. Rosie had never felt so vulnerable.

'Surely you let him finger you?' asked Julian as his wife now tucked Rosie's tee-shirt out of the way, and exposed her bosom – like two white, cherry tipped globes suspended between twin bands of black. One glance at the lewdness of her own body made Rosie try and turn her head away, but Celeste wouldn't let her. She gently urged Rosie to look downwards, then stroked each of her nipples with a fingertip, to make them harder and darker than ever.

'You did let him touch you, didn't you?' she cajoled, flicking ceaselessly, one nipple then the other, again and again and again.

Remembering, Rosie nodded, then whimpered as Julian's hands were suddenly at her crotch, working on the set of miniature press studs that held the gusset of her camiknickers in place. When he had them unfastened, he eased the sopping fabric aside, then raised her skirt and rolled it up to her waist.

Rosie closed her eyes again, aware that her face was red with shame. She felt fingers working neatly between her legs: combing open her wet pubic hair then dividing her thickened outer labia to expose the very softest parts within. Cool air flowed over her moistness and the distended bud of her clitoris, making it ache and almost cry for contact. She wiggled her hips, trying to invite either one or the other of her tormentors to touch her, but they didn't. She felt hands on her inner thighs, fingertips tracing the lines of her suspenders, someone tugging very gently on her curls.

The same someone – or maybe not – then turned their attention to her breasts, and began torturing them with little tickles, touches and licks. The very featheriest of caresses designed solely to arouse, not satisfy.

It was the same at her crotch.

'Did he touch your clittie,' murmured Celeste, while someone traced the creases of Rosie's groin, and blew on her pubic mound. 'Well, did he?' the beautiful voice persisted, while the tormenting fingertips went right inside Rosie's outer labia and performed a series of tiny fluttering strokes on either side of her clitoris. Madly engorged, the little bud seemed to pound like a drum, the beats so heavy and profound she could almost hear them. She tried to rock her body so the sliding fingers would accidently nudge into climax, but the one who wasn't stroking her – probably Julian – held her tight by the thighs and kept her still, her clitoris burning with an intense, but exquisite agony.

'Yes!' she shouted, sobbing in desperation. Just a few short minutes, and a few expert moves, had brought her to this. The very pinnacle of frustration, a state of desire so huge it was terrifying. If she didn't come soon, she was afraid of the consequences.

'And did you need him then, as you need him now?'

It was Celeste again, breaking the pattern of him, then her, then him again. Rosie groaned and struggled. She needed something now, needed orgasm by any hand, including her own or even David's.

'Yes,' she croaked, trying to jerk herself free and touch herself, because the stroking fingers would not. 'Oh God, please, I need to come!'

'Then go and find David,' purred Celeste, biting her neck just beneath the ear. 'Seek him out, Rosie. Enjoy him. He's beautiful . . . He's young and ripe. He's yours . . .'

'But he was tired,' said Rosie, confused. Her brain felt addled, her memory twisted. The fingers kept slicking and slicking, less than a quarter of an inch from her clitoris.

'Nonsense!' Celeste was laughing, pressing tiny kisses to Rosie's face and neck, licking her hot skin as the fingers squeezed gently then withdrew, and another tongue pressed delicately to each of her naked nipples in turn, wetting them, then pulling away completely.

'That's nonsense,' repeated Celeste, sweeping the damp hair back from Rosie's brow. 'Young men his age are sex machines. He's just unsure of himself. *You* have to be the prime mover, Rosie. You've got to go to him now. He's in the room at the end of the corridor on the right . . . Two doors down from you.'

All hands, all mouths, all presences slid away, and Rosie was left alone on the sofa, slumped and sleazy, her breasts and sex exposed and damp. For a few moments she just lay there – numbed and half naked – and then a small sound roused her from her stupor. Weighed down with sexual discomfort, she heaved herself upright and opened her eyes.

Celeste and Julian were lying on the rug, entwined and kissing. Celeste had one thigh jammed between her husband's legs and was rubbing it rhythmically against his crotch; while Julian had his hand up his wife's white dress, making short, stiff, stabbing movements with his arm. Their mouths were fused, their tongues working. They were already oblivious to her presence, or at least making it seem that way.

Clumsily, Rosie straightened her clothes. Her legs shook as she got to her feet. Avoiding the writhing couple on the carpet, she made her way to the door in a daze. When she reached it she turned, unable to resist another look.

Celeste's body was writhing furiously against the carpet now, and every so often her white-gowned body would lift from the floor and arch. Her partially bared thighs scissored wildly as she rose, and as her bottom seemed to float in mid-air, she wriggled like an eel on the pivot of Julian's rubbing hand. She was orgasming violently but in silence, her husband devouring her screams at the source as his own body pounded against hers. It was obvious that he was coming too.

Rosie almost ran from the room, groaning as her swollen breasts bounced. Her sex felt wide and bloated, and every movement seemed to goad her more and more. Her body was riven with longing, with a desperate need to climax. She pressed her hand to her crotch as she raced up the stairs, then almost fell as a spasm assailed her.

It was as if her sex was crying out for release, begging her for it, and on the landing she stopped, crouched gracelessly and rubbed herself roughly through her clothes.

Almost instantly a long, hard wave raced through her; the orgasm she'd yearned for, but too sudden and too soon. It felt more akin to pain than pleasure, and she grunted like an animal as she came, her pelvis pumping and weaving as she wallowed in the black depths of shame.

11

Stealth

'What's happening to me?' whispered Rosie as she slid down against a wall and collapsed in a heap on the floor.

To put it in its crudest terms she'd just rubbed herself off in an open, accessible part of the house, here on the upper landing. And she couldn't have stopped, even if someone had come by and caught her. One of the staff, on their way to turn down the beds, or perhaps Celeste and Julian, refreshed by their own swift pleasure and ready for further mischief.

And the worst of it was, she wasn't even satisfied. She'd had an orgasm, granted, but not one as powerful as she needed. She'd simply partially defused some tension; not made love – as she'd wanted to – either with herself or with any other person.

But her other person was close by now, and available, and struggling to her feet again, Rosie forced herself not to dither. Striding along the landing, she twisted the large glass doorknob, then pushed gently on the door. To her relief it swung open soundlessly, revealing the dimly lit room beyond.

Closing the door as quietly as she'd opened it, Rosie found herself in a suite not unlike her own. The same wonderful antiques, the same abundant space, and even a similar four poster bed – although this one had draperies of forest green instead of yellow.

On the bedside table, a nightlight burned, shedding its soft, muted glow on the bed and its single occupant. A figure that was sprawled face downwards; calm and still, yet at the same time subliminally restless.

David had changed.

It dawned on her again, here, just as it had in the dining room. He was a different boy altogether, sensualised somehow. Lit from within. He still looked the same, though, but with just one quantifiable difference – he wore no pyjamas tonight. He was quite clearly sleeping in the nude, with only a twist of sheet across his hips and buttocks to preserve his masculine modesty. His back, his arms and his shoulders, and his smooth, muscular legs were all naked and gleaming in the half-light.

Rosie drew stealthily closer.

Although David's face was pressed into the pillow, she could see his features in a pure, perfect profile. His bold, slightly roman nose; his crisply defined mouth; his closed eyes with their sooty black lashes so unfairly long for a man. While she watched, those lashes fluttered just once, like fans, and she took a nervous step backwards. She saw him frown in his sleep and wriggle slightly, and she wondered if he was dreaming. About sex; and maybe about her.

Suddenly her own desire seemed to ravish her. David looked so vulnerable, so available. He was something sweet and tempting she could feast on. She could have him and touch him, taste him and fondle him. Any part of him. He was an independent young man, whose trials, she suspected, had only made him stronger. But right now, she – as his tutor – still had the controlling upper hand.

Drawing close again, she carefully lifted the thin, light draping of the sheet.

His bottom was superb – neat, hard, and male – and his smooth, slender thighs were parted. Between them his balls nestled shyly, and shielded his penis from her eyes with their fuzzy, reddish bulk. In the deep, shady vale between his bottom cheeks, his anus seemed to wink like an eye; tiny, tight and alluring.

Not sure of what she wanted, but sure she wanted something, Rosie started stripping; tearing off her tee-shirt and skirt, then flinging them on the floor with her shoes. Her camiknickers had twisted during her writhings downstairs, and her nipples were peeking out the bodice. Between her thighs, the slender, fragile gusset was only half fastened in place, and her curls were poking out, on show. She could smell her own odour rising up: perfume, sweat, and the distinctive, pungent musk of a vulva that had seeped with pleasure. As she studied David closely, she saw his nostrils flare, and wondered if he'd smelt her too. She yearned for his scent in return.

Very carefully, Rosie tested the springs of the bed. It dented slightly, but the mattress seemed resilient. She took a chance, and climbed up onto it beside

David – holding her breath in case he woke. His only response, however, was to stir slightly, then still again almost immediately, muttering and nuzzling his pillow.

So far, so good.

Sweeping her hair back over her shoulder, Rosie leant over him, holding her face just an inch from his body and breathing in deeply.

She smelt the faintest hint of sex-musk, plus some kind of green-scented shower gel and the unmistakeable freshness of baby talc. It was really the weirdest of aphrodisiacs, but Rosie felt a giant surge of lust; a rushing need to explore his body, that was focused in the strangest of ways. Pressing her lips to the centre of his back, just between his shoulder-blades, she began kissing her way down his spine.

She felt his skin quiver finely beneath her progress, and when she reached the watershed between his back and his bottom, she sensed strongly that her pupil was aware of her; completely conscious, but not moving or speaking for fear that she'd stop her exploration. It seemed to signal both trust and trepidation, and Rosie vowed silently neither to betray the first, nor completely banish the second.

When he still showed no outward sign of wakefulness, she began an attack on his perfect young bottom. Covering it in kisses, she rubbed her cheeks and her nose against it, then licked at his firmly muscled lobes. Attending to every last millimetre of skin, she played around and caressed with her tongue, and at the moment when she sensed relaxation, she switched her efforts to the area of his cleft, and used her fingers for the first time too.

Prising apart his cheeks, she exposed the seductive little hole, amazed at its delicate prettiness. It looked like a small, mauve flower, the tight, crisp bud of a cultivated rose. Flexing her fingers, she opened him further and watched the miniature orifice dilate.

Alarming thoughts passed through her, odd feelings that defied her gender. It was as if she were a man suddenly: a possessor, a taker, a penetrator. She was going to have this gentle creature below her, have him and enter him. She was to use the small and sweetly puckered hole that he so innocently and openly offered her.

Using her thumbs, she stretched him even more, then moved her face in closer. She'd never indulged in play like this before, not even with Geoff. Whenever she'd touched *his* bottom, he'd complained, and she realised now that it was because he feared for his masculinity. Liking having your bottom stroked was for 'poofs' and 'queers' in his opinion, which only confirmed to Rosie that her ex wasn't quite the sexy guy he thought he was. You were wrong about a lot of things, Geoff, she thought, almost laughing against the cheeks of her lusciously surrendered young lover.

And clearly David himself wasn't hampered by such negative pre-conceptions. He was a blank slate, an open book, and she could write whatever she wanted on him. Phrases that were full and rich and strange. She could make him receptive to anything and every-thing, and as she pressed her lips to his exquisite, immaculate bottom, she relished his cry of delight.

As she kissed him, he started moving wildly beneath her: his feet kicking and scraping, his hands gouging at the sheets. His hips rose up, pressing his anus hard against her mouth, then plunged down again and circled, so he could massage the mattress with his groin.

Mastering him effortlessly, and encouraged by the sweetness and freshness of his body, Rosie opened her mouth and began to use her tongue on his flesh; licking at the forbidden little opening and teasing it with short, sharp dabs.

David was moaning continuously now, babbling gibberish, his face still pressed into the pillow as his body writhed and trembled. 'Oh God,' Rosie heard him whimper as she furled up her tongue and pushed it determinedly into him. She felt like a raider, pillaging him anew for a deeper and more telling virginity. For the second time in as many minutes she wished she was male. Or at least had a cock. She wanted desperately to penetrate him; to go in further than her tongue could reach; to feel what it was like to be inside him, and possess him in complete dominion.

As his body went rigid, she sensed him teetering on the edge of orgasm and made a split-second decision. She'd prolong the game, make more of it. She pulled back a little way, and watched his bottom and his whole back shake. He was tense as a wire, every nerve and muscle keyed up for climax. She could almost hear him screaming for release.

Half expecting him to break his silence and beg, she was pleased when he made not a sound. He had guts, and an instinctive sense of adventure, and she was proud of him. Keeping her touch ineffably light, she ran her fingers over the incurves of his cheeks and up and down his hot, tense thighs. Unbidden, his legs opened wider to expose the rich, dark bounty of his balls. She slid her hand up and delicately enclosed him.

When she squeezed, infinitesimally, she saw his toes clench and a pulse start to leap behind his knee. He made a rough sound in his throat, but otherwise stayed silent. When she leant over him, she saw that his lips were compressed in a thin, tight line, and his fine brow was crumpled with effort.

It was time. She couldn't torture him any more. Moving as smoothly and as quietly as she could, she unfastened the crotch of her camiknickers, threw her leg half across him and let her quim kiss the back of his thigh – just at the point where it merged with his buttock. Letting her weight take her down, she pressed the furrow of her sex against him, wetting his skin with her juice as she massaged her swollen membranes against the smooth, hard line of his haunch. His heat made her clitoris quiver, and as she rocked her body against him, she worked his flesh too; fondling his balls with her fingers while her momentum ground his cock against the sheet. It was as close as she'd ever get to being a man; the nearest she'd ever come to fucking him.

As her orgasm came, she inclined across his back like a willow, pressing her open mouth against the nape of his neck as her free hand searched blindly for one of his. In an instant, their fingers laced, and when David's grip grew vicelike, and he groaned, she felt his hip jerk up against her vulva.

'Oh! Oh!' she heard him gasp, as his pelvis rode the bed beneath him, and his balls leapt and pulsed in her fingers. 'Oh God,' he whimpered again, his voice just a thread in her splintering mind as pleasure sent it spinning from her body.

The next morning, as she jogged away from the house, Rosie turned and looked backwards for a second. There was a window open on the first floor, and its lace curtains fluttered cheerfully in the breeze.

It was David's room. And as she ran on the spot a few steps, then launched herself off towards the woods, she couldn't help thinking of what had happened beyond those curtains last night.

It'd been the strangest event of her sexual life so far. A union, but without intercourse, or even mutual touching. She hadn't seen David's penis, and she certainly hadn't handled it. And yet it had been under her control. She'd governed his responses completely, and possessed him in a way she'd never expected. It had been sublimely and quite beautifully peculiar, and though they hadn't exchanged a single word, she'd felt closer to David than to anyone ever in her life.

But how do I feel now? she pondered.

Taking pleasure in her own smooth stride, she decided that the word for her condition was 'great'! She'd slept well, and felt full of vitality and pep. And she could only ascribe it all to David.

After their mutual, but separate climax, she'd lain beside him for a while, listening to the rhythm of his breathing and trying to sense the current of his thoughts. He'd refrained from conversation, she deduced, because – like her – he was still mulling over what had happened. It was a pretty kinky thing they'd done between them, especially for a sexual novice. Did he have a few of Geoff's fears after all, she'd wondered. The perennial atavistic dread. The macho man's 'am I gay?' nightmare.

'Don't worry,' she told him remotely, as she pounded lightly away across the grass. 'You're a real man, my sweet. And even if you are bisexual, it'll probably make me like you even more!'

And that was another can of worms. One of several it seemed silly to open right now when the morning was so lovely and the sun so bright and uncomplicated.

When she'd woken up at dawn, and back in her own bed, the first thing she'd wanted to do was get out for a jog and explore. Last night, when she'd arrived, she'd been too preoccupied to look around properly; but this morning, out on the long veranda that ran along the side of the house, she'd been thrilled by the breathtaking view.

Stonehaven stood in the centre of its own vast park. The flat Norfolk panorama had been landscaped slightly to make it interesting, moulded into gentle rolls and hillocks that were dotted here and there with shrubs and bushes. The house itself was ringed by an elegant, formal flower garden that seemed to melt into the wilder zone around it.

Heading in the direction of the wooded perimeter, she kept her pace steady, and felt surprised by her own strength and liveliness. It was amazing. She should have felt like death warmed up after all that debauchery and creeping around the house in the small hours.

Rosie's relationship with jogging was a hit and miss affair; sometimes love, sometimes hate. This morning it was love, especially when a cooling breeze caressed her deliciously as she ran. Her clothes – a thin jersey sweat top and shorts – hardly kept her skin from the air at all, and her trainers almost flew across the turf. She felt healthier than she'd ever felt, and could only conclude that a life rich in sex was good for you. For a moment, she wished David was running beside her, but then accepted she couldn't have everything. Maybe they could swim together later? And afterwards discuss what they felt.

She also supposed she ought to get herself into the library – and do some of the work she was paid for!

When she reached the tree-line, she skirted its edge, looking for a clearing or a gap – then found a faint but quite definite path. Confident that her inbuilt sense of direction would eventually get her home, she set off boldly down the track, walking briskly but not running, so she wouldn't trip up or stumble.

Being in woods reminded her poignantly of the previous afternoon; and she smiled. It had been a cliché, but a good one. An unforgettable memory. She imagined David recounting it to some future lover, a wife or fiancée perhaps? They'd be lying in bed, in that glorious euphoria when sharing minds is as sweet as sharing bodies.

'Tell me about your first time,' the unknown woman would say. And David would smile that slow, solemn smile of his and describe a sunny afternoon on the road to Norfolk, when he'd lost his virginity to his cousin's librarian.

Why aren't I jealous? thought Rosie, pausing to peer through the trees. She'd been thinking of David with someone else and it hadn't hurt – even after yesterday's intimacy. She did want him for herself, yes; in fact she wanted him a very great deal. But she couldn't find envy in the feeling. She tried picturing him with Ladybird – and had to stop dead because the image was so vividly arousing.

Ladybird was limber and beautiful, an exotic, superbly fit animal. Her gilded body would look amazing against David's creamy pallor – once she got over her curious notions of intellectual inferiority – and Rosie longed to be there at their blending. Or even be a part of it.

Is it all that stuff with Celeste and Julian that's changed me? she wondered, enjoying the way the branches above made the sunlight dapple and flicker. She'd never even considered making love to more than one person at once until she'd arrived at Amberlake Gardens, but now the idea seemed quite natural.

As she turned the concept over in her mind, she noticed that up ahead the trees seemed thinner. Between them there was the sparkle of water, some slowly flowing river or stream. She broke into a trot again as the path became wider and more definite.

The woodland track disgorged onto a tow-path, and where they met was a large and solidly built boathouse. Made of stone and timber, it reminded Rosie of a similar structure she'd recently seen in a film. Something arty by Merchant Ivory, she seemed to recall; and in it, two homosexual lovers had embraced in a boathouse at night while all the 'straights' snoozed on unaware in the 'big' house.

I bet this place has seen some action, she thought,

pushing open the side door and stepping cautiously inside. It was an ideal trysting spot. She imagined Julian and Celeste bringing their various paramours here; either separately or in some complicated menage. There were a couple of moored rowing boats bobbing in the water, and nearby a sturdy joiner's trestle. In a flash of shocking clarity, she imagined a sleek, writhing body stretched face down across the bar, while another figure laid intimate hands on it. The picture crossed her mind so quickly that she couldn't even register their genders.

Shaken, she backed away from the sawhorse and the slowly lapping water. It was foolhardy to stand so close to the edge when she was hallucinating, so she made her way carefully to the back of the building – stepping over spare oars, coils of rope and half empty pots of varnish – and ascended the narrow staircase that led to an area up above.

Upstairs, she found a curiously cosy little set up. The storeroom, loft, or whatever it was, had been divided by a partition and made into a kind of apartment. There were a couple of easy chairs, a coffee table, a TV and even a surprisingly large bed. At the back of the room was a sink, some cupboards and a worktop, complete with a small microwave and fridge. Beyond the division was a tiny but squeaky clean bathroom – with a sink, shower and lavatory.

A love-nest, she thought with a smile, its ambience made all the more charming by the fact that from the upper level one could look down through a large, open trap-door and see the whole of the boathouse below.

Rosie looked down at the gently rocking boats for a few minutes, and tried to picture what these walls might have seen. Celeste, on the bed, entwined with lovers of either sex. Julian, ditto, if Ladybird's wild story was true.

It'd be a lovely place to bring David, she decided, her smile widening. It was comfortable, romantic, secluded, and provided she knew the whereabouts of *both* her employers at the time, well away from the Hadeys' watchful eyes. She and David could relax better here. Celeste and Julian were basically well-meaning, but their obsession with David's 'education' might embarrass him more than it helped.

Resolving to get him here as soon as possible, Rosie made her way to what seemed to be an exit. She opened a door right at the back of the room, and beyond it found a set of stone steps – on the outside of the building – that descended down to the tow-path.

She was just about to use them when she suddenly heard the sound of running. Two people running. Not really knowing why, she ducked back into the boat-house flat, and pushed the outer door quietly shut. On the lightest of feet, she crossed to the trap-door, and peered down into the area below; knowing she was trapped by her own nosey subterfuge if the newcomers chose to come upstairs.

But they didn't.

The runners were Julian and Stephen the chauffeur. They moved into the centre of the boathouse, and just stood facing each other, by the trestle. Both wore sweaty sports gear, and both were panting with exertion, but their faces bore a matching, narrow-eyed expression. The look of pure, naked lust. Without either of them speaking, they moved forward as one and began to kiss. Their mouths were ravenous and passionate, and their hands were the same; exploring each other's bodies, squeezing and groping quite freely.

Oh God, it's true! thought Rosie, stunned and breathless. She'd half suspected that Ladybird had been storytelling, but obviously she hadn't. The two men down in the boathouse were clearly lovers. Why else would Stephen be palming his employer's genitals and bending him back across his arm with the force and fury of his kiss?

The chauffeur's dominance was a shock, in spite of her being forewarned of it. She was so used to Julian being suave and confident, so used to him being the boss, and a heterosexual. It seemed out of character for him to yield. Nevertheless, Stephen was handling him in a way so crude it could only be intended to demean him.

'You want it, don't you?' Rosie heard Stephen growl. Then she watched, open-mouthed, as his big, dark hand slid down into Julian's thin shorts, and resumed the rough stimulation.

It was total role reversal. Julian looked soft-faced, enraptured, malleable. Rosie heard him whimper in his throat as Stephen caressed him, and saw him clutch at his lover's thick arms, every inch the pathetic, quivering submissive.

Rosie felt her blood stir dangerously, and her own flesh grow tense and excited. She remembered what Ladybird had described to her, and compared it with scraps of her own fantasies – the wild outrageous ones that came from nowhere. The ones that set her stroking her body compulsively and feeling guilty at the resulting orgasms. She'd always found the theory of man-to-man loving a turn on, but down below was a practical demonstration. Her hand stole slyly to her mound.

The men looked dynamic together. A poem in contrasts. Stephen was like a column of ebony, sparsely clothed in a grey vest and shorts; while Julian wore pale blue, a delicate eggshell pastel that gave his honeyed middle eastern skin the subtle bloom of velvet.

'Slut,' murmured Stephen huskily, biting at Julian's bared neck. 'Little pansy. You want me don't you? I saw you waggling your bottom . . .'

'Oh please, yes!' groaned Julian, arching even more.

Rosie had never heard a more unlikely conversation. Julian was completely in Stephen's control, completely domineered, yet she sensed there was a deep bond between them. Stephen's face was stern, but there was a strange respect there too – even though Julian was clearly quite happy to be used.

'Please,' she heard him croak, his usual extensive and sophisticated vocabulary torn away by the rawness of his need.

In a jerky, shaming movement, Stephen pulled down his victim's shorts. Julian's erection bounced up hungrily, its red tip straining and pointing towards the man who was currently its master. Rosie bit her lip, her own crotch aching, when Julian's hips began to weave.

'What's this then?' enquired Stephen, as he almost dropped Julian at his feet, then reached out to flick at his stiffness. 'What do you think you're up to? Did I say you could get like this?'

'No,' said Julian in a small voice.

'It's disgusting,' Stephen scorned. 'You need punishing . . . For being a dirty little pervert.'

The chauffeur's tone was pure theatre, grim and harsh. The men below were acting out a drama, an entertainment for their mutual pleasure, and Rosie found herself smiling as, quite suddenly, Julian started flirting.

Giving his companion a creamy, almost coquettish look, he insolently stroked his own prick and wiggled his hips like a hussy. He was playing the effeminate to the hilt this morning, and to Rosie, it was a wonder to behold. Especially when he closed his eyes, bent his knees and flirted his pelvis to and fro with an expression of pure sleaze on his face. His shorts were still pushed down to his knees, which only increased the impression of lewdness.

With the speed of a striking snake, Stephen slapped his employer's face.

'Whore!' snarled the chauffeur, his voice soft and steely as real tears formed in Julian's eyes, and Rosie could have sworn she saw his lip tremble. There was a clear, pink handprint adorning his smooth, tawny cheek.

'I'll stop you,' Stephen went on, eyes narrowed. Looking around, he snatched up a short length of cord from the assortment of nautical detritus that lay scattered across the stone floor. With unnecessary force, he grabbed Julian's wrists and tied them together behind his back; leaving Rosie wondering how there just happened to be such a convenient length of rope to hand. Did they play these games here often?

Utterly fascinated, Rosie thought of all the sights she'd seen in the past few days and tried to pick a highlight from amongst them. In her mind's eye she saw David again, masturbating; then pictured him as he'd appeared last night, stretched naked on his sleep-tossed bed, his long pale back and his firm young bottom exposed to her like an offering.

But even as she focused her attention on Julian again, and the expanse of his rudely bared loins, she sensed a movement at the edge of her vision. Something close by, in the loft itself.

She turned her head very slowly, then almost toppled head first through the trap-door when she saw David just a few feet away from her. He'd obviously come up via the outdoor steps, and the fact that he wore a tee-shirt, tracksuit bottoms and trainers indicated that he too had been out for an early morning jog. His smooth brow was creased in puzzlement, and as he opened his mouth to speak, Rosie pressed a finger to her lips to shush him, then nodded towards the trap-door. As he moved forward with a silent, almost feline grace, she wondered if she was doing the right thing. Watching was a good way to learn, but was David really ready for such strangeness?

But as he crouched noiselessly over the opening, his face showed only fascination. Rosie was torn between the urge to watch the action down below, and the desire to see David's reaction. She settled for observing the lovers. She might never get the chance again.

Stephen's hands were back on the move. With slow luxurious strokes he was examining Julian's helpless body, pushing his hand up his victim's vest and tweaking his nipples, then swooping down over his ribcage and flanks to settle on his naked hips. He didn't touch Julian's penis, but instead, slid both hands around his back, then dropped them to his trim, masculine buttocks. Julian's cock seemed to yearn towards the dark man before him, but Stephen stepped teasingly away, denying the comfort of contact.

'Oh no you don't,' he purred to his employer, and even from several yards away, Rosie saw Stephen's arms flex. He was squeezing Julian's bottom-cheeks as hard as he could, treating the taut, smooth flesh like raw clay.

Julian was panting heavily, and had sweat standing out on his brow. He whimpered like a girl when Stephen brought one hand forward, and his eyes widened and bulged. Rosie couldn't quite see what was happening: she could only deduce that Stephen was attacking his employer from both back and front now. Playing with his penis or his balls, whilst caressing the crease of his bottom. After a couple of seconds Julian's hips lurched forward, and his mouth fell slackly open.

On impulse, she glanced towards David. His face was a picture of conflict. He looked excited and intensely turned on, yet there was an edge of worry there too. Was he alarmed by the implications of what he was seeing? The connotations of having enjoyed something similar – his bottom being fondled and kissed?

It was impossible to reassure him without revealing their presence, but even so Rosie tried. 'It's alright,' she mimed. 'Just enjoy . . .' It didn't make a lot of sense, she realised, but even so he seemed to relax. He gave her a confused grin, then shrugged and looked down his own body. There was a bulge in the front of his trackpants.

'It's alright,' Rosie repeated in silence, then on impulse, slid her hand into the waistband of her shorts – seeking out her warm, moist centre. The pressure of her own fingertips was exquisite, and she rolled her hips to increase the sensation, and hoped that David would copy her.

For a moment, his eyes went as round and bright as two gold coins, and he just gaped in amazement. Then with a soundless sigh of acceptance, he laid a long pale hand across his crotch.

Down below matters were progressing. The men had shifted around slightly, and made their contortions easier to see. Stephen had a rhythmic, pumping finger at work in Julian's tight anus and he was complimenting this by holding the tip of his employer's penis in a tight, pinching grip, just below the glans. 'Sexy little queen,' he murmured huskily, then swooped down and bit Julian's neck again. Hard.

Julian was sobbing now, his face beatific. It was clear that in this quasi-feminine role he took a genuine pleasure in weeping and mewling like a damsel in direst distress. His slim hips were waving and swaying, and it seemed that no matter how firmly Stephen held on his cock, he was still about to come any minute.

Then, with a sudden, wrenching cruelty, the chauffeur withdrew both his hands, and Julian was left high and dry. His gleaming body seemed to hum with tension, and his cock stood out like a tortured, crimson prong. His eyes turned beseechingly towards his tormentor. 'Please . . . Bring me off,' he pleaded, pushing forward with his hips.

'No way,' snarled Stephen, and Rosie felt her own flesh quiver beneath her fingers – as if the chauffeur had proscribed her pleasure too. She hardly dare look at David, but minute almost subliminal rustlings told her he'd either slid his hands down inside his tracksuit, or eased his stiff sex out into the air.

'Please,' repeated Julian below them. 'Please, I need to come. It hurts . . .' His voice was pathetic and wheedling, quite unlike his usual confident drawl. Bizarrely, Rosie found this peculiar new persona a turn-on, and without thinking, began to rock against her fingers.

A strong hand settled on her shoulder, and made her still before the sound became incriminating. She looked up into David's lambent eyes, and realised that he'd edged ever so slightly closer. He was lying with his body almost touching hers and his erect penis pointing at her belly. He smiled, and she felt her quim shake again, excited by the sweet blend of shyness, arousal and conspiracy she saw on his handsome young face. Like the wonderfully quick study he was, he'd plunged into voyeurism like a pro and was as turned on by the strange sights as she was.

Stephen's voice refocused their attentions.

'Hurts, does it?' he taunted, taking Julian by the shoulders and virtually throwing him face down across the trestle. 'Well, we'll see about that!'

First gay love. Then bondage and humiliation.

Was it spanking next? Julian was draped over the hard wooden cross-piece, with his naked bottom perfectly positioned. Stephen had said – hours ago it now seemed – that Julian needed to be punished. Rosie stole another peek at David.

His golden eyes were still hugely wide, and as she watched him he bit his lip in a sort of semi-worried eagerness. He was lying in a position that precisely mirrored her own; stretched out, half sideways on, one hand supporting his chin while the other worked steadily at his groin. Rosie realised he must have read about people beating each other – Julian's library was stuffed with such literature! – but the difference between reading about and seeing for real was astronomical. She was terrified herself in a way. Her sex was already throbbing and the tableau had barely begun.

Down below, Stephen was opening up a weathered oak store cupboard and reaching inside. From where Rosie was lying, its contents were hidden, but she wasn't at all surprised when he returned to the trestle with a thick leather strap in his hand. She saw Julian's back shake, and his bound hands curl into fists when the cruel thing was drawn slowly, oh so slowly, between his buttocks. His prick was partially hidden from view by his body, but as the leather slid idly up his channel, a string of clear fluid began to snake down towards the floor from his visible and very swollen glans.

'Kiss it,' ordered Stephen, holding the strap to Julian's lips. Julian craned his head forwards and rubbed his mouth lovingly over the sturdy chunk of leather; as if it were the body of someone he worshipped and not an instrument of punishment and pain.

The chauffeur turned away, hefting the strap in his right hand, while with his left he made some small, tugging movements. Rosie couldn't actually see what he was doing, but she could imagine. And when he turned back round again, she swallowed, then blinked, then swallowed again.

Stephen had pulled down the front of his shorts and exposed his penis and testicles. They were resting on the bunched up cloth like treasures exhibited on a cushion. And they were enormous.

Astounded, Rosie looked away quickly towards David; who in turn glanced briefly down towards his own genitals, then shrugged, shook his head, and cracked a grin so droll that Rosie had a hard time not bursting out laughing.

As her hysteria began to bubble, she had to take her hand out of her pants and bite her knuckle. She was dying to giggle, almost wetting herself with the need to roll about and howl, and David wasn't helping matters either, because he seemed to be having the same problem. He was pressing his face into the rug they were lying on, his cotton-clad shoulders shaking with the effort of containing his mirth.

Eventually though, they were able to resume their surveillance, and down in the bowels of the boathouse all was dark and deviantly erotic.

Stephen stood before Julian's upturned face, his penis almost touching his employer's trembling lips.

'Kiss it,' he said, repeating his earlier command,

but in a voice that was soft and cajoling as he gently stroked Julian's black curls.

Edging himself forward, Julian complied meekly, pressing his lips and tongue to his lover's imposing sex. He went at the long, purplish bar as if he were starving, his stubble-darkened cheeks going hollow as he sucked and slurped with gusto. The noise was even audible in the loft.

Rosie wondered what David was thinking. Having his penis caressed by someone's lips and tongue must be high on any young man's agenda. It was something she hadn't done for him yet, but after this she knew he'd soon want it.

'Enough,' said Stephen, his strong voice suddenly shaky as he pushed Julian away from his prick. The pleasures of fellatio were clearly undermining his role, and Rosie admired the way he could forgo them for another man's benefit. It was all a psychodrama, she realised, because in spite of his mock subjugation, Julian was still, and always, the master. All this was his fantasy, his pantomime; a piquant and highly seasoned side-dish in the life of a sexual gourmet.

She felt David move a little closer as Stephen strode around and stood behind Julian. She and her pupil were lying face to face now, and she felt a shuddering thrill when the tip of his cock touched her leg. He made as if to pull away, but she put her hand on his hip and stilled him. Being hidden away like this was as intimate in its own way as yesterday afternoon had been – in the open, the woods and the sunshine.

Below them, Stephen swished the strap experimentally and Julian wriggled on the bar, his bare rump glistening and gleaming in a thin shaft of slanted yellow light. Rosie found the sight of it delectable, and more so for having David beside her. She shifted her position slightly, feeling the urge to touch herself again, then suppressed a wild gasp of happiness when her wish was suddenly anticipated. With a bit of a tussle, David slid his free hand up the loose jersey leg of her shorts, and then in under the elastic in the leg of her panties. He hesitated for a second, as if unsure, then seemed to get his bearings and start burrowing inwards.

Rosie moved again, to make things easier, and David responded instinctively, wiggling his finger in her secret, humid softness and making contact with the point that he sought.

Overcome, forgetting where she was, Rosie moaned when David tickled her clitoris. The urge to thrash and groan was agonising, but as awareness returned, she controlled it. Looking down, her sex still on fire, she saw Stephen pause and seem to scent the air like a puma. As unobtrusively as she could, she drew back, taking David with her, but the chauffeur didn't even raise his eyes. If he knew they were there, he was ignoring them. He had things more immediate on his mind – like Julian's naked bottom.

As Stephen lifted the strap, David's finger found her sweet spot again and she rocked infinitesimally against it. In the still claustrophobia of their hideaway, her sensitivity and her pleasure were compressed. Her vulva convulsed into orgasm, the first spasm breaking and cresting as below them the leather whistled down, hit Julian's tense flesh, and made a sound that echoed like a gunshot. She moaned again, but in perfect safety this time because down below the agonised yowls were louder.

Somewhere at the back of Rosie's mind, a cool, calm observer was surprised. Not because of the sweetness of her sudden climax – although it was very sweet and very sudden – but because she'd expected her boss to be braver. He was sobbing and gulping, juddering his hips about, and when he turned his head sideways for a moment, she saw he was actually weeping. Great, fat tears were streaming down his face, and shockingly their presence aroused her. As another blow fell, and Julian shrieked like a baby, David resumed his gentle stroking.

Already roused, Rosie's flesh leapt immediately; and as a new climax came, she rolled in tightly against her caresser, and caught his cock between her slowly working thighs. He gasped, but again the sound was lost in the cacophony from below: Julian's desperate high-pitched yells and the increasingly fierce cracks of the strap.

It was impossible to watch now, but the sounds of Julian's punishment lingered on like a strange, spicy soundtrack, and David's rubbing became suddenly less accurate.

Rosie was too sensitised to worry. Her quim was in a continuous, fluttering state of orgasm, and somewhere in the heart of their tangle, she could feel David's prick oozing warm fluid. As she sighed, it seemed to answer. It shuddered against her, leapt once, then spat semen in long, pulsing bursts. Curling her arms around him, she cradled David to her breast, and felt the force of his rapture like a wave. His mouth was moving and muttering against her shoulder, his sobs of joy muffled by her sweatshirt.

For a long while they lay just glowing and listening. The blows rained on and on, and Julian yelled harder with each one – his voice high and shrill, yet laced with a strange edge of triumph. He was enjoying himself, crazy as it seemed, even though Stephen was showing him no mercy.

Then, quite suddenly, the quality of the sounds changed. The strokes of the strap stopped for one thing, and Julian's cries metamorphosed into moans. Long, voluptuous moans. Stirring from David's hold, Rosie wriggled forward a little way and looked down, then pursed her lips to stop herself gasping.

Stephen was kissing the very flesh he'd just punished, his mouth moving slowly and wetly over Julian's reddened bottom while his big hands sensuously explored him. Julian was writhing like a snake against the trestle, but he stiffened and bucked upwards when Stephen reached around for his prick. What followed was hidden by their bodies, but Rosie could tell what was happening. Julian was being masturbated, energetically, by the man who'd just beaten and abused him.

Rosie felt David slide forward beside her, and she reached up to place her hand across his lips. The ultimate act was almost upon them – upon *all* of them – and she sensed that even after what he'd already seen, the reality of sodomy might shock him. She wasn't even sure if she could watch it herself.

But as Stephen kissed his way up Julian's spine, she

experienced it as an echo – in reverse – of what she'd done to David last night. And the process looked equally as beautiful as it had felt. She caught her breath as the chauffeur nuzzled the nape of his master's neck, then held the same breath as he moistened his fingers with saliva and transferred the slick fluid to his cock. That done, and still using his hand he pressed his glans against Julian's anus.

Julian was still moaning, but the low throaty sounds spoke only of passion and need. Rosie saw him straining backwards against the man who was mounting him, then heard his long, bleating cry of acceptance as Stephen gave a last telling push.

'Oh God, my darling, yes!' Julian gasped, and Rosie was struck by the clear sound of pleasure in his voice. He was responding to being sodomised as if it were something tender and loving; when in fact he was being ruthlessly used and crushed against a rigid wooden bar. More than this, his hands were still tied behind his back, and trapped between their two heaving bodies.

With her gaze locked on the twin, tensing rounds of Stephen's black buttocks, Rosie felt David react yet again. Nervously, but with growing confidence, he drew her hand to his newly stiffened penis, then slid his own hand back into her shorts.

And then, as Stephen pounded and thrust, and Julian shouted and wailed, it seemed quite natural that all movement should synchronise – and four people's bliss be as one.

12

De-briefing

'It's not all . . .' David paused, and seemed to debate what to say. 'It's not all fucking, is it?' Rosie smiled as she picked her way along the woodland path beside him. It was the first time either of them had spoken since they'd crept down the outside steps of the boat-house, and she was glad he'd broken the ice. And broken it so frankly!

'No, sweetheart, it isn't,' she observed, turning the smile his way. They were walking separately, because the going under foot was uneven, but she still felt wonderfully close to him.

He was absolutely right too. Entwined together in the loft, they hadn't made love in any conventional, penetrative sense, but they had given each other great pleasure. It reminded her a bit of a time not all that long ago when she herself had been back at David's stage. A time when nervous forays in awkward places had some-times yielded up magic. It hadn't happened to her much, admittedly, and certainly not as much as she would have liked, but in her heart she'd always been waiting.

And it all seemed a long, long way from her present situation, she reflected. For the past few days, she seemed to have been surrounded by people who wanted her. Men *and* women. And it was as fabulous as it was unexpected.

As they moved along in companionable silence, David seemed to be mulling over her latest pronouncement, so Rosie took her first proper chance to observe him. In the gloom of the boathouse loft, all she'd really got was just an impression. His eyes, his mouth and his prick – and a warm body clad in sports gear.

Her charge appeared even younger than ever this morning. He had his hands stuffed in his trackpant's pockets, and he was scuffing the toes of his trainers in the dirt with all the gusto of Dennis the Menace. His usually smooth hair was sticking up endearingly, and there was a long smudge of dust down the side of his arm. In the tree-filtered light, he looked nearer to pubescence than adulthood – apart from his height – and far too young for their antics by the trap-door!

For reasons she didn't want to analyse, this made Rosie want him more. He wasn't quite the innocent he'd been when she'd first set eyes on him, but there was still something untouched about him; a lingering layer of virginity that she wanted to gently peel away.

'So . . .' About to blurt out a question, she hesitated. Was he really ready for all this? Julian's peccadilloes were, after all, complex stuff for a novice. He's seen it now though, she thought resignedly, so what the hell!

'What do you think about Julian and Stephen then?'

He turned to her as they walked, and she saw an unexpected humour in his face. 'To be honest, I don't know. My mind's still in overload. Not to mention my body.'

'Me too,' echoed Rosie softly, aware of a flow of secret moisture. Ten minutes ago, she'd been satisfied, but seeing David lithe and beautiful in the morning sunshine had changed all that. She wondered if she dare stop and lead him into the trees, to finish what they'd started in the loft. It was a very tempting idea, but maybe they needed to talk a bit first? Have a de-briefing, she thought, grinning at the double entendre.

'I knew that sort of thing happened,' David went on pensively. 'I'd read about it. But Julian's the last man I'd have imagined being . . . being like that. He seems so *male*. Don't you think so?'

Rosie quivered at David's penetrating sideways glance. Did he know something? she wondered. Did he suspect about *her* and Julian?

'Yes. He's very strong and sure of himself,' she said non-committally. 'It was a surprise to see him so submissive. Although I had been warned . . . Ladybird said she'd seen them together in the gym. I didn't believe her . . . and I certainly never expected a demonstration!'

'Wow,' murmured David.

They strode on, each deep in thought. Rosie was debating whether to tell David more, and at the same time, wondering whether David was screwing up the courage to ask *her* questions. As they reached the edge of the park, and saw Stonehaven standing majestically at the centre of its gardens, his hand shot out and grabbed hers.

'Have you been to bed with him?' he demanded, his eyes like golden fire.

'With who?' Prevarication.

'With Julian.' David's pale young face was intent, and at first Rosie thought he was angry. Then she looked more closely and saw something more like passionate curiosity than ire. 'I bet you have,' he went on, letting slip the faintest of smiles. 'He's handsome, he's accomplished and clever. Obviously he's a poof on the side, but he's sort of macho with it. I think if I were a woman I'd fancy him . . .' He paused there, and Rosie realised he'd said more than he'd meant to. His smooth brow crumpled as he continued. 'And any man with breath in his body would have to be blind, deaf *and* stupid not to want you!'

Rosie was amused and flattered. 'Thanks,' she said, starting to blush and feeling the nag of desire. David's naïve yet knowing persona was an alluring sexual cocktail, and the sight and scent of his body didn't help matters. It was too late to drag him into the bushes now, but in the distance the tall house beckoned. She thought of comfortable bedrooms and secluded, out of the way corners whose darkness welcomed lovers.

But were they secluded? What was it Ladybird had said about two-way mirrors and suchlike? Stonehaven was just as riddled with peeping opportunities as the house in Amberlake Gardens was, it seemed; and she wondered suddenly if she'd been watched already. Either alone or with David.

'You haven't answered my question,' David said slowly.

There was no point in lying. David might be unschooled in some ways, but he was no fool. 'Yes, I've had sex with Julian. Does it bother you?'

When he didn't answer, and she daren't look at

him, Rosie found the urge to confess irresistible. 'I've sort of had sex with Celeste too. And I think I wanted it with Ladybird as well. I don't quite know what's happening to me, David. I've changed since I took this job. I used to be a bit of a prude, and unimaginative. And now I feel like a nymphomaniac. I mean . . . Well . . . Even after what just happened, I still feel sexy. Crazy, isn't it?'

'Join the club!' said David with feeling. He was staring at the grass around his feet, but suddenly he kicked aimlessly at a pebble, then looked with a smile so mischievous, and so wickedly yet innocently sensual that her vulva quivered wildly in response.

'I feel the same,' he said, pushing his fingers through his disordered hair. 'I seem to have travelled from nothing to everything in the space of days. I want to do it again now,' he finished, shrugging, then looking down towards his crotch, where his cock was clearly stirring in his trackpants and pushing out the thin black fabric.

'Well, aren't we a pair,' said Rosie, moving close and putting her arms affectionately round him. In that moment she just felt so fond of him, and so kindred. It was an intimate feeling, yet pure too. She suddenly felt she could tell him anything and he'd understand. Even the true reason for her employment. She was just on the point of speaking the words when he leaned forward and put his mouth over hers, pulling her body against his as he did so.

It was a long kiss, and unexpectedly assured. David's lips were soft yet forceful, prising hers open so his tongue could taste and explore. She marvelled that he could have learnt so much so soon, and know how she melted when her tongue was played with and sucked. He drew on it in a way that set up other resonances: the suckling of a nipple or a clitoris. The tips of her breasts grew hard, became delicate yet sensitive points that he caressed with the wall of his chest. And between her legs, her sex seemed to swell into a fat ball of heat that she lewdly massaged against his thigh.

As she rubbed herself, David made a sound of profoundly male satisfaction, and for a moment, Rosie's mettle was stung. So he *was* an embyro chauvinist after all, she thought, then mellowed as her sex-flesh rippled against him and he gripped the firm lobes of her bottom. She could feel his penis butting against her, iron-hard again because he was young and strong and had so much catching up to do. She swayed, her whole body boneless as she wished she was flat on her back and being taken in one long stroke.

I'm going to come again, she thought in a panic, feeling David nip her tongue with his teeth. His fingers flexed around her bottom, sliding craftily into the cleft. He'd learnt a hundred lessons in no time at all, she realised, and his ability to use initiative was devastating.

She was jerking now, dancing like a puppet and grinding her sex on his leg. She felt her juices flowing freely, seeping out onto the cloth of his trackpants and soaking it, while David's sly fingertips plagued her. He was touching her anus through her shorts and panties, pressing and prodding and rubbing as her mind filled with flash-frame images. She saw herself being taken from behind by Julian, and being tickled by his wiry pubic hair. She saw David himself, sprawled on his bed, his perfect young rump accessible to her fingers and her tongue. Then Julian again, martyred on the trestle, his eyes and his penis weeping as Stephen possessed him completely.

As each picture appeared her sex convulsed. She tried to moan, but David sucked harder on her tongue, his fingers flicking and tormenting. She felt her legs buckle, but he held her tight, her open vulva balanced on his thigh. He was controlling her pleasure with all the skill of years of experience, and the poise of an accomplished sexual roué. It was hard to believe that less than twenty four hours ago he'd been a virgin.

Rosie was awed. She hugged him hard, crushing him to her breasts, and felt her climax bloom anew as they kissed. She wanted more and more of him, and as he began to lower her to the grass beneath their feet, and their bodies momentarily lost contact, she whimpered.

Seconds later she was cooing with delight again, and wriggling in her efforts to help him strip off their lower garments. Her shorts and knickers went flying across the turf, closely followed by his trackpants and briefs – which got tangled round his trainers in their haste.

A de-briefing! she thought hysterically, then stopped thinking altogether when he entered her with a swift, vital thrust.

'Oh David, David, David,' she groaned as his lips touched her face, her neck and her ears. He was kissing her hair too, where it had come free of her ponytail, mouthing the thick silky strands and rubbing his cheeks playfully against it. She could feel him biting and nipping and nuzzling as his penis moved strongly inside her.

Rosie cried out again, wordlessly, when her flesh seemed to flutter and vibrate around him in a delicious high frequency wave. She could feel him jerking inside her, and held him tight as his whole body bucked and leapt. He was taking his pleasure in her arms, but instead of shouting or screaming, he just let out a long, falling sigh that flowed like a breeze across her throat.

It was the heat of the sun on her legs that roused Rosie. She sensed that they'd both nodded off for a moment, still joined. Suddenly, she felt concern for David's bottom. It was bare, pale, and had probably never been exposed like this before. Trying her best not to shatter the moment, she urged him to get up and get covered.

But for several seconds, he wouldn't budge. He just raised the upper part of his body and looked down into her face, his eyes huge and golden.

'See,' he said softly. 'You're not the only one . . . I can teach *you* a thing or two!' There was something so knowing in his voice, so triumphant, that she struggled like an eel to shake him off.

Goddamn the young bugger, he knew! He knew what she was here for! What her *real* job was!

'What do you mean?' she enquired warily as at last he climbed to his feet, then reached for her panties and shorts.

'You're here to teach me, aren't you?' he said, passing them to her, his manner smug and jaunty. 'You're my tutor. For sex. Aren't you?'

Rosie studied the lace inset on her panties as if she'd never seen it before, then concentrated intently upon sliding the garment on, while David put on his things too.

How could she answer, she wondered. She couldn't deny what was true. There was nothing on paper, but she had said 'yes'. And she was certainly being grossly overpaid for her library work.

'I'm a librarian, David,' she averred stubbornly as she wiggled her shorts up over her hips.

'Bullshit!' he said with relish, as if he'd just discovered the word and been dying to use it. 'I've hardly ever seen you in the library in the daytime!'

'Cheeky tyke!' she said, lunging at him. 'I've only worked for Julian a few days, and it takes time to set up all the systems and stuff!'

David was ticklish, Rosie realised as she grabbed him round the waist. Very ticklish indeed. Within seconds, he was giggling uncontrollably and squirming on the grass beneath her as she sat astride him. If they hadn't only just made love the position would have been dynamite; and even so, Rosie felt temptation stir again. His body was so strong and fit and solid as he thrashed and bounced between her legs.

'Look, you,' she said leaning over him, breathing in the fresh tang of his sweat. 'I *am* here to catalogue Julian's library, both this one and the one in London –' She hesitated, unable to resist touching his fine pale brow and his shiny fox-brown hair. 'But I admit there *is* another dimension to the job. And it *is* what you said . . .' She shrugged, thinking back and trying to remember just how she'd agreed. 'It just seemed like a good idea at the time!'

'So you really are my teacher,' he whispered, gazing

up at her, his eyes a brighter gold than ever. Between the cheeks of her bottom, Rosie felt his penis try to rise; then felt her own sex grow sticky in response. In a panic, she sprang to her feet, almost frightened that she could want him again so soon. She also had a powerful sixth sense that someone was watching them from the house, even though they were still a fair distance away.

'Yes, I am,' she said lightly, reaching out to urge David to his feet, 'but I think we'd better postpone the next lesson. I've a sneaking feeling that someone's spying on us.'

As she spoke, there was a bright flash of reflected sunlight from the direction of Stonehaven.

That's Celeste's window! thought Rosie, with absolute certainty. Oh God, what if she's got a pair of binoculars?

'Come on, let's jog,' she said crisply, starting to run on the spot. She carefully kept her distance from David, not quite sure if she could resist him if he grabbed her.

'You're kidding,' he gasped. 'I've just –' He stopped and blushed furiously.

Rosie smiled to herself, glad that he still had at least some of his shyness left.

'Look, young man,' she remonstrated, in an affected schoolma'am tone. 'If you want to learn, you're going to have to build up your stamina. So look lively!' Then, without waiting for further protest, she turned in the direction of the house and set off at a fairly fast run.

Almost immediately, she heard the thud-thud of

his feet behind her, then within seconds he was jogging at her side.

'Race you, miss!' he cried cheekily, then launched himself forward with a breathtaking energy and speed. Several yards ahead, he turned around and stuck out his tongue, then was running again in an instant, his muscular thighs pumping and working in a stride that was as long as an athlete's and as graceful as a big hunting cat's.

'You're on, lion cub,' said Rosie softly to his retreating back, then set off more slowly in pursuit.

As he ran, David relaxed and let images flood his brain. Pictures, impressions, sensations; some strange and many-faceted; others familiar, but seen with eyes that were brand new and knowing.

In less than a day, everything had changed. The thing he'd been dreaming of since his arrival in London had happened. He'd made love with a woman. Had sex. Fucked. That last word seemed hard but had its own earthy splendour; a rawness that perfectly expressed what had happened just now on the grass.

David could feel his sex bouncing as he jogged. It felt warm and lingeringly sensitive, as if his flesh were imprinted with the memory of Rosie. He imagined himself still inside her, sheathed and embraced by that living sleeve that had a mind and movement of its own. Please no, he thought in confusion, as his penis began to stiffen again, and ache from the motion of his run. It was as if he could still feel those concentric, rippling waves. Still feel the heat of her body, and still hear her shrill cries of pleasure.

To carry on running took a supreme effort of will. Desire brought a soft, giving sensation to his belly and a precarious weakness to his joints. If he stopped concentrating for a second, his legs would buckle and he'd fall down onto the sun-warmed turf; clutching at his painful erection and rubbing it to a frenzied relief.

But do I love her? he thought, deliberately choosing the thorniest question to try and rise above his tortured body.

Love for David had always been a warm, gentle feeling that he equated with safety and security. The patient kindliness of his grandparents, that inspired love. So did the wayward, contrary affection of the cat he'd had as a child.

But now these sentiments seemed meek and mild compared to the crazy things he felt about Rosie. He felt like a savage, in both mind and body, whenever he even looked at her. She was warm and gentle towards him, and he would have liked to be more that way towards her. He'd managed it in the boathouse loft, but it was difficult. And getting even more so. One hint of the shape of her body, and he was gone. The curve of a large, luscious breast, or the sweet little dink of her navel, or the long, smooth sweep of a thigh; and he was like a poker inside his briefs. The more he got, the more he seemed to need. And seeing such sights as he'd seen in the boathouse didn't help either.

From his readings and responses so far, David had deduced that he was a perfectly normal heterosexual. He liked looking at women and fantasising about

them, and he certainly knew now that he adored
making love to them. He'd never thought about men
sexually at all. Or at least not until this morning.

Seeing Julian and Stephen had excited him intensely;
both the sex act they'd shared, and the bizarre ritual
drama that had gone with it. Easing at last into a
smooth, but automatic stride, he let his mind run
unfettered and free. He wondered what it would be
like to be smacked with a strap, or to take, or be taken,
by Julian. His bowels felt hot as he imagined the
pressure within and the pain without. After last night,
he knew that his bottom and anus were especially
sensitive, and though he couldn't quite summon the
texture of the strap across his buttocks, he could
certainly understand penetration. A penis couldn't feel
all that much different to a finger or a tongue; it was
only a question of size. He imagined something very
stiff, yet velvet-skinned pushing into him, and almost
stumbled because the sensation was so vivid. Breathing
heavily, he banished all thoughts of men from his
mind, and returned his attention to Rosie.

Specifically to the concept of having her spread
out and subjugated before him. He pictured her tied
across that bar in a really beautiful dress, something
silky and blue that made her skin and hair gleam and
her eyes look like sapphire stars. Her bottom was
ignominiously bare and her panties were dangling
around her knees. This exposure seemed totally rude
to him, and far more exciting than full nakedness.
Between swathes of clothing, her skin looked whiter
and more nude. He liked the thought of seeing the
purse of her sex from behind. Seeing it moisten and

swell as he stroked her, the pink flesh glistening, and the soft leaves puffing out towards him. As he charged on towards the house, he imagined putting his hands on her buttocks, and squeezing them and mashing them until she groaned. Then he'd take a stick or a whip, and beat her bottom to fuchsia pinkness, and thrash it until her throat was raw with her screams.

What's wrong with me? he thought wildly as he reached the edge of the formal garden and suddenly hit an oxygen deficit. He'd been racing like an olympian, running from what he wanted most, and as he turned round and leant forward – hands on knees, gulping in air – he saw Rosie had fallen behind, and was running at a steady prudent pace, her limbs moving smoothly and easily.

God, she's lovely! he thought as he got back his breath and felt his heartbeat settle. His tutor was no sylph-like supermodel by any means, but her overall shape was superb. She was a modern classic; voluptuous, yet sleek. She went in and out exactly where she should do, in a series of lush, harmonious sweeps.

And it wasn't just her body. She had a pretty face too, with big, stormy-blue eyes, an impish, slightly turned-up nose, and a mouth that was as pink as raspberries. Her long hair shone, and always seemed to fall into a stylish shape; even now when it danced and lifted as she ran, or some minutes ago, when it had fanned across the grass like a halo while he'd taken his pleasure in her body. She was everything that was beautiful, David realised, and he could only thank fate for having met her. With his parochial background, and his sexually constrained upbringing, it was a miracle things had worked out so well. He could just as easily have lost his virginity to some nervous girl back in Yorkshire; someone from school, perhaps, who would have meant nothing to him. Both he and this hypothetical partner would have been too young to know what they were doing, and both would have ended up disappointed.

Instead, though, through destiny and the good offices of his unconventional cousin, life had worked out very differently. He'd been shielded from sex until he was ready. He'd been preserved until there was a warm, grown-up, incredibly fine-looking woman who was specifically around to teach him. It was the most bizarre and unlikely of arrangements, but he was desperately, desperately glad of it.

Especially when Rosie padded to a halt in front of him, and stood catching her breath as he had. Her round breasts heaved and shook in a way that made his belly twist with lust. He almost wanted to fall down on his knees and weep with gratitude. Gratitude towards Rosie for simply existing, and towards Celeste and Julian for helping him find her.

'Good grief! I must be really out of shape,' panted Rosie, hands on hips and head tilted back as she drew in deep breaths of air. The run had been exhilarating and surprisingly easy considering what had immediately preceded it. She could hardly believe she'd made violent love on the grass, then jumped up and run half a mile afterwards. She hadn't raced with David, but her pace had been good. In spite of what she'd just said, she was impressed by her own fitness. Lots of sex must be good for your stamina, she observed wryly, resolving to test out the theory some more.

David regarded her steadily. 'Your shape is wonderful, Rosie,' he murmured, as he stepped towards her, his eyes bright and golden. Rosie sensed that he wanted to kiss her again – and not leave it at a kiss for that matter – and her insides quivered at his touch.

'Somebody might be watching,' she whispered when his arms folded all the way around her, and his lips settled gently on her neck. She could feel him hard as stone against her belly, and marvelled at how quickly a young man could recover and be ready for another round of sex.

'I don't care!' he hissed, moving his hips suggestively.

'Well, I do!' she answered, fighting him, yet failing to get free. His strength was unexpected, and his arms were like tempered steel binding. Rosie felt a lovely melting, yielding sensation start to pour through her loins like honey, and was profoundly tempted to encourage him. She imagined making love right here on the stone-flagged path in full view of the house; with Celeste and God alone knew who else watching from behind the curtains. It would be outrageous, but she longed to try it.

With obvious reluctance, David finally let her loose. 'I'm sorry,' he said quietly. 'I don't know what's got into me. I . . . I feel aroused all the time.' He looked down at his tell-tale bulge.

'Come on. Let's have a swim,' said Rosie with sudden inspiration. She'd seen the pool briefly on her first look around, and right now its cool, blue water seemed the perfect solution to their heat. They could douse their unruly fires a bit, gain respite and have time to think. 'And after that, I really must show my face in the library.' She stuck out her tongue at David and his sceptical 'you're kidding!' look. 'Because no matter what you want to believe, I *was* taken on to look after Julian's books!' David was grinning now, trying not to laugh. 'As well as one or two other little matters . . .'

The poolhouse, when they reached it, was a veritable tropical paradise, part of a big, open plan conservatory that abutted onto the side of the house. At one end of the pool was a lounging area, complete with a selection of thoughtfully cushioned wrought iron garden furniture; and at the other was a tiled deck and changing complex – complete with showers, cubicles and lockers. Tubs of flowers and flowering shrubs were dotted around this area too, and the whole of the poolhouse was like some kind of 'green' environmental bubble, filled with the fresh scent of foliage and alive with the gentle, pervasive lapping of the water. A door at the far end of the complex led – unsurprisingly, given Julian's obsession with fitness – to a small but well equipped gym. There was also, Rosie noticed as they entered, a full size leather-covered massage table in the changing area. A fixture that reminded her of Ladybird, and the promise of aromatherapy.

'What a gorgeous place,' whispered Rosie, then jumped when her voice echoed off the high glass roof over the pool. 'It's like a Caribbean holiday without the hassle of flying . . .' Her voice petered out as a discouraging fact dawned on her. The water was sparkling and deliciously tempting; but she had no swimsuit. She could swim in her underwear she supposed, but it was all sweaty and sticky. Not a particularly inviting prospect.

'Celeste and Julian swim in the nude, apparently,' said David from behind her, having obviously read her mind, 'although I've never actually seen them myself.'

'But what about the staff?' Rosie queried, turning the idea over and finding it dangerously appealing. All her body and her clothing felt grubby, and there were shreds of grass sticking to her bottom, she was sure of it. The thought of plunging into all that crystalline clarity was so alluring it almost made her ache. She wanted to dive in and be renewed; made ready to do everything again.

'They tend to stay out of the way most of the time.' David quirked his fine dark brows. 'Well, you know what Julian and Celeste are like . . . They're always doing *something*!'

'Too true,' murmured Rosie, deciding that the tendency towards exhibitionism must be catching. It wasn't more than half an hour ago that she and David had been putting on a performance – rolling around on the turf half-naked, making love in plain sight of the house.

'Shall we, then?' asked David, a touch of trepidation in his voice, in spite of his previous assurances.

'What . . . Swim naked?' The water shimmered and danced and Rosie could no longer resist it. Without answering, except for a wink, she began pulling off her small amount of clothing. Trainers and socks, sweat top and shorts, pants and bra; she let them fall to the tiled floor around her. She caught her reflection in the glass of the opposite wall and saw a curvaceous wood-nymph about to descend into the water. As she half-twirled she realised she'd been right about her bottom. She was indeed festooned with stalks and grass, not to mention dark, earthy smears where she'd been slid along by David's strong thrusts.

Mindful of the purity of the water, she decided to shower before she went into the pool. She needed to urinate too, and slid discreetly into one of the several closed cubicles, set modestly out of the way around a corner. As she sighed with relief, she heard an adjacent door close quietly. Wild, plunging sex had obviously had the same bladder-stimulating effect on David, and the picture of him holding his penis and peeing had a powerful sexual resonance. Rosie had a sudden wish to be standing beside him, cradling him tenderly, kissing his neck as she directed his stream.

Banishing the bizarre thought, she finished, flushed, then made her way into the changing area. Beneath one of the open, Japanese style showers, she began to sluice off the grime and greenery. The water heat was adjustable but she kept it cool; anything to zap herself to wakefulness and shake off her strange erotic cravings. She closed her eyes, and let the water cascade over her face, her hair and her body, vaguely aware that David had stripped off too, and had stepped into the shower beside her to wash off the grass on his body.

Wet and naked, they walked together to the water's

edge, then slid in. Rosie was intensely aware of the beauty of David's body, but somehow the feeling was more tender now than lustful. She knew she'd soon want him again, but for the moment it was nice to just swim together as friends, as companions, and to laugh and splash and frolic for the sheer, high-spirited fun of it.

The sensation of swimming naked was unusual, but extremely pleasant. It was the first time Rosie had ever swum in the buff, but she decided that from now on she would take every opportunity to do so. There was a delicious but subtle excitement in the flow of water where it didn't usually flow; the silken rush as it slid over her breasts and buttocks, and the delicate tantalising drag as it filtered through her soft, pubic bush. Surreptitiously, she took a sideways glance towards David, and wondered what effect nude swimming was having on his penis.

David was a strong swimmer, and he cut through the water very smoothly, his thick hair plastered dark against his scalp like the pelt of an otter or a seal. He appeared completely unperturbed by his naked state – at least until the tap tap tap of footsteps sounded on the tiles of the conservatory, and Rosie saw his face start to colour with embarrassment.

She hardly dare look up herself, but when she did, she saw Ladybird. The fitness trainer was standing on the poolside, smiling and staring into the water, her green eyes bright with pure mischief.

13

A Scentsational Experience

Ladybird looked wonderful; sleek and beautiful in form-fitting blue lycra leggings and matching skimpy top. Her red hair was loose on her shoulders, and her whole expression was one of devilment. It was obvious that she knew they were naked, and thoroughly approved of the state.

'Hi, you guys!' she called out cheerily. 'Mind if I join you?'

'No . . . Of course not,' said Rosie, treading water in the deep end. David closed his mouth where it had fallen open in surprise, and this caused him to splutter and cough.

Ladybird seemed to take that as a yes and began peeling off her clothes. In a trice, she was magnificently stripped and walking to the edge of the deep end, where she dived in neatly and cleanly. She was no paddler either, and didn't stop to chatter when she surfaced. Using a long, easy crawl, she powered cleanly from one end of the pool to the other at a speed that made Rosie feel distinctly hippopotamus-like.

Even so, Rosie couldn't find it in herself to resent Ladybird; and as she swam along at her own slower, but not unrespectable pace, her mind was filled with the striking but all too fleeting vision of the fitness trainer's perfect golden body.

David was obviously thinking of it too; from time to time he stared across the pool intently as if his unusual eyes could see clean through the light-distorting water to the superb female shape beneath. Rosie's thoughts drifted back to his penis, and its state as he swam. Was he hard again? Turned on by this streamlined, super-fit woman?

Taking the idea further, she wondered how David would react to being with *both* of them. Given this opportune gathering, it was the next logical step. She'd been shackled by conventions of one-on-oneness herself for far too long, but now she could see new ways to love. Could he? Or was it still too soon? Too early? Considering his progress so far, she thought not. He was quite a free-thinker in the making; an untrammelled, generous soul who could give himself joyously to many.

As if reading her mind, Ladybird suddenly broke out of her series of disciplined lengths and swam across to tread water at Rosie's side.

'Are you up for that massage then?' she asked, wiping the water from her face, and grinning challengingly.

'Yes, I'd love it,' Rosie answered, feeling her heart skip wildly in her chest. 'And I think David would too.' She nodded over to where their companion was floating in a corner and watching them closely. 'Do you do men as well?'

'Try and stop me,' crowed Ladybird, striking out

strongly for the side of the pool, then climbing from the water in all her glory, clearly proud of her fabulous shape.

Rosie was slightly less proud of *her* shape, but felt a hundred per cent better about it than she had a couple of weeks ago. And what doubts she had were quashed when both Ladybird's and David's eyes widened appreciatively at the sight of her.

Their scrutiny was like wine surging straight to her belly. She felt intoxicated and aroused, consumed by a rich sensuality that made her slow her steps and almost flaunt her nudity as she walked across to the leather covered table.

'Ladybird's going to give me a massage,' she called across to David, who lingered in the water. 'Do you want to watch?'

His pale face looked flushed, and she saw him swallow. It made her smile. He was erect in the water, she guessed, and too embarrassed to emerge while they watched him.

'You can probably see from where you are,' she suggested, tacitly acknowledging his condition and making him blush even harder.

'Yes, I can,' he said quietly, then agitated the water around him as if to make sure they couldn't see his stiffness. 'I think I'll stay here a while . . .'

'No sweat,' she answered, feeling a lazy thrill of power. 'Just remember you've to come out eventually.'

David's face showed non-commitment, and he ducked under the water to avoid the issue.

'Don't worry,' whispered Ladybird, setting out an assortment of bottles and other knick-knacks on the tiled counter near the table. 'By the time I've finished with you, he'll be in such a state that he'll kill to get on this table!'

Rosie shivered. She'd never had a massage before, and the thought of Ladybird's long flexible hands working her over made her body feel hot and weak. What she'd said earlier to David was now more true than ever. She was suddenly ravenous for pleasure, and her sex felt a mile wide and yearning. Even the smallest movement was uncomfortable, and the urge to touch her clitoris made her dizzy.

'Just lie on the couch and relax,' urged Ladybird, as if sensing her arousal. 'That's it. On your front first.' The trainer had covered the leather surface of the couch with a thick fluffy towel, and when Rosie settled gingerly down, the soft nubbly fabric seemed to caress every part of her it touched. Moaning under her breath, she flexed her hips and thighs luxuriantly, then pressed her sex down hard against the couch.

She'd closed her eyes as she'd lain down, but after a second she opened them again and turned her face towards the pool. David had come to the water's edge and was staring back at her, his own eyes huge with wonder, as if he'd heard her tiny, hungering cry and correctly interpreted its cause. His gaze was so intense it was an embrace in itself, triggering heat in her vulva and her breasts. She was simmering, sizzling, at boiling point – and Ladybird hadn't even touched her. Unable to help herself, she wriggled again, holding David's almost agonised look as she rode her own surging desire.

As she began to gasp, her nostrils were suddenly assaulted by fragrance. A strong floral scent was drifting across from where Ladybird was concocting her magic – the sweet blend of aromatherapy oils that were intended for Rosie's bare body.

'Oh God, what's that? It smells beautiful,' Rosie murmured, drawing in the sumptuous vapours.

'Well, basically it's sweet almond oil, blended with a few stronger essential oils in a combination that both stimulates and soothes the senses,' said Ladybird authoritatively, drawing close. 'It's an aphrodisiac,' she whispered in Rosie's ear, moving her long hair carefully out of the way and tying it with a soft towelling cord. 'When I massage you, you'll come and come and come.' Her breathy voice sounded just as much threatening as it did promising. 'And I'll hardly even have to touch your pussy.'

'What . . . what is it I can smell though?' gasped Rosie, knowing she barely needed touch now.

'Let's see,' said Ladybird, making slick, slurpy squishing sounds as she charged her fingers with oil, 'There's a mixture of jasmine, rose maroc, sandalwood and cumin . . . It's my own favourite blend. I use it when I want particularly strong orgasms.'

This time she didn't lower her voice at all, and as Rosie looked again towards David, she saw him almost salivating with lust, his young face a taut, aroused mask. She couldn't see his hands, but she had no doubt at all that one of them was folded round his penis.

'Brace yourself,' purred Ladybird softly, then placed her slender hands on Rosie's shoulders and drew them slowly down the full length of her torso in one fluid, extenuated sweep.

The sensation of being oiled was so exquisite that Rosie trembled all over. The epicentre of the shivers was in her groin, but as Ladybird coated her scrupulously, the warm, slippery substance made every part of her tingle with pleasure.

Closing her eyes again, Rosie groaned without shame. Her yearning for genital contact seemed to double and treble as the oil sank into her skin, yet perversely, she wanted the wait to be drawn out and prolonged. Ladybird began the real massage on the back of her neck for starters, humming a tune as her fingers skimmed and circled. As she went lower, along the shoulders and down the back, Rosie was possessed again by a massive need to touch herself, to slide her hand between the couch and her belly and drive her fingers into the core of her sex. Just the thought created tension in her arm, which Ladybird was instantly aware of.

'Bad girl! Mustn't touch!' she hissed, as if Rosie's craving had been written on her flesh.

'Please . . . Oh God, I'm dying,' whimpered Rosie as her masseuse moved on and began to concentrate on a small patch of skin just an inch above the crease of her buttocks.

Rosie cried out, louder this time. It was as if that minute area was a button – a switch – connected by a fine hot wire directly to the tip of her clitoris. She whined and wriggled, unable to stop herself, electrified by the giant wave of feeling. Her hands clenched automatically at her sides, shaking as she fought to control them.

'Very well then,' said Ladybird, her husky voice revealing that she too was affected by the odours.

'Here, David, make yourself useful!' she called out, and almost immediately there was a commotion in the water.

Half delirious, Rosie opened her eyes, and saw David moving towards her from the pool. His penis was sticking out before him, superbly erect, with a stream of water flowing lewdly from its tip. Rosie remembered her peculiar fancies in the lavatory, and moaned again at this new rush of yearning.

As he reached the side of the table, Rosie felt two sets of hands touch her body; Ladybird's guiding David's. She lifted her belly to give them access, then screamed out in an instantaneous climax when a wedge of laced fingers rubbed her clitoris. Dimly, she felt Ladybird withdraw and resume her uniquely skilled massage, while David's hand remained, and worked diligently in the chink of her sex. His narrow fingertips seemed to have absorbed Ladybird's talent somehow, and the masturbation he gave was slow and delicate, yet still sufficiently forceful to bring Rosie to peak after peak.

Amazed, she heard her own shouts and yells echoing off the glass roof of the poolhouse. Her crotch was a well of burning pleasure, and her whole body alive with juddering swells of blissfulness that swept out from her vulva in circles and were stirred by Ladybird's kneading. She felt as if she were going to expire, orgasm herself into oblivion, and when she knew she could take no more, she begged her tormentors to cease.

Whimpering and snuffling into the couch, she was aware of them gently complying, then kissing her – one after the other – on the heavily oiled lobes of her bottom. In a brief lucid instant, she wondered where David had got the idea to do something so ritualistic, then surmised that he'd merely copied Ladybird. Whatever, the tender little gesture was beautiful.

For many minutes, Rosie floated in a spaced out, slack bodied haze. It was as if she'd been a bomb of sensation that had gone off with a bang, then left perfect inner silence in its wake. She could hear the ripple of the water, and small sounds of movement nearby, indistinct and unattributable. She could feel the diffuse heat of the sun on her back, filtered by the creeping vines that grew up the inside of the glass, and also by the glass itself, that seemed to offset the fiercest of the rays and admit only beneficent light.

Pleasure such as she'd experienced wasn't easily gotten over, but at length, she pushed strongly with her hands and sat up as gracefully as she could.

A charming sight met her eyes. David and Ladybird were kneeling on a pile of towels – and she was slowly massaging his back. They were both still naked, and David still erect; yet there seemed nothing overtly sexual about their actions. David was stretching his shoulders from time to time, and making small sounds of contentment – but clearly only from the easing of knotted muscles.

'Ha! It lives!' said Ladybird pertly, pausing in her slow digital glide across David's scapulae.

Rosie managed a lopsided grin. Her body was fully satisfied now, but there was still a heart-tugging attractiveness about the couple before her. If she'd had the energy, she would have wanted one, or more probably both of them, but instead, she accepted a temporary hiatus. There would be other days, and all just as delicious.

'Do you want this table now?' she asked, her voice coming out in a soft, almost mouselike squeak.

'Yes,' answered Ladybird, rising lithely. 'But only if you can stand, sweetheart.'

'I'll try,' Rosie said, then slid her feet cautiously to the floor. When she straightened her legs and tried to stand, her knees felt like water and she swayed. In a flash both David and Ladybird were beside her. David pulled up a nearby stool and helped her to sit down on it; while Ladybird draped her around the shoulders with another of the freshly laundered towels.

'Are you alright now?' the beautiful trainer asked, crouching down to touch Rosie's cheek. David just stood to one side, an expression of concern on his fine young face, while his erection was as solid as ever. It jutted out imposingly in front of him, pointing towards them, although David himself seemed barely aware of it as he looked worriedly in Rosie's direction.

'Believe me, I feel fabulous. Never better,' she replied, feeling her strength and vitality flood back. She fixed David with a long, steady look. 'And I seem to think it's your turn now, if I remember rightly.'

'Right, my boy, up onto that couch,' said Ladybird with a fair degree of authority. Whatever doubts she'd had about relating to David were now obviously gone. She looked strikingly confident and physically stunning. In the realm of the senses, she was queen, supreme and empowered by her skills.

With a sure, natural elegance, David did as he was told, but then hesitated, kneeling on the couch. Rosie covered a smile with her hand, although really it wasn't funny. To squash a hard-on like that beneath him would be painful. Poor devil, she thought, watching him stare bemusedly at his own stiff manhood.

'On your back, Sonny Jim!' said Ladybird, reaching out to touch the offending member. 'We'll need full access to this . . .' She tapped his penis playfully and he gasped. Rosie saw his face contort, and his flanks quiver with effort. Slowly, and with extreme care, he lay down on his back, his splendid but unruly young cock pointing proudly at the distant glass roof. As he closed his eyes and settled back into stillness, Rosie could sit no longer, but rose to her feet and moved in closer to the table, knotting her towel around her waist as she walked.

Ladybird said nothing, but winked broadly, reaching into the sports holdall she'd placed on the counter earlier. From its depths she pulled out a bunch of the same soft towelling ties that she'd used for Rosie's hair. Her green eyes glittered like shards of emerald, and Rosie sensed a game beginning.

She bit down on her lip and held in a gasp, when Ladybird began arranging David's body on the couch – with his arms bent back above his head, and his legs widely parted. Rosie had noticed that there were metal rings bolted to the four corners of the couch, but she'd not really thought about their purpose. She'd supposed they were something to do with shifting the weighty contraption around, but realised now that they weren't.

They were for bondage. To secure some unwilling – or willing – subject to the table for the purposes of erotic stimulation. Even as the idea dawned, Ladybird nodded pointedly in the direction of David's feet, and handed Rosie two pieces of towelling, while taking two more for herself.

David had been strangely passive on the table, but as he felt their efforts to secure him, he began to struggle. 'What's happening?' he demanded, his right leg kicking and snaking in Rosie's grip.

'Keep still, David,' commanded Ladybird, her voice steely and strange.

Rosie was impressed, then suddenly realised that this role wasn't new to her friend. Ladybird had done this before, obviously, and her tangible aura of dominance – and the way she'd co-ordinated the restraints – suggested that she was intimately familiar with the more esoteric uses of this particular table.

I wonder who it was last time? thought Rosie as she fastened the ties around the ankles of a chastened and motionless David.

Julian? Very likely. He obviously liked that sort of thing. Or perhaps Celeste, who seemed quite catholic in her sexual tastes and probably loved anything slightly decadent.

Rosie's fingers faltered and she fumbled with a knot. What if Ladybird had chosen to tie *her* up? Then done exactly the same exquisitely arousing things that she'd done earlier? As she finally managed to make the tie safe, Rosie imagined it was her own body stretched helplessly on the couch. She could almost feel David's finger on her clitoris, rubbing it gently as she bucked and heaved in her bonds, torn apart by overpowering sensation.

And more shocking than even the fantasy of being tied, was the realisation that she actually wanted it. Watching Ladybird scrupulously wash her hands, then begin mixing her oils again, Rosie made a silent vow to sample these strange delights as soon as she was able – which in *this* household could be a matter of hours rather than days, she concluded wryly.

'Can you dry him off for me, please,' asked Ladybird as a new and equally delectable aroma-blend seemed to fill their immediate environment. This mix seemed more robust somehow, sharper in its top notes, and decidedly male. Combining oils and their perfumes was clearly an art form, and one that Ladybird excelled in. Picking up a fresh towel from the heap, Rosie made a second mental note. She'd like to learn this skill too, just as soon as she could think straight again.

David shuddered as she pressed the soft fabric to his skin. Instinct made her avoid his genitals though; mainly because his prick was so stiff and inflamed that the slightest of touches might trigger him. She'd come quickly herself under Ladybird's scented minis-trations, and been glad of it, but she wanted David's experience to last longer. She wanted his pleasure to endure and be extended to its utmost limit. This was yet another whole new world for him, and she didn't want it rushed or hurried.

Smoothing the towel over David's body, she dried his face, his torso and his limbs. He kept his eyes tightly shut throughout the process, but his strong-featured face was revealing. His mouth narrowed with strain as she neared his groin, and he stirred restlessly, tugging at his bonds. On a whim, she leant over his prick and blew on it, and immediately he cried out, his hips bucking up towards her.

'Naughty!' said Ladybird chidingly, but to which of them, Rosie couldn't tell. The scent of the oil was overwhelming – it made her feel giddy and daring. It filled her head with smells that were hot and animal and spicy. She caught a citrus note somewhere in the blend, and found its bite both exciting and euphoric.

'Stand by . . . He'll need you,' said Ladybird calmly as she poured the potion onto her hands, then moved closer to David's quaking body. With the lightest of strokes she began annointing his arms and shoulders, then worked smoothly across his chest and his ribcage.

The massage was brisk and businesslike, and it was hard to tell which element affected David most: the kneading or the pungent aromas. He began shifting around on the couch and moaning in a long, sub-vocal chunter. As Ladybird reached some particularly sensitive spot, he'd squirm like a wild thing and gasp; then relax again when she moved on to somewhere less critical.

Quite soon though, most parts of his anatomy seemed critical. Feet and forearms, shoulders and kneejoints – wherever Ladybird patted and circled and rubbed. His hips were in constant lifting motion and his penis swayed and jumped, and ran freely with a clear, shiny fluid. Rosie felt her own resolve weakening too. She wanted to reach over, glove him gently in her fingers and bring ease to his rampant stiffness. She longed to hear him wail with rapture and gratitude, and see his grimacing face grow soft and calm. So focused was she on David, that Ladybird's sudden, faint cry, and the stilling of her deftly moving fingers came as a complete and rather piquant surprise.

'Oh God, Rosie, you're going to have to help me,' she whispered, leaning weakly against the table. David's eyes flew open as he absorbed the slight jolt, his face a picture of puzzlement and lust.

At a loss, Rosie glanced towards the bottles and the bowl with the oil in. Not quite sure what to do, she made a start towards it.

'Not that, *me*!' gasped Ladybird, swivelling around against the table, parting her long, sleek thighs and bracing her feet on the floor. 'Help me come, Rosie,' she begged. 'I know you're not sure about this, but please . . . just put your hand here and let me do the work.' On the word 'here' she flaunted her slim pelvis forward and made her moist sex open and pout between the delicate red curls of her motte.

Remembering how she'd felt in the gym back in London, Rosie didn't hesitate. She moved close and slid her hand between Ladybird's legs, gasping at her friend's heat and wetness. Instinctively, she waggled her fingers and rubbed them from side to side across Ladybird's large bud-like clitoris. The other woman groaned heavily, and true to her word began to work herself roughly and rhythmically on Rosie's rigid fingertips. Her slim hips rocked and swayed, then after only a few seconds, she let out an uncouth gurgling grunt and jammed her hand in hard over Rosie's, almost hurting her.

'Yes! Yes! Yes!' chanted Ladybird, in the age old cliché of orgasm, her hot flesh rippling and her juices trickling and flowing. The spasms were deep and distinct to the touch, but as they faded, she slumped forwards, her slender body finding momentary support against Rosie's. Then, just as quickly as she'd demanded her pleasure, it was over, and the trainer stood straight again, bouncing lightly on her toes and clearly ready to proceed.

'Let's get on then, shall we?' she said, pouring fresh oil into the palm of her hand as if nothing unusual had happened.

Returning her attention to David again, Rosie saw a man tormented by need. His handsome face was a mask, his skin white and stretched, and there were great jagged spots of high colour daubed across his elegant cheekbones. His penis was vivid too, harder and more angry-looking than ever. Ladybird's casual climax had only exacerbated his lust, and he seemed only a couple of breaths away from coming.

'Please,' he entreated softly as Rosie leant across to stroke his sweaty brown hair off his face. As her fingers strayed, tempted by the beauty of his features, he craned up towards her and sucked her thumb into his mouth, pulling on it urgently, like a comforter. It was the first time a grown man had ever done such a thing to Rosie, and she felt a thin twist of pleasure between her legs, that seemed to flutter in time to his suction.

'I think he's ready,' said Ladybird suddenly, her fingers lying flat on David's belly. Rosie realised she was meant to do something. She drew her thumb out of David's mouth, moved behind his head, and pressed her hands against his tied-down wrists. Her hold on him was ineffectual really, but the gesture was primarily symbolic. She felt the muscles in his forearms tighten as Ladybird slowed her oily stroking, very delicately took hold of his cock, and at the same time – with her free hand – reached down between his legs to hold his balls.

'Dear God,' gasped David as Ladybird began handling him with the measured precision of a surgeon. Her grip – and her syncopated motions – remained constant even though he struggled; and within seconds he was shouting and groaning and jerking his body on the couch. Without his bonds, Rosie couldn't have held him, and she expected them to snap any moment. Oil, and his own thick fluids were squelching and squeaking through Ladybird's fingers; the noise revealing and graphic as she worked on his hard, red member. Rosie was utterly captivated, and felt her own sex drip and swell too. Especially when Ladybird's fingers slid down to the cleft of David's bottom.

'Kiss him,' she ordered curtly, nodding to Rosie and rotating her grip on David's prick. As she did so he screamed, his dark flesh leaping visibly and his rich creamy seed jetting out. Rosie wanted to watch, and to taste it, but obediently she dove around to his side and pressed her mouth down onto his.

As she pushed with her tongue, his lips yielded, even though he still tried to shout out and rave. Moulding his mouth with her lips, she drew his joyous cries inside her, absorbing the sound as if it were his very life itself. She felt like a vampire goddess, devouring his rapture and feeding on the essence of his orgasm. She wondered casually if Ladybird was sucking his penis, but found she didn't really care. His sweet young voice was born of his brain, his heart and his soul, while his semen came merely from his baser parts: his cock and his blind, aching balls.

As he finally grew still, she let her mouth rove over his face, kissing his chin, his cheeks and his eyes. With him quiet at last, she straightened up and watched Ladybird finish her ministrations. There were strings of silky whiteness on David's thighs and belly, and these she massaged into his skin like an unction. It was as if the product of his magical loins was the final ingredient in her spell.

Rosie moved to stand beside Ladybird, and stared downwards. Still bound to the couch, David looked angelic, his face and body both divine and wasted. His skin was slick and gleaming, and his hair – usually so neatly combed – was all tousled into spikes and points where he'd tossed and strained in his ecstasy. He seemed only semi-conscious, but he was smiling – a perfect, innocent, beautiful grin that turned Rosie's innards to fire all over again. His cock was flaccid now, but still held a marvellous promise – as if at any second it might stretch into the long, magnificent baton she'd felt move and swoop inside her as they'd squirmed and bucked on the grass. It seemed like a lifetime ago now, but as she glanced up towards the glass, and the sky beyond, she realised it was only an hour or two. If that.

As she remembered their sunlit frolic, she wanted it again. Wanted to be back there, kissing him, tasting his tongue, breathing his joy into her mouth as he came and she came too. She looked down at his soft, sticky cock and wished it a hard hot pole that she could mount and ride to glory. She thought of their first time, on the way to Stonehaven, and of how she'd taken exactly what she wanted back then.

But if David was too tired to perform now, wasn't there always Ladybird, whose sexual power was prodigious? The beautiful trainer had said Rosie wasn't ready, but maybe she'd been wrong? Maybe now was the right time to experiment?

Then, suddenly, Rosie's anticipatory musings were shattered. She heard a high, clear voice calling her name. Someone was approaching, and looking for her. They weren't here yet, but they weren't far away either – probably in the passage that led to the main hall.

'Rosie? Are you there?' Celeste's bell-like tones rang out, much closer now. 'There's somebody here to see you!'

Rosie glanced desperately towards Ladybird, and then saw a truly extraordinary phenomenon.

It was like watching Wonderwoman, or Supergirl – naked. Rosie had simply never seen anyone move so fast or in such a highly co-ordinated fashion. In a flash, Ladybird had the ties off David's wrists and was handing him a terry-cloth robe from the selection piled nearby. To Rosie she just nodded significantly, and made folding and tucking motions.

Her heart beating wildly, Rosie picked up the cue and lashed her towel somewhat higher around her body in a makeshift but decent sarong.

By the time the double doors to the passage swung open, both she and David were clothed – although he still looked blank-eyed and dazed. Smiling broadly, Celeste swept into the room, preceding whoever the visitor was, and as she did so, Ladybird walked naked to the side of the pool and executed a smooth, almost world class dive straight into the water of the deep end.

Rosie would have liked to have congratulated her friend for her incredibly quick thinking. She would also have liked to have given David a little shake, to help him wake up. She would even have liked to have taken a closer look at Celeste, who appeared to have only just risen from her bed, and was wearing a sheer silk kimono that revealed far more than it hid.

Rosie would have liked to do all these things and more, but the sight of a familiar figure – stepping out from behind Celeste – stopped her dead and froze up her limbs.

The 'somebody to see her' was Geoff.

14

Metamorphoses

He's still as handsome as ever, thought Rosie, studying her ex over the rim of her glass. So why does it seem as if he's changed?

They were sitting in the library, at right angles to each other on matching buttoned-leather couches which were duplicates of the ones in London. Celeste had suggested that they retreat amongst the books for a private and undisturbed chat.

The introductions had been brief and disjointed. Rosie had been shocked mute for a few seconds by Geoff's unexpected arrival; but to her surprise, the impact had faded quickly. She'd even felt a bubble of excitement; a frisson of power as she'd stepped forward, smiled easily, and said 'hello'. With a poise that seemed to come from nowhere, she'd found herself playing the hostess, with the usually all-dominating Celeste mysteriously demurring to her.

And that wasn't the only change. For the first time ever, she'd looked at Geoff and seen him completely out of his depth. He had, and still did seem completely at a loss, and it amused Rosie no end. She suddenly realised that she was now quite at home in the bizarre Hadey menage; that it was perfectly natural to be amongst people in various stages of undress, some with their faces still flushed with sex. She almost giggled when Ladybird popped up out of the water to say 'hi' and displayed her beautiful breasts. Geoff nearly choked, however, and then was overcome by a fit of furious coughing when Celeste's kimono started sliding sideways and showed a flash of her black pubic hair.

The only person Rosie had been mildly worried about was David – but even he nonplussed her ex boyfriend. He held out his hand and offered a courteous 'how do you do', his expression as grave as that of an alien prince inspecting his guard of honour. Rosie felt the giggles surge through her again, then an instant later, felt a wild flash of anger. David's composure had been so exquisite she could have kissed him, yet she'd also noticed Geoff's swift but familiarly dismissive expression at the sound of a second northern accent.

Bastard! she'd thought silently, making an inner vow to get him for that. Although even now, some quarter of an hour later, she hadn't quite worked out how.

Geoff was still in a state of semi-shock.

A few minutes ago, Celeste had tottered in, swaying theatrically on her flimsy high-heeled mules, and carrying a bottle of wine and two glasses. 'I thought you'd like this,' she said, her voice soft and suggestive, then sashayed out again, her robe drifting clear of her bare white bottom as she wiggled and simpered outrageously. Rosie had had to cover her grin with her hand, and was still smiling now, thinking of the other woman's complicity. She'd seen Celeste glide like a mannequin in far higher heels, and in even trickier dresses. The whole performance had been an attempt to deliberately unsettle Geoff.

And it's bloody well worked! thought Rosie, taking another sip of wine and appreciating its sparkling fruitiness. She suspected that the wine itself was another ploy. Although it probably wasn't something she'd drink herself, Celeste had brought them Rosie's favourite sweet Italian spumante – as if tacitly stating that in this house, *her* preference was the correct one, and not the dryer, more sophisticated product that Geoff might have expected. Draining her glass, she reached discreetly for the bottle. Her stomach was empty, and she'd been giddy with sex to start with, but she didn't care. Against all the odds, and when the mood should have been high trauma, she was thoroughly enjoying herself.

'Who is that woman?' demanded Geoff peevishly, running his fingers through his thick blond hair.

Rosie had to admit he looked particularly attractive this morning. He was wearing a soft fawn shirt, and chinos; the sort of colours that had always suited him. Designer casuals were perfect for his upwardly mobile image, and his sleek golden boy style. For a moment, Rosie thought of being in bed with him, and despite all the unkindness of his betrayal, she still found the idea appealing. She considered seducing him to assuage the desire that had been building again – just before his arrival – then stopped dead in the middle of her thought-stream.

Oh God, the changes were more profound than she'd realised. It's *me*, not him, she thought wildly, smirking into her wine, then sipping again. *I've* changed. *I've* got the advantage now, and the snivelling weasel's scared of me. She put down her glass, realising that alcohol was now superfluous, and regarded Geoff steadily and silently.

'Who is she?' he repeated, clearly rattled because she hadn't answered promptly, as she'd always done.

'Celeste?' She paused, drawing out his wait like toffee. 'She's Mrs Brent-Hadey . . . My boss's wife. Isn't she beautiful?' She imbued the short description with as much sensuality as she could muster: echoes of Celeste's touch, her lips, her voice and her perfect, available body. She could feel her own sex responding to all the inferences, and hoped that Geoff would be as affected as she was. When she looked down at his linen clad groin and saw the beginnings of a bulge, she wanted to leap up and down and shout 'gotcha!' – but instead she just looked him in the eye, and studied him as intently as she could.

This was so much fun.

'And those others?' he persisted, his voice slightly higher than usual. Shriller. 'Who the hell are they? What's going on here, Rosie? I thought you were here to work?'

Rosie stayed quiet and calm, turning her attention inward, and as she did so, somewhere in the house, someone started playing the piano.

Oh, David, she thought, I hope I'm not hurting you.

She imagined him puzzled and confused by her sudden disappearance with Geoff, then seeking solace in his artistic gift. She remembered passing through a small music room last night, and saw David in it now – at the piano, in just his trackpants, venting his frustration on the keys. The music was violent and passionate; she didn't know what it was – maybe Beethoven or Tchaikovsky perhaps? – but there was fire and lust and longing in it. She wished she was there beside him on the piano stool, ready to embrace him and offer him her body the instant the last note died away.

Meanwhile, back here in the library, she seemed to be winning a game of sorts. She had an upper hand she'd never had before, and the thrill of it, combined with the diffuse, background presence of David, made her more lustful than she could ever have imagined.

'I am here to work,' she answered, with a slight smile. 'But you know what they say about "all work and no play" . . .'

'What do you mean by "play"?' Geoff was flushed beneath his tan now, and he took a long, deep gulp at his wine – no longer bothered, it seemed, by its unfashionable fizzy sweetness.

Rosie crossed her legs before she answered, remembering an actress in a film doing something similar, to unbalance *her* inquisitor. Given the angle she was sitting at, she doubted if Geoff could actually see her pubis, but the possibility alone made him swallow.

'Well, David and I had been for a long run together, and then we had a swim.' She leaned back, and saw

Geoff's eyes lock onto the upper edge of her towel now, where it almost hung from the points of her breasts. 'After that, Ladybird arrived, and as she's an aromatherapist, we all spent some time giving each other massages . . . With perfumed essential oils.'

Again, the erotic potentials weren't lost on Geoff. 'But you were all naked!' he spluttered.

'You can't do massage with clothes on,' she pointed out blandly.

'What, even with the boy?'

'The man,' said Rosie softly, touching her tongue delicately to her lower lip. The old tricks were always the best. 'David is a dear friend of mine. We've become very close over the last few days.' She paused again to let the significance sink in. 'And anyway, Geoff, what does it matter to you? You were the one that said we should split up.'

'I –' he began, but changing pace rapidly, Rosie cut him off.

'What are you doing here, Geoff? How did you find me?'

Two questions at once seemed to throw him, and he put his glass down clumsily on the table, almost spilling his wine. 'I rang the library and they told me where you were working in London. And when I went there, they told me you were in the country with the Hadeys. It's not all that hard to find!'

'But why?' she persisted silkily, then adjusted her towel.

'Because I knew I'd made a mistake. We were good together . . . we shouldn't have split up.' As he spoke, he shifted uncomfortably in his seat, his eyes darting from her breasts to her legs and back again. At his own crotch, the bulge had visibly grown.

'Split up? Eeh lad, I thought you'd chucked me,' Rosie replied, making her voice a blunt, northern caricature. 'What about your new girl? Mizz "Happening" in PR?'

Geoff had the grace to look shamefaced. 'It fizzled out. She was too pushy. She was after my job, not me. The PR department was just a stepping stone. And so was I.'

Rosie said nothing. 'Serves you right' would have been too childish, and inappropriate for the mood she was trying to build. As she considered her best response, she realised that the piano had just fallen silent, and in her mind she followed David to his room. She imagined him stripping naked; imagined herself naked too, falling to her knees before him, kissing his body, mouthing his cock to ease his –

'Rosie, please, listen to me! Can we give it another chance?'

The interruption made her angry. Would Geoff never realise he wasn't the centre of the universe? That other men could interest her?

'We could be good together, I promise you,' he went on, oblivious to the fact that she'd barely even been listening to him. 'You could be the best possible thing for me right now. The new managing director comes from Leeds. I thought we could invite him and his wife to dinner. You know, impress him? Show him how settled we are?'

Rosie felt another huge swathe of anger. You pig! she yelled silently, wanting to rage and fume, but channelling the force of it inside her. Making it steel her resolve, and stoke the fires that burnt for others. Geoff was still a handsome brute, and if things had been different, she might have found a way to forgive him. But now he'd revealed himself to be just the same user he'd always been. And it was time to make him pay for using *her*!

'So it's not my voluptuous body you're after?' she enquired, keeping her voice smooth and pleasant as she slid across and sat beside him, then let the towel fall artfully from her breasts. It was a move worthy of Celeste herself, and the shock on Geoff's face – the instant naked lust – cried out for a polaroid camera.

'Rosie!' he hissed, glancing nervously towards the door, then looking back hungrily at her breasts.

'Ah . . . Maybe it *is* my body after all?' she said quietly, reaching for the bottle again, and making the towel fall completely apart as she poured herself another glass of wine. 'Not just the fact that I could make you look good with your boss?'

'No! Yes! I don't know . . .' Geoff seemed mesmerised by her lush, pale curves. He was licking his lips, making fists with his hands. His stylish, creamy chinos were pushed out grossly at the crotch, as if her flesh was new and exotic, and he hadn't already made love to her dozens of times in the past.

'God, I can't think straight!' he stormed. 'You're so beautiful, Rosie. I'd forgotten . . . I want you so much it hurts!'

'So you want me, do you?' she said, a delicious idea forming. A scheme Celeste would have adored. 'Why don't you show me how much?'

'Oh yes, Rosie,' he murmured, launching himself towards her, his movements uncoordinated and desperate.

Rosie held him off – even though she was tempted. He *was* a good lover. Selfish sometimes, granted, but he did have a certain brute flair.

'No, that's not what I mean,' she said, smiling obliquely, then letting her gaze drift down to his crotch. 'I said *show* me . . .'

Geoff frowned and looked downwards too, as if not wanting to believe what he suspected.

'Rosie?'

She nodded slightly, lifting her eyes to meet his.

It was a pivotal moment. Her true metamorphosis. Rosie was reminded of the heroine of the erotic novel she'd been reading. That contemporary classic she'd dipped into in London and brought with her here to Stonehaven. There had been such a moment for Josephine – the character in the book – when she stopped being a woman who let fate jostle her, and became one who took life in her own two hands and made it do what she wanted. Josephine hadn't faltered when the time had come, and she, Rosie, wouldn't either. She looked at Geoff unblinkingly, her expression controlled yet amused.

And then he shuddered. A long hard shake from head to foot as *his* change became irrevocable too. Rosie watched impassively as he fumbled with his belt, unbuttoned his stylish trousers, then reached into the folds of his boxer shorts.

His cock was rigid as he eased it out, the skin red and stretched and gleaming. A picture of need. Of abject male hunger. Of surrender – at last – to her supremacy.

'Very nice,' she said quietly, turned on but not tempted any more. His penis was just a toy to her now; something to play with. Or for *him* to play with because she wanted him to. 'Why don't you stroke it a bit? It looks as if it needs it.'

'Rosie! What's the matter with you?' he demanded, his voice unsteady.

Rosie didn't answer. Instead she leaned over and kissed him slowly on the mouth, slightly off centre. She pushed her tongue inside, then flicked it like a snake's, goading his but giving him no chance to push back. His lips were still parted as she drew back. They were moist and slack, and his eyes looked stunned. Rosie nodded briefly towards his cock and like an automaton, he took it in his hand and started squeezing.

It looked so incongruous. A crude, earthy act performed by a man so smooth and self-aware. He almost seemed not to know how to masturbate, and curiously that added a certain charm. Rosie felt arousal building but kept her expression mask-like and unrevealing. Her body was simmering, but she reserved the knowledge for herself; to make use of it later with one who better deserved it. She kept her legs neatly closed, although it cost her real discomfort. Rather that than show her flesh all shiny-wet and swollen.

Geoff was wriggling his bottom now, and his face was flushed and sweaty. 'Please,' he gasped, his teeth gritted as he pushed his pelvis towards her.

'Please what?' she murmured, reaching for her glass

and taking a small sip. She barely tasted the wine; the action was only for effect.

'Please, Rosie, I need you,' he groaned. 'I really want you. You're so gorgeous. Please, give me a blow job.' He jiggled his penis winningly in her direction, trying out his old sexy smile and failing miserably.

Rosie winced inside at the crudity of his language, but on the outside remained quite still. She studied his erection sardonically, narrowing her eyes as if it were some particularly tedious cataloguing chore, and pursing her lips to increase the disapproving image. Finally, she put her glass down with a soft, decisive clump and steepled her fingers before her naked and still oily breasts.

'But I don't want that, Geoff,' she said simply, nodding downwards at his cock and the fist that enclosed it. 'And I don't especially want *you*. At least not at the moment.'

It was only a partial lie. She didn't want Geoff, the man who'd treated her so shabbily; but she did want a man. And there was no denying Geoff was a virile and good-looking one. Even with his face full of horror and incredulity.

Steeling herself magnificently, she rose gracefully to her feet. 'Goodbye, Geoff,' she said softly. 'Maybe I'll see you when I get back to town? You could introduce me to that new boss of yours. I've always thought Yorkshiremen were sexy . . .'

'But, Rosie,' stammered Geoff. To his credit, his erection remained solid, despite his obvious frustration. 'You can't do this! You're kidding . . . You're not going to leave me like this, are you?' He looked down at his body.

'I can and I will,' she replied with a blithe heart. She'd been worried about a moment such as this, but it, and Geoff had been almost childishly easy to cope with. 'Any problems, use this,' she suggested, picking up the towel and tossing it neatly across his hand and his penis.

She turned, then, and walked away from him; secure in her beauty and confidence. She could hear him protesting vehemently behind her – berating her, the house, and all its other inhabitants – but she couldn't be bothered to listen. Geoff and his voice were the past, and the future was far more alluring.

As she showered and dressed in her room, there was just one picture in Rosie's mind: David, when she'd turned to look at him as she and Geoff had left the poolhouse. While the water was running, she suddenly imagined she could hear music again, then saw that pure, pale face of his, and how it looked when he played the piano. She saw his solemnity and the concentration in his sovereign-coloured eyes, but when she turned off the shower, the music was gone, and she saw only his confusion once more, and the hard lines of pain and disappointment.

And yet, despite this, David had been the epitome of grace under pressure. He'd clearly suppressed what he'd felt, and been completely amenable and polite. There was no question of him not knowing who or what Geoff was but he'd shown no animosity. Rosie didn't quite understand how such gentlemanly behaviour could be erotic; but it was. She thought of his quietness, his preternatural stillness, and felt her body grow hot and needy in spite of her cool clothes, her soft, fresh perfume, and the fact that her just-washed hair was still damp where it hung on her shoulders.

She'd made a special effort to look good. Her delicate lavender skirt and camisole were light as air, almost transparent, and she wore virtually nothing beneath them. She'd rifled through her makeup box, then studied her face in the mirror and decided that in this case, less was more. Her complexion had a glow of its own, even though it was nearly as pale as David's. She'd caught a little sun this morning, but that only accounted for *some* of her radiance. The sheen on her skin and the twinkle in her smile were down to sex. To highlight the colour of her eyes, she'd applied a soft grey blue line around them, and darkened her lashes, then finished off with a soft cherry tint on her lips. She'd done nothing with her hair, except run a comb through it, once. Its natural gloss and thickness were all the ornament it needed.

'You look nice,' said Ladybird as Rosie reached the bottom of the stairs.

The fitness trainer was in clothes now too, but only minimal ones, noted Rosie with a grin. A red lycra halter top and cycling shorts looked surprisingly good with Ladybird's vivid hair, and they clung to her body like paint.

'You don't look so bad yourself,' Rosie offered, feeling momentarily shy. What had passed between them by the pool had been sweet and intimate, but the fact that she'd begun making love with women as well as men was going to take some getting used to.

But it would be well worth the effort, she thought, looking sideways at Ladybird's long thighs.

'Where is everybody?' she asked, suddenly realising it must be lunchtime. She wasn't hungry, but she did wonder what it would be like to sit around the table with the residents of Stonehaven after what she'd seen – and done – this morning. Then another thought occurred. Oh God, what if Geoff hadn't gone yet? What if he was still hanging around somewhere, determined to get his own way?

'Well, your blond friend went tearing off about half an hour ago.' Ladybird waggled her beautifully groomed eyebrows. 'He was burning rubber like crazy and there was gravel flying everywhere . . . What on earth did you say to him?'

'I think he was a bit annoyed,' said Rosie calmly. 'He showed me his willy, and I said I didn't fancy it. What can you do when a man can't take "no" for an answer?' She tried for deadpan, but a snigger still broke through.

'You turned down good manflesh? Shame on you!' Ladybird waved an admonishing finger.

'I'd seen something I liked better,' Rosie countered, thinking of David, and how he'd looked on the massage bench, aroused and writhing. She wished he was still there right now, waiting for her.

Ladybird smiled knowingly but said nothing.

'What about the others?' asked Rosie, pleating a fold of her skirt between her fingers, then noticing the other woman eyeing its sheerness.

'David was playing the piano, but he seemed to be making a bit of a meal of it, so now he's gone for a walk, I think. I saw him heading in the direction of the river,' Ladybird said very pointedly. 'And if you want to know where Celeste and Julian are, just follow me.' Her green eyes glittered, and she took Rosie by the arm and led her towards the conservatory.

When they reached the open door, Ladybird touched a silencing finger to Rosie's lips, then crept forward like a cat burglar, utterly noiseless in her high-tech trainers. Rosie followed her. Very carefully.

As they approached the pool, under cover of a thick bed of shrubs, they heard a medley of two familiar noises. The rhythmic slapping of water against tiles, and the breathy, disjointed moans of a woman being soundly pleasured.

Julian and his wife were in a corner of the shallow end. Celeste was lying in the water, clinging onto two handholds, while Julian was standing between her outspread thighs, thrusting hard, with an expression of determined passion on his face. With one hand he was gripping his wife's hip tightly, and with the other he was bracing himself against the pool's edge. Rosie had never seen him look more male.

It was a stunning contrast to his performance earlier, when he'd cried and cringed before Stephen, but as Rosie was rapidly coming to understand, there was a sexual shapeshifter in everybody. She'd been stuck in one role herself for far too long, but now she wanted adventure. Be flexible and daring, try the strange, the outre, and the new.

Lucky David, she thought suddenly, who could be free and adventurous from the beginning, and not have to go through all the conventional mindgames she'd gone through with Geoff and his ilk.

But as she was about to draw away, and go looking for her fortunate pupil, a noise from the pool made her stay. It was Julian, crying out fiercely.

He was half-groaning, half-shouting, his slim hips a mad pumping blur as the water flew and danced in his wake. Rosie saw his hand slip on the side of the pool and just as it did, Celeste responded with an age old female gesture. She tried to enfold her climaxing husband in her arms, but with nothing at all left to anchor them, the couple went down beneath the surface in a wild, thrashing tangle of limbs.

The commotion was enormous. For a moment, it looked as if someone had thrown David's piano into the water, but eventually two bodies surfaced, still embracing and kissing and fondling, despite a lot of spluttering laughter. They were no longer joined at the groin, but they were pressed together so closely they seemed glued to one another. As they rocked and swayed, their hands ran affectionately over each other's bottoms, and they kissed and nibbled and nuzzled like a pair of sex-crazed animals.

It was an affecting sight. Rosie felt both aroused, and touched in another, deeper way. Julian and Celeste were both unprincipled libertines, yet clearly they were profoundly in love. They would both happily share their bodies with others, but at the heart of things they were devotedly married. Rosie imagined them old and grey together yet still behaving outrageously. Behind her, Ladybird sighed, as if she'd seen the same picture too.

What happened next was even more like a romanticised movie. Julian suddenly lifted his wife up in his arms and placed her gently on the side of the pool. Then, while she gazed at him lovingly, he climbed out of the water, picked her up again and carried her to one of the thickly upholstered mattresses that were set out nearby. As he lowered her onto it, Celeste locked her arms around his neck and drew him down on top of her, kissing his face with great fervour as he arranged his body over hers.

Julian's penis had been softened by his orgasm and his chaotic dousing, but as they watched, Rosie and Ladybird saw it stiffen again and butt against Celeste's rubbing thigh. It changed, before their eyes, from tender quiescence to a rampant, demanding shaft that shone dark and red against his consort's smooth pale skin. As Rosie touched Ladybird's arm and led her away and out of the conservatory, he was just entering Celeste yet again.

'Beautiful, eh?' said the fitness trainer when they were out of earshot, and Rosie noticed her eyes were misty. She felt a bit that way herself. Sentimental. That, and incredibly aroused and hungry to enact such a scene of her own. With David.

'Yes,' she agreed quietly. 'It's the best of both worlds. Sexual freedom, but with trust and love as well. I envy them.'

'Me too,' murmured Ladybird, then shrugged and smiled, her expression good-natured. 'But I'm going to make the most of what I've got,' she said philosophically, smoothing her hands over her sleek red-covered hips. 'Seeing as David's out walking, Julian and Celeste are busy, and you're here, that means Stephen's on his own somewhere. I think I'll see if he needs a little company.'

'Go for it, girl,' said Rosie, and on impulse, leant over and kissed her friend's soft mouth, feeling an instant of piquant temptation. 'Good luck,' she whispered as they drew apart. 'Not that you'll need it. You're far too gorgeous for anyone to resist . . .' She let her voice trail away, but knew that Ladybird had understood the subtext. Their own particular time would soon come – on a day when a man wasn't quite what either of them wanted.

Rosie's heart felt light as she set off out across the grass towards the distant tree-line, and beyond it, the river and the boathouse. Every instinct she had told her David had already gone there, and in her delicate, filmy clothes and with her body fresh and perfumed, she felt like a bride going expectantly to her groom. Wrapped in that sense of romanticism again, she thought how neatly the lovers in the household had divided themselves into couples. Such conventional arrangements wouldn't last long, she was sure, but for now it was a happy situation.

And the sight of Julian and Celeste had primed her perfectly. She'd been vaguely aroused to start with, having denied herself Geoff, and now she was hungry – ravenous for David's almost, but not quite virgin beauty; for his strength and his gentleness; his eagerness to learn, and his startling ability to absorb sexual wisdom at a speed that left her gasping. When he came into his prime, he was going to be quite a phenomenon; and even if she wasn't around to enjoy him then, Rosie felt privileged to be the one who had him now.

As she approached the boathouse, her nerves began

to dance and tingle. She halted for a moment on the track, and ran her hands over her breasts, her belly and her loins. Sliding them up the inner slopes of her thighs, she caressed herself slowly through the fabric of her skirt. Her body felt warm and alive. Totally ready. Her sex was open and moist, her nipples hard and puckered; the moment couldn't have been more right to offer herself. Walking forward, still stroking herself, she made her way to the foot of the outside steps.

The boathouse loft was receiving more sun now. The light was filtering in through the windows that looked out onto the river and the room had a soft, golden ambience instead of its earlier gloom. When Rosie entered, she was struck for an instant by a sense of peace and stillness, and almost thought the place was empty.

But it wasn't, because like a vision from her fantasies, David was lying motionless in the centre of the large low bed. His eyes were closed and his face was as pale and smooth as a graven image. He had one hand pressed lightly to his groin, and around him lay a dozen or so books. They were strewn on the bed and on the floor, and all open at blatantly erotic illustrations. Rosie recognised *Les Baisers d'Amour* and several others she'd brought from London.

She'd half expected him to be naked – undressed and ready for her – but instead he lay on the quilt still clothed, the only bare part of him his feet. His trainers were on the floor, among the books, and presumably he'd not bothered with socks. Without the rest of his nude body to distract her, she couldn't help but notice the slenderness and elegance of his toes, and the vulnerability of his insteps and ankles. She was tempted to drift forward and kiss him there, but as if he'd tuned into her thoughts and intentions, he opened his eyes and regarded her steadily. His hand flexed slightly at his crotch.

Now he was looking at her, Rosie hardly dare approach him. He looked perfect and almost unattainable, even though she could now see his erection quite clearly. It was a promising bulge in his stone-faded jeans; and he'd no doubt been stroking it as he waited for her. His shirt, a soft cloud-white thing made of cheesecloth, was unbuttoned half way to his waist. She could easily imagine that just a moment ago, he'd reached inside and caressed his own nipples.

'I was thinking of you,' he said without preamble. His voice was quiet, but very calm and strong, without any hint of uncertainty. As she watched he clasped himself slowly and deliberately, announcing a readiness that balanced her own.

Shaking now, Rosie walked up to the bed, and stared down at him. 'I'm flattered,' she said, nodding down at his tumescence. She felt far more nervous now than David apparently did, and her fingers trembled as she edged a book out of the way and sat down on the bed beside him. She nodded questioningly at the volume she'd just moved. It was open at an antique, colour-washed drawing of a man and a woman entwined in the *soixante-neuf* position, licking each other's genitals with tongues that were long and flexible.

'Just doing my homework,' he muttered, sitting up.

A bit of colour had come into his face now, as if her nearness had affected his confidence. 'I didn't quite know if I'd see you again . . .' he added after a moment. 'I thought you might be gone by now. I heard a car . . . and I wasn't sure if you were in it or not.'

'A fortnight ago, I might have been,' she said, letting her fingers cruise his denim-clad thigh. 'But not now.'

David shifted slightly, rucking the quilt beneath him, but he managed to meet her eyes. 'I thought he was your boyfriend. He seemed very possessive. He didn't seem to like us all being together.'

'He *was* my boyfriend. But he was only possessive when it suited him,' Rosie observed, thinking how true the statement was. 'But I'm not into that any more. All that "I'm your one and only" stuff . . . I've seen a better way. I want to be free to care for anyone I choose. Any man. Any woman. No limits . . . and no lies.' She grinned at David, hoping he'd understand, then felt a plume of almost physical elation when he smiled back shyly and reached down to cover her hand with his, just an inch or so from his groin.

'That sounds very sensible,' he answered, squeezing her fingers and slyly edging them upwards.

As her hand closed over his manhood, Rosie sighed with pleasure. This was an instance of masculine pride she *could* accept – and enjoy without capitulation. He was beautiful and he knew it; as strong and virile as the young male lion she'd likened him to from the very beginning. And yet in spite of this, she sensed that David would never try to manipulate her, as others had done, or make her do things for his benefit at the expense of her own wants and needs.

Beneath her fingertips, his sex seemed to radiate life and heat. She could feel the clear shape of him through the denim of his jeans, the thick, hard line of his yearning. He moaned as she traced his trapped erection; then suddenly he sat up and wrapped his arms around her, kissing her and pressing softly for entrance with his tongue as she rubbed and fondled at his crotch.

The kiss was a revelation, a summation of how far he'd progressed in his studies. His mouth bore the taste of his growing power; licking, nipping and sucking at her as he eased her backwards and down onto the pillows, then rolled on top of her. Still kissing, he reached between them and drew her hand away from his penis. Pressing his loins against hers, he circled his hips where he lay, massaging her body with his weight and with the solid mass of his flesh. He was imposing himself on her at every point of contact, yet Rosie did not feel oppressed. She welcomed the dominance of this man, encouraged it, crying out around his firm intruding tongue as he slid his hands between her and the bed, and cupped her bottom through her tissue-thin skirt.

They kissed for several minutes, rocking their pelvises against each other in a dry imitation of sex. Their tongues swirled and stroked around in each other's mouths, exchanging moisture and faint murmurs of passion.

'You're beautiful,' gasped David, lifting his face from hers and looking down into her eyes. Rosie felt a soft, weakening sensation in her belly as if his hot golden eyes were melting her right down to her vulva. The flesh of her sex felt as warm and yielding as jellified honey, and against the division of her labia, his penis was a long, rigid bar, probing blindly in search of her niche. Her clitoris was swollen and inflamed, and it throbbed insanely beneath the down-bearing pressure of his sex.

As her legs began to shake, and her breath caught in her throat, David lifted himself away from her, his expression intense, almost possessed. Rosie groaned. She was almost coming. She *needed* to come. Yet David plainly had an inner agenda.

With exquisite grace, he rose to his feet and slowly began to strip off his clothes. His shirt he unbuttoned meticulously, exposing his smooth skin inch by inch, then letting the white cloth swish sensuously down his arms and catching it behind his back as a model would. Rosie smiled inside, wondering how he could instinctively perform so well. She doubted if he'd ever even seen a female stripper, never mind one of the newer breed of male ones.

Beneath his faded jeans, his underpants were black and very brief. His stiffness was altering the shape of them and jutting out boldly before him as he shim-mied his way free of his denims.

Rosie wanted to leap up and grab him, run her hands luxuriantly over his body and enjoy its strength and vitality. She wanted to pull off his neat black underpants and caress the beautiful organ beneath them. She wanted to kiss him, revel in him, devour him; yet instinct held her back. This was David's show, his moment, and it would be selfish to under-mine him. Instead she just held out her arms.

With a small, composed smile, David slipped off his briefs and lay down beside her again. He seemed unembarrassed by his nakedness, and untroubled by his swaying erection. Still smiling, still calm, he began unbuttoning the front of her camisole, popping the tiny pearl spheres from their buttonholes with all the care he'd used on his own buttons. His movements were measured and tantalising, and it was all Rosie could do to hold back, and not rip open her clothing herself and offer her naked body to him.

When he flipped open the two wings of soft fabric, David sighed. She was bare beneath the camisole, and she saw his eyes grow heavy with lust as her breasts gleamed whitely in the sunlight. Bowing his head like a penitent, he started kissing her nipples – first one, then the other – wetting them with long, moist swipes of his tongue and nipping with his hard, straight teeth.

Rosie could hold back no longer. With a cry of relief, she clasped at his head, rumpling the smooth, sleek line of his hair and fondling his ears and his neck. The sensation of being bitten was delicious, and it shot towards her groin like a dart. She moaned and pushed her hips towards him, tugging at her skirt as she did so. The floating lavender garment had a loose elasticated waistband, and in seconds they were sliding it down her legs as a team. When it reached her feet, David sat up and flipped the skirt away with a flourish; while Rosie kicked off her shoes and sent them tumbling over the edge of the bed.

All she had on below the waist was a minute white silk g-string – an almost transparent triangle of fabric that seemed to enhance far more than it covered. Her soft, bushy pubes peeked out from satin bound edges, and the silk itself was damp with her dew. She reached down, about to strip it away completely, but surprisingly, David stayed her hand.

'Leave it,' he murmured, touching a finger to the small white scrap. 'It looks pretty.' The exploratory fingertip pressed, and then wiggled; working the gossamer-light cloth through the tangle of her hair until it lay against her hot, liquid core.

Rosie dug her heels into the bedspread as a huge wave of pleasure overcame her. She was climaxing and she could not contain her hunger any more. She pulled David against her as she came, crushing his caressing hand between them and grabbing at his back, his buttocks and his flanks – any part of his warm body she could reach. His penis was jammed against her leg, hard and fiery, burning like a thick, living brand.

Rosie's eyes were shut but she could still sense David's golden gaze; it felt like a shimmer of heat on her cheeks where his face hovered just above hers. His breath was tickling her chin, his gasps faint and light as he buried a hand in her hair, then swept his mouth down forcefully on hers, sealing her lips with a kiss, his timing instinctive and perfect.

'I don't know how much I can teach you, David,' Rosie said presently, when her mind and her voice were her own again. She was lying on her side, facing David as he lay facing her. She was relaxed and replete, her body loose and satisfied, and she was holding his penis in her fingers, stroking its still-enduring hardness with slow and teasing swirls.

'It's like I said in London,' she continued, letting

her hand loosen as he shuddered. 'I'm not all that experienced myself. I only really started to learn when I came to work for Julian.'

'Well, we'll just have to work it out together then, won't we?' he said faintly, his hips rocking back and forth as he struggled to control his reactions. 'Have intensive tutorials . . . Read books . . . Ask the experts . . . There are enough of them around,' he observed, grinning wickedly, then gasping with pleasure as her fingers closed round him again.

He was truly a wonder, this pupil of hers, decided Rosie, as the devil in her own belly stirred. 'Where shall we start?' she asked, leaning forward and kissing his cheek. As she did so, she stroked the groove under his glans with her fingernail, and smiled in slow, female triumph as he hissed her name through his tightly gritted teeth.

'There's a book on the floor,' he gasped, his head lashing from side to side on the pillow as she squeezed with one hand and stroked with the other. 'It was open at a picture . . . Teach me *that*! Now! Please!'

Rosie glanced down at the picture of the top-to-tail lovers, kissing each other's sexes in an entanglement as old as yin and yang. Then she looked back to the resplendent young maleness in her hands, and felt her mouth water and her vulva slicken in readiness.

Oh yes, my gorgeous boy, I'll try anything! she told him silently, curling down towards his crotch to lick his penis, while his strong hands pulled her hips across his face, then dragged aside the thin silk that covered her.

He tasted salty and delicious as she sucked him,

and his penis seemed to swell and fill her mouth. Yet as thought began to blur, a single question assailed her, popping in her mind like a lightbulb the very instant she surrendered to his tongue.

This is glorious, my sweet, beautiful David. But is it you who's being taught here . . . or me?